A BREATH AWAY...

The Spirits knew she had tried in vain to remember her life as a white child. After a while, it mattered not. Conway might not ever accept that, but it was truth.

She kicked and pushed against Conway's chest. Pressed against him, she found it difficult to breathe and impossible to ignore his heart beating strongly beneath her hands.

Looking up, she forgot what she wanted. With his lips only a breath away, she went still. The desire for him to kiss her again stole her resistance. Her limbs turned to mush.

Perhaps he divined her wish. He lowered his head, and just before his lips closed over hers, he muttered, "Damn you."

Doubtless, she was. Damned to live the rest of her life as a Comanche squaw. Damned to live without the love of this man. *Only this man,* her heart cried.

Conway tilted his head, his lips slanting over hers. Hot, moist, heady. Delicious. Wrapping her arms around his neck, she burned and gave herself up to the heat coursing through her.

WRITTEN ON THE WIND

JOYCE HENDERSON

LEISURE BOOKS NEW YORK CITY

To my mother, Ethel Pearl Douglas,
who, alas, didn't live long enough to see my
work published. Though anxious for my well-being, she
watched me spread my wings and fly at the tender age
of seventeen. She cheered me on then, and I like
to think she's cheering me on even now.

A LEISURE BOOK®

November 2005

Published by

Dorchester Publishing Co., Inc.
200 Madison Avenue
New York, NY 10016

ISBN 0-8439-5621-6

The name "Leisure Books" and the stylized "L" with design are
trademarks of Dorchester Publishing Co., Inc.

Printed in the United States of America.

Visit us on the web at www.dorchesterpub.com.

ACKNOWLEDGMENTS

My thanks to my agent Marlene Stringer of the Barbara Bova Literary Agency. Your hard work on my behalf paid off.

I couldn't ask for an easier or more knowledgeable person with whom to be associated than my editor Alicia Condon. I do my thing, she quietly does hers and voilà, the next thing I know my books are on booksellers' shelves. Thank you, Alicia.

Chapter One

Texas, 1860

"We got ever' last one a them red varmits," a voice drawled.

White Fawn caught back a gasp. The man with the disembodied voice thought she was dead. She lay still. It made no difference. She could not move, felt as though a log lay on her chest.

"Seven of 'em," the voice repeated. "Eight if'n you count this here boy."

Something nudged her left leg. With her long hair tangled across her face, she took a chance and slit open one eye. Late afternoon light filtered through her hair. No more than a foot away, a brown, scuffed boot and the hem of a duster loomed.

"Scalp 'em all," another voice said.

White Fawn snapped her eye closed and froze. *No! I am alive!*

Suddenly, a portion of the weight lifted from her. Wetness splatted her cheek. He had scalped One Bear!

Not a log, but One Bear's body held her down. The brave she was to have mated with after the full moon. His warm blood seeped through her hair and trickled into her ear.

In the next instant One Bear's upper body dropped and grazed her shoulder. Still, she dared not breathe. Holding herself as still as the fawn for which she was named, she resisted the urge to flinch when fingers tangled in her hair. *No. Please* . . .

A shot rang out, kicking up dust next to her head. Dirt and small rocks stung her face. Her head hit the ground with a jolt, her ear glancing off a rock.

"Leave the boy," a deep voice ordered.

"Where'd you come from?" The first voice whined above her, his sour breath nearly gagging her.

"I don't war on kids," the deep voice said, "and neither will you."

Whiny Voice muttered, "Kid, hell. He was ridin' with 'em. He's as dangerous as the rest of 'em."

"Was. He's dead. Come on. You need to bury the rancher and his woman."

"And this vermin?" the third voice asked.

"Leave 'em. The buzzards and crows will take care of them."

"Who the hell are you?"

"Matthew Conway."

"Ranger Matt Conway?" Whiny Voice sounded astonished or awed.

"Former ranger. I'm ranching now, and I've not had a bit of trouble with Indians for more than a year. Now this." His voice rang with disgust.

"Well, hell. They was attackin' these folks—"

2

"I'll accept that, but I'm telling you to get a move on. Bury the rancher and his wife."

White Fawn took a shallow breath as spurs jingled across the dry ground. They were leaving. Thank the sun god. Her chest and shoulder ached and her forearm was afire. A bullet must have gone through her arm.

She froze again when a man asked, "You savin' bullets, Earl? Your slug went clean through one redskin and got the kid."

Whiny laughed. "Lucky, I guess."

Risking another peek, White Fawn slitted open both eyes. Three men, one taller and broad in the shoulders, walked away toward the house that still stood in the waning light. Had these men been a few minutes later, the cabin would have been in flames. Little Elk had just nocked a flaming arrow when the first shot rang out and his body flew sideways off his pony; his bow and arrow plunged to the ground.

White Fawn fought back tears. She must escape. One Bear's pony was nowhere in sight. Neither was Pepper. Without one of the ponies, she would never find her way back to the main camp.

Four days they had ridden from Eagle Feather's camp searching for horses. One Bear had vowed to bring back no fewer than ten on this raid. They would have, too, had these Texans not gotten in the way.

She heard a scraping sound and opened her eyes again. The three men shoveled the rock-strewn soil, trying to dig graves. The big man stabbed a long-handled shovel into the earth while the other two jabbed ineffectually with spades.

Demons from hell, all three. Only her size and Pan-

3

ther's borrowed buckskin leggings had saved her from being raped. They thought her a boy. Eighteen years ago or more, she was unsure how many summers had come and gone, Eagle Feather had saved her from a squaw set on mutilating her. She reminded him of his little daughter lost to a white man's bullet a few months before she had been captured. He had adopted her.

Closing her eyes, she prayed: *Help me. Please help me.* She wasn't sure to whom she prayed. She did not quite believe in the spirit world the *Nermernah*, her Indian people, revered and feared. Her white father, who was no more, must surely have prayed to a god. That god had not intervened many years ago. Why would he answer her now?

Something woke her. Cold, amazed she had dozed, White Fawn still lay on the ground. Carefully, she opened her eyes to darkness. Breath stalled in her chest when she heard a *chink*. A bridle, and hooves shuffled nearby.

"Move out." The deep-voiced Texan spoke within spitting distance.

"We could bed down in the rancher's place."

"You could, but you won't. I want you both gone from here."

"You ain't my boss, Conway."

"No, but I have a Colt that lends me a loud voice when I'm of a mind to speak."

Nervous laughter followed. White Fawn listened as the horses' shod hooves grated close by, then gradually receded into the distance. As they picked up their pace, the men's voices became no more than whispers on the wind.

Her only company now was the ceaseless wind that soughed through the trees. White Fawn finally moved her free right arm when she heard the lone cry of a wildcat in the distance. It surely would smell blood, and she would die if she didn't find shelter.

Brushing her hair from her eyes, she turned her head. Pain arrowed down her back. "Ah," she moaned and feebly shoved at One Bear's body.

His dead weight did not budge. Though not a big man, little more than six inches taller than she, he had a barrel chest. Drawing a shaky breath, she pushed harder and raised her left arm at the same time. Pain flamed in her forearm and shoulder, but she persisted. She must free herself from One Bear and find shelter. She was freezing.

She thanked the darkness that concealed her companions' bodies. Tomorrow would be soon enough to see them. She would not have time to properly mourn these brave warriors. Her breath hitched when she thought of Eagle Feather's sorrow when he learned of the young men's deaths.

It seemed to take forever before she finally wiggled from beneath One Bear, then struggled to stand. The moon and stars swayed and dipped when dizziness nearly toppled her.

Taking a steadying breath, she bent her injured arm against her waist and cupped it with her right hand. She would stay in the rancher's house the rest of the night, clean her wound, and decide how to return to

Eagle Feather's camp. Though they might come back, the Texans had not tarried to round up the fifteen horses that had bolted. Maybe she would find one after daybreak.

His night vision as sharp as a predator's, Matthew rode behind Earl and Cecil. Earl incessantly bumped his gums, and Cecil absently answered. Matt said nothing.

"I'm gonna get me one of them forty-fours." Earl sucked his teeth. "Did all right with my piece, though."

"Lucky shot," Cecil insisted.

Matt snorted and slowed Trooper. He'd done the same job these men were so proud of. A job he hadn't liked and left none too soon. Killing Indians occurred with increasing frequency, and he was sick to death of it. If they'd stop their depredations, carnage like today would cease.

True, when he first took up a gun six years before, bloodlust drove him. If the damned savages hadn't mutilated his pa and raped and killed his ma while he was out selling horses, maybe he wouldn't have taken up a gun. Even now, tears stung his eyes at the memory of his mother's body sprawled on the ground, skirt ripped to tatters. The blood . . . He blinked away the gruesome image.

For some strange reason, though his kid brother Morty had been killed, he'd been spared mutilation. Maybe that was why to this day, Matt wouldn't allow kids to be scalped by men he led or came upon. Kill them cleanly to survive, but no butchery.

As much as his heart still ached at his loss, as much as his mind rebelled, in an odd sort of way Matt admired the Indians. Comanches were kinda like him—loners, light travelers, scorning authority of any kind. Every Indian he'd seen or challenged had been his own man. Fearless, free, a lover of the land, and killer of wildlife only when necessary for food, clothing, or shelter.

"Hello, the camp!" Earl called.

Matt's head snapped up. Hell's fire! Time had slipped by while he woolgathered. He snorted derisively, and rode Trooper into the light cast by a fire. He glanced toward the east. The sky's gunmetal color heralded dawn.

"Cap'n Matt!" Isaac Bettencourt grinned.

Matt shook his head. Would the boy ever stop calling him that? For six months now he'd been plain Matthew Ian Conway.

"What you doin' out here?"

Matt gestured to the two men who had dismounted before being asked. "Came upon these fellas right after they'd shot Comanches."

"How many?" Isaac asked.

"Eight," Earl said before Matt could respond. "That coffee smells mighty fine. Got enough to share?"

Hesitating, Isaac cast a quick glance at Matt, who shrugged as he lifted his leg over the cantle and slid to the ground.

"Uh, sure. But you gotta provide your own cups."

"We can do that." Cecil introduced himself and Earl.

Isaac stepped close to Matt and spoke quietly while the two men secured their horses beside Isaac's mount and packhorse. "Earl Murdock? Ain't he the fella Colonel Gates drummed out of the corps?"

7

"Yeah. And I'm keeping an eye on him—or asking you to. I need a couple winks."

"Sure thing, cap'n." Isaac picked up a tin cup and the metal coffeepot. He filled the cup to the brim and handed it to Matt.

The coffee scorched hot and strong down his throat. Damn, Isaac made good coffee. He gestured to the two men. "Actually, they got seven warriors and a boy."

Cecil crouched next to the fire and sipped from his cup. "We was too late. They'd already arrow-shot the rancher and his wife."

Death in Texas at the hands of Indians was an almost everyday occurrence. Matt didn't like it, but he understood. Comanches, or *Nermernah*—People, as they called themselves—tried to protect the land they had traveled for God knew how long. What he would never accept was their penchant for mutilation. Indians admired a man who "died well." But damn, he was still alive, and he'd suffered. Comanches were masters at exquisite torture before allowing a man to die.

What was good for the goose was good for the gander. If Comanches attacked him and his, he'd respond in kind, .44 belching fire as fast as he could pull the trigger.

Hot though it was, Matt swallowed the rest of the coffee in a few gulps and handed the cup back to Isaac. "I'm going to get some shut-eye before the sun glares."

"Right." Isaac dropped the cup next to the dwindling fire. "I'll bed Trooper for you, cap'n."

Isaac Bettencourt was not yet eighteen when Matt had met him six years ago. Though only a couple of years older himself, he'd been less than enthusiastic about allowing Isaac to join his "band of merry men," as he called the Texans who rode with him in those days. But Isaac could shoot straight and made camp as quick as a seasoned man. Matt's protective instincts welled up toward the younger man as they would have for Morty, had he lived.

Tossing his bedroll on the ground, Matt rolled out the blankets and collapsed, so tired his bones ached. Before sleep claimed him, thoughts of the Indian kid nagged. From his size, the boy appeared to be about Morty's age when he died. Hell's fire, he'd go back and bury the Indian proper, like he'd done for his kin.

Knees drawn up, White Fawn crouched in the corner of the one-room cabin, her arm cradled against her midriff. In the near-impenetrable gloom, unease chilled her bones. Surely she had sheltered in a dwelling like this while a toddler, thinking the sturdy walls would protect her. But of those two or three brief years she had no memory.

As she gazed about the small enclosure, thoughts of the big man haunted her. Half a head taller than the others, with broad, muscular shoulders, he had been frightening to watch. Dangerous, that one.

Unable to stop thoughts of death, she stared bleakly. First Little Elk had died, then two more braves had fallen from their mounts. That was when she had tumbled from Pepper's back, the wind knocked out of her.

"Your hand!" One Bear had screamed.

Without thought, she had raised her arm. One Bear

grasped her wrist as he rode by. The next instant she was behind him, arms wrapped around his bare torso. Escape had been uppermost in One Bear's mind, but he had failed.

Besides the bullet wound, her shoulder ached. She did not know how it had escaped dislocation from his powerful upward jerk. She shivered as her hand wandered to the amulet that rested between her breasts. Drawing the leather thong from beneath her buckskin tunic, she stared at the metal. Her eyes widened in disbelief when her thumb rubbed across . . . the bullet! The spent lead that had passed through One Bear and injured her was imbedded in the amulet.

"Eagle Feather," she murmured. Once again he had saved her. Their little band's head chief had given it to her as a mark of affection and possession. Claimed as his daughter, she would be harmed by no one. Not even Yellow Bird, who hated her even now.

Those many years ago, the Indian woman's man had died in the raid in which White Fawn had been captured. Before Eagle Feather had stepped in, the distraught woman had slashed White Fawn's legs, intent on killing her, irrationally blaming White Fawn for her man's death. She took a deep breath to chase Yellow Bird's vengeful face from her mind.

As she tucked the amulet beneath her soiled buckskin garment, her heart constricted. Grief would revisit her band and that of the braves who had joined One Bear on the raid. Four warriors she knew well had traveled to the spirit world. Three from Elk Horn's band lay dead as well. Would Eagle Feather change his longstanding declaration for peace and take up his lance to avenge them? Though she could find no blame if he did, still, she wished the killing would stop.

Noting the light had strengthened, she glanced around the dirt-floored cabin that had been home to the poor couple now lying cold in the ground. A bed, two chairs, a table, and a trunk were the only furnishings. Next to the fireplace on the rear wall, two waist-high shelves held crockery and a metal pot. A second pot sat on the hearth, and a third hung over dead coals.

Last night's supper. Her stomach growled. She had not eaten since . . . yesterday morning. And then only pemmican. Tears filled her eyes at the sight of stew. Grease floated on the cold mixture, but she needed food to gain strength.

Dipping her grimy hand into the pot, she swished aside the congealed grease and scooped up pieces of potato, onion, carrot, and meat. She shoveled it into her mouth, one handful after another, until she gasped for breath. Slow down, she cautioned herself. It had been a long time since she had eaten beef. It might make her sick.

Sitting back on her haunches, she peered at her dirt- and blood-encrusted arm. A black robe had taught her how to cleanse a wound. He called himself a priest, and insisted she address him as Father Anselmo. Unbeknownst to Eagle Feather, she had also learned the white man's tongue.

While a *puhakut,* shaman, scoffed at her for such foolishness, she had persisted with the practice when she was allowed to treat an injury. In time, she came to respect the shaman since his herb decoctions, chants, and smoke wafted by feathers worked as well, sometimes better than her efforts. Still, she believed the priest's admonition that wounds became putrefied if not kept clean. She was in danger of losing her arm, perhaps her life, if she did not wash the wound and use a poultice.

A sense of urgency swept her. Pony or not, she had to find her people. After a couple more handfuls of stew, White Fawn sat back and absently wiped her hand on her leggings.

She stood, swayed, and waited until the dizziness passed, then walked to the door and cracked it open. Light flooded in, along with crows' raucous caws.

Moving back to the hearth, she peered into the deep pot on the floor before the fireplace. She ducked her head and sniffed, then gingerly dipped in her grease-covered hand. Clean water. Drawing out a cupped handful, she greedily sucked it up.

After drinking her fill, she again rose and made her way to the trunk against a wall. As she reached it, she glanced up into the face of a stranger. "Aiyee!" Jumping back, she covered her eyes. How had that girl gotten into the cabin?

Quaking, White Fawn spread her fingers and peeked between them. She could no longer see the face. Her brow creased in bewilderment as she lowered her hands and glanced around. There was no one here. But she had seen someone!

Again she crept toward the trunk, her eyes fixed on the square on the wall where the face had been. She froze, staring in fear. Her black hair disheveled and dirty, a girl with an equally dirty face peered back at her. Rounded violet eyes appeared as frightened as she.

12

"Who . . . who are you?"

White Fawn narrowed her eyes. The violet eyes narrowed as well. She took another hesitant step as memory teased her mind. A looking glass? Father Anselmo had one, but it was a tiny, broken sliver, smaller than the palm of her hand. As she leaned closer, the image came nearer, and she knew. She was seeing her entire face for the first time other than in wavering river water.

Dumbfounded, she gazed at her image and murmured, "White Fawn."

The black robe had written another name in his book, one he had insisted upon addressing her by. "One day," he said, "white people will find you and take you back, Rebecca."

Tears flooded her eyes and those of the image. "White Fawn," she repeated.

She was Indian now. From the moment of her capture, it was too late to go back. In the ensuing years, more than one white captive had told her that they were dead to the white man, never to be accepted again. Even a child became a pariah after living with Indians.

She raised a shaking hand and touched her cheek, watching her image in the mirror. *"Filthy savages!"* one white woman had screamed as she died rather than be forced into a brave's lodge.

White Fawn had been very young, though already part of the *Nermernuhs'* world, but those words lingered in her mind for a long time. Still did. Yet Eagle Feather had proved kind, and his first wife, Bright Star, accepted her as her own.

She watched her finger trace her jaw in the mirror

image. "Fil . . . thy savage," she whispered. She was certainly that, her face grimy from several days without washing. Her back stiffened. Her people were not filthy. Unlike some of the bands they encountered, most of hers bathed regularly, at least once a week.

Resolved to cleanse her arm and find a way home, she rummaged inside the trunk. Finding a cloth, she went back to the water bucket. Outside, birds' wings flapped, followed by a cacophony of screeches.

She trickled water over the damaged flesh and gingerly rubbed at the mud. She would not get the wound clean this way. Looking with bleak eyes at the bucket, she knew of only one way. She plunged her hand into the water nearly to the elbow. Air whooshed from her lungs; she sucked it back in, gulped.

Slowly, she moved her arm back and forth in the water, that slight motion like glass shards on her wound. After several minutes, she lifted her arm. Most of the soil was gone, though the ragged gash where the bullet had torn flesh was ringed with a thin ribbon of mud. At least the shot had missed the bone.

Fresh blood welled. She needed a poultice. What to use? Bright Star had promised to teach her but never got around to it. Another memory crowded her mind. Father Anselmo had said alcohol was better used to cleanse wounds than to drink.

Scratching sounded on the outside wall. She froze, eyes rounded in fear, and waited. Trapped. She could not tear the cloth loose, crawl through the window, and escape without being heard.

Foolhardy to have ignored the birds' warning sounds. A narrow shadow slanted at the base of the door; another joined it. In the next instant, a brown rabbit, whiskers twitching, stuck its head around the door frame. She released the breath she had not realized she held and stifled a shaky chuckle. It was enough to startle the rabbit, gone in one bound. It served to galvanize her.

She could not stay here. If the white men came back, she would die. She spied a bottle tucked behind stacked cups on a shelf. Pulling the cork with her teeth, she sniffed it as she had the water. It smelled like the vile liquid a *Comanchero* had traded some braves for two beaver pelts. The black robe had poured it on the ground rather than allow them to drink it.

Looking from her arm to the bottle, she realized she must pour it over the wound. Holding her arm out, she tipped the bottle.

A scream ripped from her throat. Her body shook. She gagged as stars flashed before her eyes. The bottle slipped from her fingers and she crumpled to the dirt floor in a dead faint.

Matthew Conway grabbed his gun, rolled off his bedroll, and dived behind a rock. His body flattened on the ground, he cocked his .44. At the sound, Cecil jolted awake, rolled over, and cocked his own gun.

Beyond him, Isaac, equally alert, lay flat.

The men remained motionless, listening, eyes searching. Though it was well past sunup, Matt saw nothing. Heard only Murdock's snort as he turned in his bedroll.

Cecil looked over. "What?" he mouthed.

Matt shrugged and listened again, unsure what had

wakened him. He tensed at a crackle in the brush on the far side of a line of cedars. His finger eased against the trigger.

Isaac had made camp in the lee of the cedar break as a buffer against the incessant wind whistling from the north. Spring had arrived, and it had become noticeably warmer as each day passed.

Twigs snapped.

Trooper whinnied, and the other four horses shied, straining their tie ropes. Suddenly, a black-and-white head appeared from behind the trees, then the entire body of the speckled horse.

Matt remained immobile. Though he knew the Indians at the ranch house were all dead, that didn't mean others hadn't tried to join the raiding party. If there were more Indians, they'd be killing mad had they discovered the dead at the cabin.

"Conway," Cecil Barnes whispered, "that's the pony the Indian kid was riding."

Matt nodded. "Stay put."

He slithered backward on his belly into the brush and gathered his feet under him. Crouched over, he worked his way around the line of cedars and again dropped to the ground. Inching forward, he separated the brush obscuring his view. Grass as tall as small trees waved in the morning breeze, dotted by more cedars and the occasional oak. His dark eyes searched for anything out of the ordinary: thick ground cover swaying in the wrong direction, a break in the sea of three-foot grass. Nothing.

After a few tense minutes, he holstered his gun and

stood. The pony was alone and had apparently caught their horses' scents. Matt walked back to camp.

Cecil rolled over, looked up at him, nodded, and holstered his gun, as did Isaac.

At that moment Earl shot out of his bedroll, grabbing for his gun. "What's going on?"

Murdock would be dead by now had Indians been afoot, Matt thought, but he didn't say so. Instead, he inclined his head toward the pinto that had moved in next to Trooper and Cecil's horse. "We've got company."

No more than fourteen hands, the little mare had made herself right at home between the bigger geldings. Her dainty head lowered, she helped herself to the scattered grain.

"Pretty." Scrambling to his feet, Isaac started toward the horse.

Matt raised his hand. "Wait."

Isaac looked a question at him.

"We don't smell right. She'll spook if you're not careful."

The younger man cast a sheepish grin. "Right. I forgot."

How could he forget? Comanches he'd been downwind of smelled to high heaven. They bathed infrequently, if at all. The horse would know that in a blink of her soft brown eyes.

Striding to his saddle, Matt took up his lariat and moved in unhurried steps to the far side of the horses. He crouched beside Flash, Isaac's incongruously named mount, and waited.

The mare smelled him, that was a fact, for she

snorted and sidled backward. Which gave Matt the opportunity to flip his circled lariat to the ground. After some nervous stomping, the smell of the grain drew her back.

Matt waited until she lowered her head to lip up the oats, then swung his arm up and, in the same motion, ducked beneath Flash's neck. Flash reared back. So did the pony. But he had her. The rope cinched tight around her neck when she reared, hooves flailing the air.

Furious and frightened by the lariat, she screamed and reared again and again. Small though she was, Matt had his hands full. He stiffened his legs and leaned back as she dragged him across the camp, overturning the coffeepot and towing him right through the circle of rocks Isaac had ringed to contain the fire the evening before.

"Atta girl," he heard Earl say. "Give 'im hell!"

At the same time, Isaac called, "Hang on, cap'n."

Matt felt skin break on his bare hands, and the rope slipped through his bloodied palms. Then, as suddenly as her battle had begun, it stopped. She quivered with fright, nostrils distended, head high, rope taut.

Matt's chest heaved. "Hey, now, little lady. No one's going to hurt you." His soft, coaxing voice did not a particle of good.

Like hell, she might as well have said. She dropped her head down, twisting in an effort to dislodge the rope. Her front hooves came off the ground again, but not as high as before. Instead, she crow-hopped toward him and whipped her tail around, flinging her hooves sideways.

18

Matt leaped straight up in the air to get out of her way. When his feet hit the ground, she neighed and yanked back. He thought his arms would pull right out of their sockets. From the corner of his eye, he saw something sail into the air. By the time he figured out what it was, it had settled over the pony's face and neck. She neighed, her body shaking.

"Better?" Cecil asked, sounding as though he merely inquired about the weather.

Matt drew in a breath before he could answer. "Thanks."

Cecil was okay. He'd tossed a blanket over the mare's eyes, effectively blinding her. She would calm somewhat if she couldn't see.

"That's a danged good-lookin' piece of horseflesh," Murdock said and started toward her.

"No!" Matt snapped. Earl stopped in his tracks. "Don't go near her. She's nuts with fear." Hell's fire, didn't the man have a lick of sense? Why Cecil Barnes would ride with Earl, Matt couldn't fathom.

"Yeah, but . . ."

Matt shook his head and drew gently on the rope. The mare took a hesitant step, obviously afraid to move when she couldn't see. "Come," he coaxed and wound her in a couple of steps.

He backed up and talked quietly, drawing her away from the other horses. When he was about five feet away, she stiffened, wanting no part of this odd-smelling stranger.

"Okay," he said around a grin. "Isaac, get the sack of oats from my gear."

19

The boy hotfooted it to Matt's belongings. He up-ended the oats into a pile under the mare's nose. No more than a hatful remained, but it would do.

She reared, then settled and lowered her head. Grain was obviously a powerful incentive for this horse. Without moving closer, Matt snagged a corner of the blanket and ripped it from her neck and face.

She twisted her head from side to side, eyes rounded and wild. When he didn't move, she eyed each man in turn. Her whole body shimmied, head to tail, as a wet dog would shake. Satisfied that the men weren't com-ing closer, she nosed the oats several times before deigning to eat.

Matt grinned. Spirited, she was. But the kid had rid-den her, so she must be well-trained. She was too small for him and would need the right person on her back. Too bad Lupe, his housekeeper and foreman's wife, didn't ride.

He shrugged. The mare was a beauty and he'd keep her.

Chapter Two

White Fawn came awake to the soft call of a mourning dove. Disoriented, she blinked. Her cheek lay against the cold ground. When she moved pain shot up her left arm, bringing her to full awareness of the bullet wound and where she was. How long had she been unconscious?

She sat up and glanced toward the door that stood open. Still daylight, but shadows from the trees to the west stretched across hard-packed earth in front of the cabin. Late afternoon. The crows no longer screeched, but she heard the swish of birds' wings. Until that moment, she had not realized how acute her hearing was. Eagle Feather's training had not been in vain.

She examined her wounded arm. Fortunately, the slash across her forearm had not made contact with the ground when she fell.

Sliding her feet beneath her, she struggled up. A wave of nausea hit her as she swayed on unsteady legs. *Not again!* Gritting her teeth, she fought the swimming sensation in her head, took slow, even breaths until her stomach settled.

She needed to bind her arm. Rummaging through the trunk, she found a length of muslin. Too large. She wished for the scissors the priest had given her. Surely the woman who had lived in this isolated prairie house must have scissors, too. Delving deeper into the trunk, she carefully lifted out folded garments and piled them neatly on the ground.

She looked down at her buckskin tunic splotched with One Bear's blood. She had worn it for . . . quite awhile. Other than the sun and the moon, the change of seasons, she had no way to mark time.

Finding an oblong metal box, she pried it open and found the scissors for which she searched and, surprisingly, a knife. Stored in its own thigh-tie sheath, it would be easy to conceal beneath her garment as she traveled on foot or on horseback.

She didn't know how to use the bows and arrows scattered outside. Now she had a weapon to protect herself, and, more importantly, to skin rabbits. Bright Star had taught her how to snare them. Berries, wild onions, cactus, and rabbits would nourish her for some time to come.

After cutting the muslin into a long strip, she awkwardly wrapped the material around her arm in a thick pad and then tied it with one hand and her teeth. She found twine in the trunk, which she could use for fishing line if nothing else, as well as a wool blanket, a coat, and a small satchel. Though the days were warm, nights cooled quickly when the wind came from the north, as it had last night.

She paused, reflecting. White men looked upon Indians as no better than the lowliest animal. Thieving red-skins. "I am now one of them," she murmured.

Casting a sorrowful glance about the room, she knew remorse that the people who lived here had died. This had been the first raid she had taken part in. One Bear had insisted she accompany them, to cook and help with the horses. Not once had she hurt a captive. Not once had she killed anyone. But now she was forced to steal.

Resigned, she began putting the garments she could not use back into the trunk. And the knife . . . well, she hoped the only use for it would be skinning rabbits.

With a length of the twine, she tied the coat and blanket into a tight packet. Then she stuffed the re-maining muslin and the scissors into the satchel. Slip-ping her arm through the satchel's strap, she hefted it against her side, then picked up the blanket bundle. The door creaked when she opened it a bit wider and stepped into the waning light.

White Fawn stopped in her tracks. The blood leeched from her face; her violet eyes widened until she thought they'd burst.

No! "No!" she screamed, and flew from the shade of the lean-to roof, flinging her hand in the air. "Go away!" she cried.

But it did no good.

"Buzzards and crows will take care of them," the big man had said. They were everywhere. Vultures and crows perched on every one of the bodies littering the beaten ground.

As she watched, a huge, ugly vulture dipped his head

into One Bear's open chest. Another clawed Little Elk's ear from his head, then speared it with his beak. Two birds perched on Elk Horn's body fought over a piece of flesh. Covering her mouth with a shaking hand, she retched.

Gagging, unable to watch anymore, unable to disperse the birds, she whirled and ran. It made no difference where. She plunged through the brush, but the images and the horror followed her.

Pushing on until her lungs nearly burst, she stumbled and collapsed on the ground. Tears tracked her cheeks as she sobbed, gulping air into her burning lungs. *Spirits of the* Nermernuh, *God of the white man, Ranger Conway had known what would happen and not cared. Had left her People to that!*

Face turned to the sky, White Fawn keened as she had heard the women of her village do following the deaths of those they loved. Yes! Comanches loved; they laughed; they prayed; they bled and died.

She did not know love for One Bear, but they had been friends. Bright Star had assured her that she would grow to love him once they mated.

"They were *nerms,* humans, Ranger Conway!" she screamed. "One day you, too, will be carrion!"

After a time her sobs subsided. Her throat hurt. As if coming out of a trance, White Fawn glanced about her with dull eyes. She sat in a copse of cedars. The sun's last rays lit the western sky. It would be full dark before long, and she could not stay here. She would head toward the river white people called the San Saba, farther into *Comancheria*. Back the way she had traveled

24

for four days. Surely she would find a hiding place along the riverbank until daylight.

The whites claimed they could settle on vacant land. "It is not vacant," she muttered, the land seeming strangely lonely tonight. Without One Bear. Without Little Elk and the others.

A hawk sailed overhead; its scree sang on the wind as though it called to her. For as long as the People could remember, they had traveled this prairie as free as that hawk. If the land belonged to anyone, it belonged to them, the *Nermernuh*. So did the hawk, cougar, bear, and buffalo.

She glanced back the way she had come, and shivered. If her people did not burn it, that house would not remain empty. The Texans would return. If not the men she had seen yesterday, then others.

Raising a clenched fist, she vowed to the heavens, "I will survive!"

But not if she encountered those men again. Two of them appeared no bigger than One Bear, shorter than Eagle Feather. But the one called Conway . . . Goose bumps pebbled her skin as fear gripped her. She pushed away his memory. Surviving and finding her way home if pitted against that one would be . . . miraculous.

A helluva day. Matt's arm ached as he drew on the lead rope for what he was certain was the millionth time. The mare followed—she had no choice—but she'd maintained tension on the damn rope the entire way. Tying her off on the saddle horn hadn't lasted a mile. She'd weaved about, the rope drawing across his thigh like a saw scraping flesh, then nearly knocking him out of the saddle when she crow-hopped to his left, the rope cinched taut across his hips.

He glanced over his shoulder, his gaze colliding with the mare's dark eyes. A humorless grin bracketed his mouth. "Might as well give in. You won't win. Skirmishes maybe, but not the war."

As though testing his mettle, once again the pony tossed her head, nearly yanking the rope from his hand. At least he'd had sense enough to wear his gloves after this morning. Still, the insides of both were stiff with dried blood.

Suddenly, Trooper neighed and stopped dead. The mare did the same, as if in chain reaction. Matt's knees automatically clamped tighter against the saddle leather. "Now what?"

Then the smell registered in his brain. Rotting flesh. The Indians' bodies had lain all night and in the sun today.

After bidding Cecil and Earl so long and inviting Isaac to visit his ranch next time he was nearby, Matt had headed south. It was only a mile or so out of his way to swing west to the little cabin.

Images of the little Indian fellow had drifted through his mind all day. He'd lain almost hidden beneath the Indian who'd tried to save him. Father and son, perhaps, or a kid brother. Matt grimaced. Idiocy, maybe, but he felt compelled to go back and bury that boy.

"Whoa," he coaxed, and stroked Trooper's withers to calm the nervous prancing. "Nothing to fear, boy."

Circling the lead rope around the saddle horn to free his hands, Matt pulled his blue-and-white bandanna from around his neck and tied it across his nose and mouth. To block the smell a little.

He reclaimed the lead rope and nudged Trooper's flanks. Nickering a protest, the gelding danced sideways and threatened to buck, but a touch of Matt's spurs settled the horse to a slow walk.

Shortly, the cabin came into view. Matt's dark eyes took in the grizzly scene. "Oh, shit!"

Sending Trooper into a trot, he ripped off his hat and waved it in the air. "Ya!"

Wings flapped as dozens of birds took flight. He rode directly toward the prone bodies . . . what was left of them. The birds didn't go far. One after another settled on tree branches. Beady eyes watched Matt dismount.

He led both horses to the hitching rail located on the east side of the little cabin. He looped Trooper's reins around the bar a couple of times. The pony, though, would bolt if given half a chance, so he tied her more securely.

Turning back, he lifted his hat again and waved it in the air. The birds stayed put, which didn't surprise him. They'd feasted all day and weren't about to scatter because one puny man interrupted them. *God-a-mighty*. He strode to where he remembered last seeing the kid. There was nothing left of the larger Indian's face. His chest had been clawed open; bits of flesh still clung to the bones. He studied each body in turn.

"Son of a bitch."

It wasn't the first time he'd seen the remains of men preyed upon by birds and other animals. But it *was* the first time he'd seen such fresh kills, and the job unfinished. He shook his head with regret as he strolled back to the first body. Even though it would have taken him, Cecil, and Earl all day to bury this many, they should have. Even Comanches deserved better than this.

As he stared at the corpses, it took a moment before reality registered. The kid wasn't there beneath his companion. "Hell's fire." Earl's bullet had found its mark all right, but only one Indian had died. And *he* hadn't checked. Stupid!

He turned in a circle, searching the surrounding area. How badly was he hurt? He'd had the whole night and day to escape. Maybe still close by, or long gone. Afoot, injured or not, he couldn't have gotten far. Matt dropped his gaze to inspect the ground. The soil was scrabbled where the kid had managed to climb from under his companion. Moccasin tracks led to . . . the cabin!

Whipping out his gun, Matt snorted with self-disgust. He could have been a dead man by now. *Should* be dead by now. Serve him right for such carelessness. Through narrowed eyes, he stared at the house. The door stood ajar. He was sure it had been closed last night.

Belated thoughts of survival sent him running toward the mounts tethered out of the line of fire from inside the cabin. He stopped behind the mounts. Nervous from his approach, they stamped their feet. Ducking under Trooper's neck, Matt sidled up to the building and pressed his back against the planks, then peered around the corner and listened. All he heard was the shuffle of the horses and the clink of bridle.

He straightened against the building, looking toward

the bodies. Not one of them had carried a rifle, only bows and arrows. That wasn't as reassuring as it might have been. Hell, some Indian kids as young as five could nock and loose an arrow with surprising accuracy. Though small, the kid could be in his teens, as able as a grown warrior.

No doubt about it, the youth was dangerous. But Matt wondered, if pushed to it, whether he could kill a boy. Capture him, maybe. Matt didn't have to do anything, but he would. Alone out here, that kid could, probably would, kill whoever crossed his path.

If he did manage to catch the little rascal, that brought up the question of what to do with him. Take him to Steven at the orphanage in Austin, maybe. "Lots of maybes and what ifs," he muttered, then shrugged. *Cross those arroyos when the time comes.*

He glanced behind himself, then began to circle the cabin. There were no windows at the front or on this side of the house, but there might be somewhere else. Besides, he'd rather have the waning light at his back than in his eyes if he had to face an Indian. Any Indian.

Careful where he placed his boots, Matt worked his way around the cabin, finding only one window, but it was covered. Hell's fire. Nothing was ever easy. Drawing to a stop at the west corner of the structure, he chanced a look around the building's edge. If that kid was inside, he was smart. Quiet and dangerous as a riled rattler.

Matt jumped when a crow cawed. His finger tightened on his gun's trigger. Drawing in a breath, he shook his head. He'd come within a whisker of firing.

29

Be just dandy if he shot himself in the foot. Frowning, he inched a boot out to creep toward the doorway. Do no good to stand here until the light was gone. If the boy was inside, he needed to see him.

Matt's breath came hard as he reached up and yanked the bandanna below his chin. Gut-wrenching odor or not, he was so tense that he felt strangled trying to breathe though the material. Soundlessly, he placed one booted foot ahead of the other in excruciatingly slow motion.

Next to the open door, he took another deep breath. Time to slap leather or get off the horse. Pivoting on his left foot, he raised his right leg and kicked the door, surged into the dim cabin, and dropped to the ground, rolled, then came up on his knee. His .44 pointed, leading the way; his gaze swept the room.

Empty. The damn cabin was empty.

"Hell's fire!"

A drop of water splatted on White Fawn's cheek, then another and another. When she turned her head, a drop hit her between the eyes. She blinked. Rain. Peering up through the brush she had burrowed under the night before, she saw nothing but gray sky.

She thanked the Spirits for the warm coat and blanket she'd taken from the cabin. The thought brought back the horror of the evening before. She shivered. Today she must begin the trek north to find her People.

She cast a baleful eye heavenward. The welcome spring rain was now her enemy. With the sun hidden by clouds, it would be difficult to find north. Bushes crackled on the other side of the river, and her thoughts stood still; her eyes widened in fear. Cautiously, she parted the green leaves obscuring her view.

A doe, head up, ears alert, looked directly into White Fawn's eyes. Frozen, White Fawn watched a tiny fawn teeter from the scrub behind his mother, his spindly legs quivering with each step. He must have been born this morning and had yet to learn his mother's stealth. He lowered his delicate head to drink and toppled headfirst into the river.

Unable to contain her mirth, White Fawn chuckled loud enough to alert the doe. She barked, whirled, and in two bounds was swallowed up in the trees and brush. White Fawn watched in astonishment at the quickness with which the fawn leaped away, no more than a step behind his mother.

She smiled. Rare to see deer that close, and a fawn at that. Surely it was a good omen.

Crawling from beneath the shrubs, she stretched, and the blanket slipped to the wet ground. She scooped it up, folded it, and retied it with the twine. Picking her way to the river's edge, she knelt and drank her fill of crystal water from cupped hands.

She had nothing with which to carry water. No horse, no sun to guide her, no food. Her stomach growled as if in answer to her musings.

But first things first. Turning the coat sleeve back, she unwrapped her arm and breathed a sigh. The wound was clean, no streaks indicating putrid skin. Stealing herself for the shock, she submersed her injured arm in the cold water. The current swirled against the damaged flesh. She held it underwater until her arm was numb.

Picking up the strip of cloth, she discovered both ends of the cloth had trailed in the mud. "Aiyee." In the bag, she found the scissors and snipped off the soiled ends.

After rebinding the wound, she gathered the duffel and blanket. Hungry she was, but she decided to move on before attempting to snare a rabbit. The rain might make a fire difficult, but it wouldn't be the first time she'd eaten raw meat. Perhaps she would find berries along the way as well.

Matt had found evidence that the Indian boy had been inside the cabin and had decided not to bed down there. He'd taken advantage of the remaining daylight to ride north until full dark, then made a cold camp. A good five miles from the rancher's place, he'd imagined he still smelled decaying flesh.

Following the boy's trail had been as simple as following wagon tracks. Where there'd been no moccasin prints, he'd found broken branches. Good thing. If the rain kept up, the footprints would wash away, though right now it was little more than a drizzle dampening his hat and coat.

Matt had tracked one hell of a lot of Indians in past years, and never, until now, had they been easy to follow. Another piece of luck had him sighing with relief this morning. The mare had decided to tag along with little resistance. Still, he grasped the rope rather than tie it to the saddle horn.

He wasn't happy to be riding into *Comancheria* rather than south toward the comforts of his own ranch. But he couldn't leave that kid to wander loose.

God only knew what trouble he'd get into, or what damage he might do if he encountered white people. Though he appeared less than bright, Matt had tracked too many Indians who were crafty as hell.

The Indian *was* crafty. He might have been unconscious for a while, but he'd played possum for hours, and Matt had fallen for the ruse. Disgusted, he grunted.

Trooper danced and tossed his head when a doe crashed toward them. Matt drew rein and waited. Spying him, the doe veered off. A fawn followed a few paces behind.

What spooked her? Perhaps he should scout on foot a little way. Dismounting, he tied Trooper and the mare to sturdy saplings. He listened. The only sound was rain dripping. A bear or cougar might be nearby. Either one would send the doe into flight. To leave the horses untended didn't sit well, but he had little choice. The San Saba was close. Maybe the kid had bedded down near the river.

Though the ground was getting soggy, Matt made little noise, and found bare ground rather than walk on leaves or grass. After a hundred yards or so, he heard the river's lazy swish against rocks. He bent low and moved toward bushes, then knelt behind them and peered through leaves.

Other than the river's song, it was quiet. Birds had holed up to avoid the pelting rain, and small game had made themselves scarce. He searched up and down both banks. Fifty feet to his right, he noticed an easy crossing where the banks sloped on each side of the river. As he recalled, the San Saba was three or four feet deep at most in this area.

Matt worked his way up to the crossing and waded in. Shoot, the water didn't even come to the tops of his boots. He sloshed across and then frowned. Crouching, he picked up a piece of white material . . . and another. Two pieces that had been cut, not torn. Both were mud-splattered and one of them was smeared with dried blood. His eyes narrowed. If the kid had left these, he was injured.

He searched the ground. It took a while, but he found a couple of telling moccasin prints and crushed grass and leaves where the kid had spent the night. Hell's fire, he was a little squirt. Matt spanned the length of one print with a spread hand. No bigger than from his thumb to the top of his middle finger.

The rain poured more heavily now. Matt pushed back the brim of his hat so water would cascade down his back rather than cause a miniature waterfall in front of his nose. He gazed northward. The kid would be miserable traveling on foot in this weather. Maybe he'd find him before nightfall. A slim hope, perhaps, but he didn't relish riding too far into *Comancheria* alone.

Too late, he wished he'd shared his plans with Isaac. The young man would have been helpful.

He walked a zigzag path for a while. Yep, fresh trail.

Matt retraced his steps to the horses and mounted up. He'd better keep his eyes peeled. He didn't know what weapons the Indian carried, and he didn't relish the thought of an arrow thunking into his chest.

Far to the north in the *Llano Estacado,* where few white men had ever ventured, Eagle Feather sat cross-legged in his lodge. His once piercing black eyes, now clouded with the age of fifty summers, stared through the open flap of his tipi. Wide blue sky arched over the land, gray clouds rimming the southern horizon. If the Spirits smiled, rain would nourish the earth before it slept. Little rain fell here where his People had roamed for generations before life had stirred in him.

His heart sat heavy in his chest. The sun had risen ten times since he had watched White Fawn ride off with One Bear. He should not have allowed her to go. A vision had disturbed his sleep and left him uneasy. White Fawn's pony traveled in tall grass, her rope bridle gone, her back bare. The only daughter left in his world was in danger.

Though proud of his two sons, who sat to his right and left, quiet and respectful of his troubled thoughts, the violet-eyed girl had long ago wormed her way into his heart. His favorite. He had thought on it many times but had given up trying to understand. It was truth. Perhaps she had been a gift from the Spirits after losing the daughter of his blood.

The girl he had taken to his heart was a good rider. He had taught her himself. An apt pupil, she had broken the pinto herself. Time and again she climbed back on until Pepper settled down.

"My father." Straight Arrow interrupted his thoughts. "We will search for her if that is your desire."

Where would they search? Vast lands lay south where One Bear had gone. "I am thinking on it," he said.

Smoke from the small central fire curled lazily toward the tipi's top opening. Eagle Feather squinted through the smoke at his first wife, Bright Star, the mother of his two older sons, who sat to the right of the doorway.

"She is in danger."

Bright Star nodded, for she had never gainsaid him in the twenty-five winters since he had taken her to wife. Willow Branch, his second wife, sat to the left of the opening, and his third son, who had seen fifteen summers, stared at him with a fierce countenance that brought a faint smile to Eagle Feather's lips.

His vision quest three years behind him, Beaver Heart adored White Fawn. The love between the two was as though they had sprung from the same loins. Beaver Heart's words did not surprise him.

"I will go with you. We shall find her." The boy glanced from Straight Arrow to Black Crow, then riveted on him, as though daring each to deny him.

Eagle Feather decided that if he mounted a search, he would allow Beaver Heart to go with him.

It troubled him to leave his relatives and friends without guidance. Only twenty lodges made up the band. Eagle Feather had kept his People from war for many seasons. Death stalked those who challenged the white man. Though each warrior could go his own way, the heads of each lodge had listened to him for a long time, and they had prospered.

Only One Bear had challenged his message of peace. The proud owner of fifty horses, he wanted more. When he took White Fawn to wife, One Bear had vowed to deliver ten horses to Eagle Feather. An impressive gift.

To restock quickly, One Bear raided. Wild horses roamed the plains, mostly in twos or threes. Catching them often proved more difficult than raiding white men's mounts. Mounts that were, for the most part, already broken.

Little Elk's woman, She of Small Voice, had come to him asking about her man. She, too, worried. Too many suns had risen since the raiding party had left. The vision rested like a rock in his chest.

Coming to a decision, Eagle Feather spoke to his eldest son. "One must remain with our people." He saw the protest in Straight Arrow's eyes, so he continued before the young man could voice his dissent. "Black Crow and Beaver Heart will ride with me. You must stay, my son."

"You would travel so far?"

Old he might be, but Eagle Feather intended to find White Fawn, and he would do so without bloodshed. He glanced at Black Crow, who smiled, and then at Beaver Heart. "You will not kill white men unless attacked."

"Father—"

"Beaver Heart, if you cannot abide by my words, you shall remain here with your brother."

"As you say," his son acquiesced, though the glitter in his dark eyes made Eagle Feather doubt his conviction.

"And you?" he asked Black Crow.

"With stealth we shall proceed, my father. May the Spirits gift us with success."

Across the dirt floor, his two women bowed their heads, acceptance of his decision apparent. Eagle Feather prayed inwardly for the strength he would need. If he failed and died, his family, his band, cast adrift, would doubtless wage war against the white man.

Chapter Three

In late afternoon Matt came across the remnants of a makeshift camp. The boy had killed a rabbit. Discarded bones lay near a mesquite bush, the ground cover beaten down where he had sat.

Matt tipped his head back. Blue sky now shone through broken clouds. The rain had come and gone, leaving a much-needed earth soaking. Perhaps the rain had been widespread and drenched his place, too. If spring rain failed to materialize, his well level would suffer. By the end of summer, his stock would be mighty thirsty. Though several thousand head roamed free, he needed water for the pigs, horses and chickens in the pens and new barn, and in corrals now under construction.

Movement caught his eye. Slipping to the ground, he peered into the heavy brush forty feet away. Four-legged or two-legged animal? Matt tied the horses and crept toward a stand of trees on the far side of the clearing.

Then he heard running footsteps. Two-legged. Picking his way into the brush, he knelt beside moccasin prints he'd been following all day. Frozen in place, he listened.

Trooper whinnied. He leaped up and ran toward the horses. The kid must have distracted him with noise, then circled back. As he broke into the open, Matt saw the Indian. He'd already untied the mare, the rope looped in his mouth Comanche fashion. The boy grasped a hunk of mane and began to swing himself atop the horse.

"No, you don't, you little varmint!"

The boy glanced Matt's way and lost his momentum. Dropping the rope, he fled, but Matt, right on his heels, dove forward, arms outstretched, and clasped buckskin-covered legs. His forearms plowed into the soil as they slid headlong on rocky dirt.

"Oof!" the boy grunted as Matt's weight pinned him to the ground.

But not for long.

Boneless as a snake, he writhed around to face Matt. Black hair covered his face, but his hands were busy as hell. Clawing the air, he found Matt's throat. Fingernails raked his skin. He grabbed the Indian's hands and pressed both to the ground above the boy's head.

"I won't hurt you if you'll be still!"

A waste of breath. The boy kicked his knees against Matt's butt and again twisted between his legs.

"Stop it!" he bellowed. Why bother? Fat chance the kid understood him. Far superior in height, Matt slithered backward, forcing his captive's flailing legs flat to the ground. "Damn you," he gritted between labored breaths. "Cut it out!"

Suddenly, the youth obeyed. His head turned to the side as he sucked in air, and his chest heaved. For such a little squirt, he'd been as hard to subdue as a bobcat. He panted like one, too, no doubt gaining a second wind, for in the next instant he resumed writhing.

"Stop it!" Matt emphasized his order by lifting the boy's coat-covered wrists and slamming them hard into the ground.

It worked. He stilled. The much-too-large coat he wore lay open, skewed off one shoulder.

Matt stared at the kid's chest, eyes wide in disbelief. Firm breasts rounded beneath a buckskin tunic.

"You're a girl!"

Of course! An Indian might don shirts in the dead of winter, but those who'd died in the raid wore only breechclouts.

Matt sat on her thighs, his knees cradling her hips. Like all her kind, she stank to high heaven. Squaws occasionally went warring with their men, but rarely with such a small raiding party. A girl, he thought, dumbfounded. *Hell's fire. Tricked by a girl!*

"What the hell are you doing here?" Stupid. Did he expect her to answer . . . in English?

Her breathing had slowed, as had his. Her head was turned to the side, and black hair covered her face. Matt pulled her hands together over her head and clasped both in his right hand. He gathered her hair and moved it off her face. Though dirty as hell, the strands felt oddly fine; they weren't gummed with bear grease.

She sucked in a breath as she turned her head, eyes tightly closed. Probably expected him to kill her. Well, he hadn't intended to kill the boy, and he for sure wouldn't kill a girl.

Opening her eyes, she glared at him. He blinked once, twice. A frown furrowed his brow. *Violet?* An Indian with violet eyes?

"God-a-mighty. You're white!"

She planted her heels and thrust her hips up but couldn't budge his weight.

"*Naduah Nerm,*" she said, her voice breathless.

Woman of the People, he translated. "Like hell. You're as white as I am, little girl."

"*Naduah.* Wo . . . man," she whispered.

Surprise widened his eyes at her halting English. "Maybe," he conceded, but she sure hadn't grown very tall.

The coat's cuffs caught beneath his viselike grip around her wrists, he looked her over. Though small, her breasts rounded enticingly beneath the buckskin. He was certain his hands could span her narrow waist. Blood smeared her tunic. Probably the brave's; she'd fought too vigorously to be injured.

"You understand me, don't you?"

She said nothing, only glared at him with eyes dark with anger . . . and fear. Understandable. He, along with other Rangers, had killed a large number of Comanche. But he wouldn't apologize for that. No, sir.

Despite the grime on her face and neck, her skin was lighter than his. Her eyes tilted exotically at the corners like a cat's.

He tried again. "You speak English."

41

She shook her head.

"You just did."

"Little."

Though her efforts were futile, she again tried to buck off his one-hundred eighty pounds.

How long had she been a captive? She'd insisted she was a woman, but how old could she be? Sixteen, seventeen, maybe. Must have been with the Indians for years. But if that was true, how could she still understand him? Youngsters captured by Indians generally forgot English by the time they were retaken or ransomed.

She strained to free her wrists.

"Stop it!"

Heaving a sigh, she stilled again. So, what to do with her? If he took her to Steven Voight in Austin . . . He shook his head. Every woman he knew who'd been returned to the civilized world had either slit her throat or escaped back to the Indians. Not a one had been accepted back into white society.

The girl squirmed under his weight as Trooper stamped a foot. Matt looked up. Somehow, the pinto had gotten loose and stood no more than fifteen feet away, eyes trained on the girl. He glanced skyward. Darkness would be upon them in less than an hour. He needed to find a place to make camp.

The girl returned his glance warily. She wouldn't be docile, but he didn't want to hurt the little mite.

"I know you understand me." He paused. When she remained mute, he said. "I'm going to let you up, but don't try to run." *Oh, sure.* She'd be gone like a shot if given half a chance. Well, what the hell. He could catch her again.

42

Her wrists still snug in his hand, he worked his legs until he could get his feet planted beneath him, then stood. When he jerked her up, she flew to her feet, weightless as a bird. He frowned at that thought. No doubt she'd seen the buzzards' carnage on her friends' bodies. He was sorry for that, but it was too late to worry about it. Being sorry wouldn't bring back her life as a white child either.

Hell's fire, she'd been in the thick of that war party. Stop the maudlin musing and get on with it, Conway.

Suddenly, she dug in her heels and pulled back as hard as she could. Even through the coat's cuffs, he felt her delicate wrist bones grind beneath his grip. With little effort he could shatter them.

"If you don't settle down, you'll hurt yourself."

She quieted, but he could feel the tension in her body, poised for flight should he let go. He'd have to tie her. Ridiculously easy to drag her behind him. Still, she balked, stiffening her legs as he had against her pinto.

When Matt approached, Trooper backed as far as the reins would allow, ears pricked. Nervous from him bellowing at the girl, no doubt. "Whoa," he coaxed.

Pulling the girl close, he wrapped his other arm around her waist, hoisting her against his side. She draped over his arm like a sack of grain. Almost his undoing.

She kicked and pounded his thighs with her fists. He squeezed, cutting off her air. It worked long enough for him to rummage in his saddlebag for a length of rawhide. Unceremoniously, he dropped her, captured both her hands, and circled the leather around her

43

wrists before she could get a second wind. And all the while, he wondered what to do with her.

"No!" Her frustration sent the pinto dancing away.

"Afraid so. Until I figure out what's to be done with you."

Matt dragged her to Trooper. Yanking a short leather strip from the saddle horn, he tied it around the girl's neck, trailed it down her back, around her waist a couple times, and cinched it. He easily evaded her attempt to kick him in the shins. Feeding the rope through his hand, he mounted Trooper and kneed him toward the pinto. Though forced to follow, the girl strained against the rope, snapping it taut.

Catching up the mare's rope, he glanced from the girl to the mare and then at his occupied hands. Trooper was well-trained, but Matt couldn't ride with only his knees to guide him. His heart thudded as he did something he thought he'd never do in his lifetime. He looped the rope around his saddle horn, tethering the girl like an animal.

He'd heard stories of how Indians made captives walk behind their mounts as they were marched to villages. Usually stripped bare, sometimes forced to walk for miles, stumbling, falling, dragged until they were again allowed to regain their bare feet. That he wouldn't do. But tying her on the pinto could be a mistake. A big one.

When he looked down at her, she was busy pulling at the leather around her wrists with her teeth. He jerked the rope, which nearly brought her to her knees.

"Quit!"

She scowled but lowered her hands. Clearly, she understood him. Twilight was upon them. A breeze had kicked up, sending the scent of sagebrush into the air. Spying his hat lying where they'd fought in the dirt, he groaned. He lifted his leg over the pommel and slid to the ground. Fortunately, Trooper stood as though nailed to the spot.

Mare in tow, Matt retrieved his hat and clamped it on his head. As he remounted, he recalled the stream he'd crossed, a good-sized offshoot of the San Saba. He could camp there, then head home tomorrow. He reined Trooper and started off at a walk. The girl resisted and said something in Comanche.

"Look," he snapped, "until I figure out what to do with you, you'll come along. You might as well do it quietly."

She shook her head and spat something in Comanche, jabbing her bound hands toward a clump of brush.

"What?"

She chewed her lower lip with extraordinarily white teeth, then raised those incredible violet eyes. "Blanket." She pointed again.

Of course! She had a bedroll stashed. It took a few minutes to find it and a small satchel. Stolen, no doubt. After securing them with his gear, he remounted and nudged Trooper to a walk. He wouldn't drag the girl.

As he rode, he thought about the Mexican couple who worked for him. They were more like family than help, and he dreaded Xavier and Lupe's fit-to-be-tied reaction to his latest insanity. It would be far better for all concerned if he tossed the girl on the pinto and sent her on her way. His sudden determination not to do so made no sense. She might have white skin and light eyes, but in every way that counted she was Comanche.

Fear knotted in White Fawn's chest like a clenched fist. Panting, unable to draw a deep breath, she stumbled behind the the big man atop his gray gelding. She gazed north, fearful she would never see Eagle Feather, Bright Star, and Willow Branch again. Or her brothers . . .

Her ankle turned on a rock, and she wrenched her head forward to watch her step. The white man drew rein and looked back at her. His deep brown eyes missed nothing as they flicked her length, then settled back on her face. Her breath stuttered until he turned and once more sent his horse forward.

Maybe he would take her back to the cabin and add her body to the warriors'. Perhaps that would not be so bad. She would simply be dead, no longer trussed up like an animal.

Her wrists hurt where the man had held them earlier, though the snug rawhide did not bite into her flesh. Actually, it was hard to tell what part of her hurt the most: chest, shoulder, or the wound that burned beneath her coat sleeve. He had not discovered it, and she would not tell him.

A while later, he dismounted, tied Pepper and his mount, then stalked toward her. In the dark, his body loomed over her, more frightening than in daylight.

"We'll camp here." He led her to a tree. "Sit." He wound the rope around her waist and tied it out of reach behind the tree trunk.

46

Shortly, a tiny flame grew to dance amid a small pile of sticks. Unless someone was very close, the glow would not be seen through the dense grass and brush.

It made no difference. No one looked for her. Perhaps Eagle Feather would send out a search party. But he was an old man and liked his comforts, such as they were. Lost in despair, she turned her thoughts to Beaver Heart and Black Crow. They might ask to look for her, though Straight Arrow would not. He had never said much, usually ignoring her presence. She jumped when the man spoke.

"You probably need a minute alone."

She had not relieved herself since morning. Add that discomfort to her fear, and it was no wonder her stomach hurt. He knelt in front of her, his back to the fire. She peered up at him, unable to see his shadowed face. Only his overpowering size.

"Listen, girl. Wandering in these parts is dangerous for more reasons than you can count."

Starting with you.

"Bears and cats roam here, not to mention snakes. I'll untie your hands but not the rope."

She blinked. She hoped he would not follow her into the brush while she squatted.

"The lariat is long enough for you to get out of the light behind some bushes, but I'm hanging on to it. Sorry, I don't trust you."

Suddenly, she remembered something she had forgotten during the day. Her thoughts had circled futilely in an effort to figure a way to escape. Now she felt it. The man had not discovered the knife strapped to her thigh.

Matt studied her stoic expression. She certainly gave nothing away. Other than the fact that she hated his guts. Loosening the rope, he pulled her up. He was struck again by her tiny size. The top of her head didn't reach his chin. As he stuffed the thong in his duster, she watched him, eyes wide and wary, then rubbed her wrists.

This was a helluva note. It was one thing for a man to take a piss around other men but quite another for a woman to do so.

He inclined his head. "Over there." He turned her around and nudged her shoulder to send her ahead of him. Pausing, he gave her a good amount of lead until she stepped behind the natural cover. "That's far enough."

She sank out of sight. Living with the Comanche, she had probably squatted wherever and whenever the spirit moved her. He doubted modesty was a Comanche trait. He waited for several minutes, then felt the rope tighten.

"You through?" When she remained quiet and didn't appear, he frowned. "Hey . . ." *Girl? Woman?* He'd have to ask her name. "Hey," he repeated, and started toward the bushes.

Unprepared, Matt staggered when she suddenly leaped up and came at him. Then he saw it. A blade glinted in the firelight, the haft clutched in her hand as she lunged.

"Damn!" He sidestepped, but not quickly enough. The blade caught his coat sleeve midway between his elbow and shoulder. Pain shot up his arm as steel grazed flesh. "Shit!" Blindly, he reached for her as she attacked again. Catching her wrist, he raised his arm, jerked her off her feet and, circling her waist with his other arm, crushed her against his frame as he went down on his side.

Clawing at his fingers, she bucked and kicked. God, did she kick, catching him in the shin twice. He was glad of her moccasins. Had she worn boots, she'd have cracked the bone.

"Ah!" she yelped when he bent back her hand. It would take very little to break it. Her fingers straightened. The knife plopped on the dirt inches from her flying hair.

Here they were again, his body pinning hers to the ground. The girl didn't have a prayer of overpowering him, but he couldn't help admiring her spunk . . . if it killed him. And she'd certainly intended to. A few inches closer and the blade would have plunged into his heart.

He levered himself up enough to allow her to breathe and looked down into furious eyes. Hate laced with fear speared him as deftly as she'd tried to do with the blade. In spite of it, he grinned. "You missed."

Though his arm burned like a son-of-a-gun, he'd be damned if he'd let her know that.

Either his grin or words provoked a string of Comanche he couldn't understand. Spittle sprayed from her mouth. "Hate you!" she screamed. "Off me!"

"Well, well, you do speak English."

She stilled. Tears sheened her eyes. Frustration, no doubt. He'd feel the same in her position.

Despite the God-awful odor from her unwashed body, Matt found himself inexplicably responding to her soft form. He didn't know what this woman had endured at the hands of the Comanche, or what she'd seen in his eyes, but abject fear leaped into hers.

"No!" she wailed, pitiful as a small child.

As though he'd been dropped in an icy river, his blood cooled. What the . . . She had curves in the right places, but dammit to hell, she was a girl, young and vulnerable. At his mercy.

Matt scrambled to his feet and drew her up at the same time. "Hey, I said I wouldn't hurt you. I meant it." He scooped up the knife and waved it in her face. "But you're not going to skewer me either."

Shaking, eyes round as she scanned his face for the truth, she crossed her arms and hugged herself. Slowly, her gaze traveled over him. He looked down. His dark-stained coat sleeve revealed the injury.

He glanced at her again. Hell. She was barely keeping tears at bay, and her lips trembled. She thought he meant to kill her.

An owl hooted. A twig snapped and popped in the fire. The girl jumped. Her fingers clutched the too-big coat covering her slim torso.

Dangerous she was, but dammit if she'd settle down . . . No matter that his body had betrayed him a moment ago. Somehow he needed to reassure her.

"What's your name? I can't call you *girl* or *hey*."

Stubborn as a Missouri mule when it came to speaking English, she gave her name in Comanche. "White Fawn?" he translated.

She nodded. He wondered if a squaw or brave had

given her the name. A brave . . . How many had she lain with?

"Mine's Matt . . . Matthew Conway. We Conway men are big galoots, but we don't harm women." Now, there was a barefaced lie. Though he never deliberately aimed at women or children, he'd seen plenty cut down in the heat of battle. Hell's fire, it was necessary. Dammit, they were fighting a war. The Comanche knew it, too. And why was he trying to comfort her after she'd tried her damnedest to kill him? He must be losing his mind.

Turning on his heel, Matt jammed the knife in his belt and drew on the rope. Docile for the moment, she followed. Maybe she'd come to the conclusion he wouldn't be bamboozled. Being slammed to the ground had to hurt.

Matt took care of the horses and generally ignored the girl. She had to be as exhausted as he. Surely she'd sleep. If she didn't, he wouldn't either. Silently, she took the hardtack he handed her. Damned if he would hunt game in the dark. He'd rustle up something more tasty for breakfast.

The fire had dwindled to embers, and still White Fawn lay wide awake. Matt—Matthew Conway had trussed her securely to the tree. After she'd eaten, he'd retied her hands. Tears welled as she stared through the branches overhead. Between the leaves stars sparkled, distant and brittle as ice crystals.

She shivered, though she was not cold. Besides the coat, the white man had thrown the blanket to her. Bedded down on the other side of the fire, he lay on his back, his head propped on his saddle. He had removed his gun belt before lying down. Unholstered, his gun lay at his side, his hand resting on the grip. Asleep he might be, but she had the feeling the slightest sound would bring him to his feet as quick as a snake's strike.

What did he plan to do with her? How could she escape? These questions repeated over and over in her tired mind. She squeezed her eyes shut. It had been sheer folly to try to kill him. As frightened as she was, as much as she hated what his companions had done to her tribesmen, she did not really want to kill him or anyone else. She simply longed to find Eagle Feather and be comforted by Bright Star.

Comfort . . . Oddly, Conway had seemed to want to provide that for her. *"Hate you!"* Turning on her side, she drew up her knees and pulled the blanket tight over her shoulder. Ice trickled through her veins as she stared at the big man.

Though she had yet to lie with a brave, she knew what the heat in the man's eyes foretold. Of late, One Bear had looked at her like that. The same gleam had lit Eagle Feather's eyes when he gazed at Bright Star or Willow Branch. After bedding down, she often heard rustlings and moans from whichever wife he took to his blankets for the night.

Though the chosen woman looked content the next morning, White Fawn knew men could use women cruelly. Rape, it was called in the white man's language. She knew of white women who had died after Indians finished with them, and of Indian women who suffered the same fate from white men.

Though she didn't believe One Bear would have used

her thusly, she had never looked forward to lying with him. Nevertheless, she would have. It was expected of her. She would have mated with him and borne his children. She loved children. That part she had looked forward to.

Her thoughts returned to Matt—Matthew Conway. In the one moment a rare smile had transformed his handsome face, he had seemed . . . gentle. She knew firsthand that he was big and strong. He picked her up or slammed her to the ground as easily as he would swat a mosquito.

The man had proved more dangerous than she had imagined. Her fear had come to pass.

She was in his power.

Chapter Four

As the sun lit the sky to orange the next morning, while Matt bathed in the river, the rabbit he'd shot earlier sizzled over a small fire. The pool he'd chosen, formed in a wide spot in the river, was surprisingly deep, over his head. Cold and refreshing, the cleansing water gave him a chance to take a closer look at the nick on his arm. It was an inch long and shallow, and already on the mend. He'd been lucky. Soap stung the scratches where she had marked his neck.

Before climbing out of the water buck-naked, he peered at White Fawn. Assured she still slept with her back to him, he leaped ashore. Several days ago he'd foregone his Union suit because the weather had turned warmer. He shrugged into a clean shirt, then pulled on his jeans. As he picked up his belt, White Fawn turned to her back, threw the blanket to her waist, and stared at the tree overhead. As if a poker had been rammed down her back, she sat up abruptly.

"Good morning," he said.

Mute, as usual, she nodded, which was as cordial as

she'd probably get. White Fawn was not one to talk much, even in Comanche, so she wasn't apt to be congenial. Instead, she'd probably be as full of spit and fire as a cornered cougar when he told her that he expected her to bathe.

Picking up his dirty clothes, he ambled over to his saddle. He rolled the dirty garments and stuffed them into one saddlebag, then drew out his last clean shirt.

He shook it out and stared at White Fawn. Seated, her back pressed against the tree trunk, she eyed him as he approached. Matt squatted in front of her. Maybe if he smiled it would put her at ease and make what he had to say more palatable.

All his smile accomplished was the rounding of her expressive eyes, a clear signal that she awaited execution. He untied her hands. "White Fawn, I, uh . . . want you to change into this shirt after you take a bath."

"No," she whispered. Glancing from him to the river and back, she shook her head for emphasis.

"Look, you stink," he said bluntly. "I'll let you ride the pony today, but I have to tie you. That means I have to get close to you. You stink," he repeated, unsmiling this time, and *she* had the nerve to look offended. "Take off your moccasins."

She didn't move. Her gaze darted around, as though she hoped to find help. He reached for her foot, determined to have his way. She shinnied her back up the tree, and shook her head so violently, he expected it to come unhinged.

"God-a-mighty, I'm only asking that you bathe and wash your dress." He extended the shirt to her. "You can wear this until it dries."

If he'd thought this would be easy, he was barking into an empty hole. He sighed, dropped the shirt, and reached for her. She came alive like that cougar he'd thought about. Fight! Hell, she could wiggle faster than a sidewinder. His chest heaved by the time he got her moccasins off, found and removed the knife sheath tied around her leg, and then untied the rope.

She whirled to run. He clamped a hand on her shoulder and swung her into his arms with ease. "You need a bath. You'll wash that dress," he bellowed as he carried her to the riverbank.

"No!"

He tossed her in, several feet from the bank.

"No! I no sw—" She landed with a mighty splash, sending water high into the air.

Matt clamped his hands on his hips, satisfaction lighting his eyes. She would take a bath or he'd know the reason why, by God. Her hands broke the surface, clawing for something solid. The rest of her remained underwater. Just as well. A good soaking would do her good.

Gloating, he soon began to wonder why she didn't poke up her head. He lowered his arms, waited. Her words finally registered.

"Hell's fire!" He ripped off his shirt and dove in.

Fortunately, the water was clear as a looking glass. He saw her immediately, dog-paddling, going nowhere. He tangled his fingers in her hair and hauled her to the surface. As he unwound the heavy, wet tresses from his hand, several strands pulled from her scalp and remained tangled around his fingers like cobwebs. He hoisted her against him, her head upon his shoulder.

She coughed and sputtered in his ear as he swam the

three strokes it took to touch bottom and stepped up on the bank. He lowered her to the ground, an arm around her waist. She leaned over his forearm as water gushed from her mouth.

"Why the *hell* haven't you learned to swim? For that matter, you could have *walked* to shallow water," he fumed.

"No reason." She gasped and straightened.

"Why doesn't that surprise me?" he snapped. He released her, and she slumped to the ground, still gagging. Head hanging, her face hidden behind the fall of dripping hair, she reminded him of a drowned cat.

"Is no quicker way kill me, Mr. Ranger?"

"If I wanted to kill you, I'd have done so before now." His glare of displeasure that she'd think him low enough to kill a girl was lost on her; she didn't look at him. "I wanted you to take a bath. I *still* want you to. Why do you think I'm a Ranger?"

She swept the wet hair over her shoulder and lifted her head. Matt blinked. Though rivulets of dirty water slipped down her throat, her face was rather clean, and she was . . . pretty. White Fawn no longer had the milk-white skin some women prized. Her skin had been kissed by the sun to a burnished hue that spoke of health, and freedom to roam.

"Shoot good. Ride good," she said.

Collecting his muddled thoughts, he said, "I was. Now I'm a simple cattleman."

She narrowed her extraordinary eyes. "No *simple*, you."

Matt picked up his shirt and shoved his arms into the sleeves. Maybe she was right. Few people were simple, but one thought had driven him since his folks died: to make a go of the ranch his father had carved out of the Texas soil. True, he'd sandwiched in a two-year stint with the Rangers. In the meanwhile, his dream of a thriving cattle ranch had been carried on by Xavier and hired hands.

Matt glanced down at the wet jeans hugging his thighs. He'd have to wear the dirty pair until these dried. No way would he sit a saddle in wet pants.

Suddenly, he swung around, remembering—and smelling—charred meat. "Dammit!" He leaped the few yards to the fire, grabbed for the green stick the rabbit was impaled upon, and burned his hand. The rabbit hit the dirt.

He looked up at the sky, frustration steaming in his brain. *Will nothing go right today?* He was hungry. The girl must be, too, and now . . .

"Brush off the dirt, Mr. Ranger," she said quietly.

The last straw! Matt rounded on her and took a menacing step in her direction. "Dammit, if you don't get in that water to bathe, I *am* going to drown you!"

Duck-walking backward, she put up her hands, eyes wide. Oh, great. Now he'd *really* scared this slip of a girl. Still, he bellowed, "Stop calling me *Mr. Ranger*. My name is Matt . . . Matthew Conway!"

She nodded agreement, again giving him the impression her head would fly from her shoulders. She backed into the stream until she was waist deep. "I do." She dipped her hands into the water and scrubbed her face; clearly, she knew he'd been pushed far enough. "I do," she repeated.

He picked up the soap and tossed it to her. "I'm going to turn my back." He pointed at the clean shirt on the ground. "Put that on when you finish. But, by God, if you run, if you give me any more trouble . . ." He let the threat hang.

He could see the wheels turning. *You are bigger than I, so I'm forced to do your bidding. But I do not like it.*

Too damn bad. Matt turned his back, pulled on his socks and boots, then salvaged what he could of the rabbit. His ears attuned to her splashing, he listened carefully; all was quiet from that quarter after several minutes.

"Are you decent?" When she didn't answer, he glanced over his shoulder. Air whooshed from his lungs. White Fawn looked like a water nymph, small and . . . desirable.

She sat by the tree, bare legs tucked under her. His shirt engulfed her body, the sleeves rolled several times. She held a pair of scissors poised to cut off a long hank of hair.

"What the hell do you think you're doing?"

She jumped, dropped the scissors and glanced his way. He kicked them out of her reach. Now that her hair was cleaner, it was beautiful. Why would she cut it?

She grabbed for the scissors. "Mourn people!"

"Mourn your people, my foot!" He'd heard of the practice. Indian women did more than cut their hair; they cut their arms, whatever body part was handy. Jesus, all sorts of self-mutilation. A helluva way to mourn the dead. He wouldn't allow it.

"Braid it," he snapped.

She did, glaring even as her fingers worked.

Matt used the scissors to cut a piece of leather from

the thong he'd used to bind her hands and tossed it to her. As she tied the end of the braid that hung to her waist, he spied the scissors' tin. Secreted in her blanket, no doubt. Hell, she could have stabbed him with those, too.

He picked up her soggy dress and shook it. As he spread the wet skin over a bush, he frowned. A little hole . . . Looking at her, he visually measured from the base of her throat to her heart. *Holy shit.* That bullet had gone through the warrior and . . . Motioning at her chest, he asked, "Where?"

Blank for a second, she finally reached inside the open collar and drew out an amulet. Flattened beyond recognition, a spent lead was embedded in the circle of metal. The impact must have felt as if it had buried itself in her breastbone.

He glanced up and found her expression stoic. No wonder she mistrusted all white men. If not for that amulet, she'd be dead. Add that to the times he'd tackled her, then thrown her into water over her head . . .

"Eagle Feather gift," she whispered, fingering the dull metal.

Eagle Feather. The one who'd tried to save her? Though young, Comanches often took girls barely in their teens to their blankets. His fingers curled into fists. Had she resisted? Probably not. A *naduah,* a woman, in every sense of the word. Envisioning her beneath an Indian, he felt bile churn in his belly.

A bird's squawk and fluttering wings jolted him. He cleared his throat and flattened his hand on his own chest. "Are you hurt here?"

She said nothing, still gazing at the gift she apparently treasured. He didn't pressure her. A useless question, anyway. Even if her chest was sore, she fought well enough.

Still, there was the bloody cloth he'd found. "Are you hurt anywhere else?"

Again hesitant, she slowly pushed up the shirt's sleeve. A quarter-inch-deep slash creased her forearm. Any lower and the bone would have shattered.

He'd arrived in time to see her riding behind the warrior on the horse, her arms wrapped around his torso. The bullet must have plowed through her arm, then lost enough power as it passed through the warrior's body to stop in the amulet.

"That should be bandaged so it won't get dirty," he said in a gruffer voice than he'd intended.

She pointed to the duffel. He found cloth like he'd picked up by the stream.

They ate what he'd salvaged of the rabbit, the only sounds those of waking wildlife. Matt poured coffee into his one and only tin cup and handed it to her. She shook her head. Lord, the silence this girl—woman—maintained was enough to drive him nuts. Though he avoided chattering females, one this quiet taxed his nerves. He gulped the brew and burned his tongue. Cursing under his breath, he broke camp. If he intended to be home tomorrow, they had to move.

White Fawn stared at the rump of Matt-Matthew's big gelding, her tied wrists poised over Pepper's mane. She clutched the coarse horsehair. He had refused to put the reins in her hands. A rope surrounded one wrist, trailed down to circle one ankle, under Pepper's belly to her other ankle, then back to her other wrist.

Even if she dared try to loosen the knots with her teeth, it would take forever. She was trapped.

With the sun now past its zenith, she gazed longingly over her shoulder. Two days they had traveled south, farther and farther from the *Llano Estacado* and her people.

Eagle Feather. He and his tipi had become her refuge. Her gaze settled on the Ranger's broad shoulders. She shook her head. She must stop thinking of him as a Ranger. Matt-Matthew was his name.

At her mention of Eagle Feather, his expression had become fierce. He appeared ready to strangle her.

Speaking English had proved less and less difficult. If she were to convince this man to let her go, she would need his language. Fear and despair nearly overpowered her when she thought of how white people would look upon her, would treat her.

She would be better off dead.

She stared, mesmerized by the play of muscles beneath his dusty white shirt, then looked at the one he had given her. The shirttails covered her knees, the tops of her moccasins hidden beneath the hem. Such a big man.

She remembered her reaction when she had seen him without a shirt. River water beaded on his muscular chest and belly, caught like diamonds in the V of dark hair that arrowed down to his trouser's waistband.

"You will experience desire one day." Willow Branch

had chuckled at White Fawn's discomfort with the subject she dwelled upon as the time approached for White Fawn to mate with One Bear.

"I don't think so," she'd argued. She definitely had not looked forward to a life of servitude, her lot had One Bear lived. Though he would not have mistreated her, a Comanche woman's work was endless. It was simply the way of life among the People.

Even knowing that Eagle Feather would give her to another warrior—and he would—eventually, her wish to return home remained strong. Unless she chose to become a warrior woman, for which she did not have the stomach, she would be dependent upon a man.

She looked at Conway again. Unbidden thoughts of mating with him flitted through her mind. Her gaze skittered away uncomfortably. She did not fully understand her awakening body, the desire Willow Branch foretold. One thing she knew with certainty: Conway was a threat to her.

"Are you thirsty?"

Her thoughts were snuffed like a doused fire. Engrossed in her musings, she had not realized Pepper had plodded to a halt. Conway's horse angled crosswise on the trail, blocking her.

Yes, thirsty, and not just for water. Not just from dust in her mouth and unrelenting sun beating down on her back and thighs.

Nudging his mount closer, he reached for the Army-issue canteen tied to his saddle.

She wiped the mouthpiece and gulped her fill. The warm water washed away the dust clogging her throat.

"Thank you." Handing back the canteen, she wiped her mouth with the back of her hand.

He took a long drink himself, surprising her when he did not wipe off the mouthpiece. Heat settled in her stomach. What would Conway taste like?

"We'll be at my place in a couple of hours."

No. "Why take there?"

"That's the safest place."

"No belong there. Eagle Feather . . ." His expression darkened, but she pressed on. "Indian now. Wish return my people."

"Don't think so. You may have lived with them a long time, but you're as white as I." His mouth thinned. "I'm not sending you back to those savages."

Heat suffused her cheeks. "People no savage! Eagle Feather kind. Counsel no war."

"Yeah? Then why were you riding with a raiding party? Those arrows weren't toys. Your *people*," he sneered, "were bent on thievery and destruction."

"One Bear no have kill white man, no shoot him. Eagle Feather no ride to war." Because this white man would not believe her, she shook her head when he asked another question.

"What's your name?"

She bit her lip. She had already told him.

"Your *white* name. I know you have one."

He cocked his head, reminding her of an inquisitive bobcat she had once seen. She had laughed, thinking him cute, poised over a hole, intent, until . . . She shuddered at what the cat had done to a defenseless prairie dog.

This man was even more dangerous than that bobcat.

Her white family was no more. She would not tell him the name the priest had given her. "White Fawn name, Conway."

A chuckle bared his teeth, so white compared to One Bear's. Breath stalled when she again wondered what he would taste like. So confusing! One moment she was angry with him, the next . . . He did not even like her! Fear of him should override any such thoughts.

"Conway, is it?" When she did not respond to his question, he shrugged. "That'll do for now. Beats Mr. Ranger." He paused. "I'll find out eventually."

Pepper stamped a foot. Trooper snorted and sashayed sideways. Conway squeezed the gelding's flanks with his powerful legs. "Ho," he cautioned, his gaze still on her.

"Know not where live long ago. No how many years been since left white world." According to Bright Star, White Fawn would have been with them for eighteen summers.

The smile never left his lips. She could not halt her wayward thought. *So handsome*. His dark eyes bored into her as if to divine her thoughts.

Silently assessing, he shrugged again. "We'll see. I'm pretty good at what I do."

"Say rancher."

His eyes fairly danced when he laughed. "That, too."

Breaking from the trees surrounding his home, Matt reined in Trooper. Every time he returned after days away, gladness stirred within as he looked upon the dogtrot house he'd rebuilt. Alone. Grieving following the deaths of his loved ones.

He'd cleared the burned rubble, then built a larger house. This time there were windows in every room, high off the ground so Indians couldn't easily enter.

Satisfied, he noticed that the barn had been completely finished and his men were busy building a corral adjacent to the pitched-roof barn. Even as he watched, Lars Gunnerson, the big Swede, picked up a post as easily as though it were a matchstick, balanced it on his shoulder, then stepped forward and dropped it into the hole. Two feet of the eight-foot pole disappeared into the ground.

The instant Matt nudged Trooper forward, both his men dove for rifles propped against already standing fence, swung around, and leveled the rifles at him. When they recognized him, grins creased their sun-baked faces.

"Hey, boss!" Hoby lowered his rifle. Gunnerson, always more cautious than the younger man, who followed him around like a son, was slower to drop his.

"Hoby." Matt rode toward them. Lars nodded but said nothing. His pale blue eyes narrowed as he took in the horse and rider behind Matt.

Lars had lost two brothers in an Indian raid and was not pleased to see White Fawn. Though she still wore Matt's shirt, her moccasins screamed Comanche.

"Jesus, where'd you find her?" Hoby asked, his brown eyes wide with wonder.

"A few days' ride north of here." Matt didn't hide the direction they'd ridden. White Fawn had looked back often enough to know they'd headed south.

Matt glanced at her as Hoby walked nearer. Though she often looked frightened of him, now she was petrified, her gaze locked on Lars. Of the three men, the Swede was the proverbial gentle giant. Though he hated Comanches, he'd be the last to threaten her.

"Holy shit!" Hoby exclaimed. "She's got blue eyes."

No. Her eyes are violet, Matt thought.

She raised her leg, shifting her weight as far from Hoby as the rope would allow. White-knuckled, she clutched the pony's mane.

Matt found Hoby eyeing her with unbridled lust. Though young, she would be considered fair game. Without regret, white men forced Indian women to submit. If white women managed to survive captivity, those same men often forced them to their beds or killed them.

"Hoby," Matt warned, his voice flinty.

The man reluctantly left off his perusal. Blinking, he backed away from Matt's glare.

Comanche she might think herself, but Matt would protect her. He'd looked upon her almost as lustfully until he'd considered how young she must be. "She's just a kid. You're not to touch her, Varner."

"But, boss . . ."

Dark eyes steady, Matt slowly shook his head. "I'll say it only once more. You are not to touch her."

Hoby's grin was anything but amused. "Shit, she's probably spread her legs for half . . ." He clamped his mouth shut at Matt's expression. Hand raised defensively, Hoby backed away. "Okay, I get the message, boss."

If she'd lain with half a dozen Indians, she'd still come to no harm in his care. She had spunk to spare. Probably hated his guts. But she respected his greater strength and expertise with a gun.

"Back to work." Lars nudged Hoby's shoulder.

At that moment, Mutt set up a ruckus that would wake the dead. The huge dog sailed off the porch, followed by Susy and several of her equally noisy pups.

Spooked by the cacophony, the Indian pinto reared and neighed. Had White Fawn not been clinging to the pony's mane, she'd have doubtless fallen. With bound feet and hands, she'd have hung helplessly beside the horse's churning legs.

Matt managed to keep his own seat and wind in the mare. "Mutt, shut up!"

The dog quieted in mid-bark. It took the pups a minute more to get the message. Still, they sniffed around the horses' hooves, their brown and buff-colored butts high and tails flying.

"Git!" Matt snapped.

Susy and Mutt backed off, but not the untrained pups.

Lars raised a foot and clipped one in the rump. Though not hurt, the pup yipped and scuttled away, tail tucked between his legs. The pack followed, headed back to hide under the house. Susy ambled after them, but Mutt planted himself next to Lars. Matt could only guess at Mutt's breed. Mastiff, shepherd, and maybe lab thrown in for good measure. Tongue lolling to one side, eyes on Matt, he appeared to await further orders.

From the corner of his eye, Matt saw his housekeeper step to the edge of the porch. But he turned to White Fawn. "You okay?"

The girl nodded, then mulishly jutted out her chin and stared straight forward.

"She speaks English?" Lars asked, astonished.

"She doesn't say much in Comanche or English, but she understands."

Reining Trooper toward the house, Matt glanced toward Hoby again. The revelation that White Fawn spoke English had further piqued his interest. Damn, what the hell was he going to do with the girl?

And now he must face Lupe, who would think . . .

Well, who knew what she'd think? The woman never reacted the way he expected. Not quite old enough to be his mother, she nevertheless treated him like a wayward son.

Frowning, hands planted at her waist, she turned dark eyes from him to White Fawn, then back to him. "Trouble follows you like a blue norther, Matt. Looks like this time you've lassoed it and brought it home."

"Maybe you're right." He grinned, glad to see the well-educated, no-nonsense woman.

Neither she nor Xavier cared two cents for Indians and would as soon see every last one dead. Hell, most of their lives they'd been one step ahead of Comanches intending to scalp them. Not until the Cruzes had moved in with him had they known a modicum of peace.

Lupe had a soft spot for kids, and White Fawn looked like a child. But they'd never been blessed with children of their own. Surely Lupe wouldn't be stiff-backed and mean to the girl.

"Where's Xavier?"

Lupe hiked her chin toward the south. "Couple of the hands thought they saw several cows close to dropping calves. He'll bring them to the barn if he finds them."

Matt pushed back his hat. That was one of the problems when cattle roamed open country. If they got into any kind of trouble, it was devilishly tricky to find them.

"Matt?"

His gaze snapped back to Lupe.

"You plan to sit there the rest of the day? You've got that girl trussed up like a goose. An unhappy goose, from the looks of her. Get her down and come in."

Lupe was right. White Fawn, stoic as ever, stared forward with nary a blink. But she wasn't just unhappy. More likely, she was mad as thunder at him for bringing her here. But if he let her go, she'd hightail it to the Indians. She did *not* belong with them. And he didn't give a good grunt what she thought.

He slid off Trooper and began untying her wrists, glancing up and meeting sparkling eyes. Yep. Fearful, frustrated, and mad.

When the rope fell away, Matt clasped her arm and pulled, expecting her to swing her leg and slide to the ground. She didn't. Instead, she grabbed for the horse's mane, missed, and toppled sideways, landing with a thud on the ground.

"Hell's fire!" he exclaimed.

At the same time, Lupe yelled, "Matt! What are you trying to do? Kill her?"

"No!" Matt crouched, slid his hands under White Fawn's slight body, and lifted her as easily as one of the pups.

He looked down at her nestled against his chest. Eyes closed, hands clenched, she hadn't made a sound. Not when she grabbed for the mane. Not when she hit the ground. Not when he picked her up.

She fit as if made for his arms. Her warm womanly scent teased his hunger. Those wayward thoughts made him angry—at himself.

"Dammit, are you all right?"

"Great, Matt. Reassured by your *gentle* tone. She speaks English?"

"Hell, yes. When she speaks." He glared at White Fawn. "You could have told me you needed help dismounting!"

She glared right back, still mute in his arms. This girl would try the patience of God. And, God knew, *he* was no saint.

Lupe rolled her eyes heavenward, walking into the breezeway past Matt's room to the second door on the right. Mockingly, she swept her arm for him to carry the girl inside. "I guess this will have to do. It's the only room we have."

True. Matt occupied one room and Lupe and Xavier slept in another. A fourth served as a parlor and dining room.

Lupe cooked in the open under a lean-to attached to the back of the house. Though she never complained, Matt had vowed to enclose it this summer. He knew it was miserable and cold in the winter. Wind whipped around the building. Just keeping a fire going in the stone fireplace was a chore.

"Are you going to put her down?"

He grimaced. God-a-mighty, his mind was mush today. White Fawn scowled at him. No surprise there. "Can you stand?"

She nodded. He slid his arm from beneath her legs and allowed her feet to touch the ground, though he still clasped her against his chest. When she looked up, frowning a question, he muttered, "Got your feet under you this time?"

He sighed when she didn't answer, didn't nod. Did nothing but stare at him from the most beautiful eyes any woman had a right to. Too hard on a man's . . . heart.

Withdrawing his arm quickly, he turned to Lupe, who eyed him with disapproval.

"Why is she wearing your shirt? Where are her clothes?" Before he could respond, she raised an admonishing finger. "Matthew Conway, have you been fast and loose with this child?"

Matt closed his eyes, took a steadying breath and looped his fingers in his belt. "No." Opening his eyes, he gritted through his teeth, "Dammit, Lupe, you know I wouldn't—"

"Clean up your mouth. I've heard nothing but foul language since you—"

"All right!" Exasperated right down to his boot tops, he flapped his arms. "I haven't done one thing but make her take a bath. She stank enough to blind a man. She's wearing my shirt because her tunic was wet. It's still wet, dam— . . . It's still wet."

Aware of White Fawn's interest, he saw her gaze dart from him to Lupe. He knew she thought Lupe was getting the best of this conversation.

White Fawn bared her oh-so-white teeth in a derisive smile.

She might as well have hit him in the chest with an arrow. His entire body shut down. *Breathe*. His mouth suddenly as dry as the prairie, he couldn't moisten his lips to save his soul.

White Fawn wasn't simply pretty. She was beautiful.

He whirled about and gained the door in two strides. "Find something decent for her to wear after you make her bathe again. And keep an eye on her. She's wily as a wolf!" He slammed the door.

The entire house shook on its foundation.

Chapter Five

Looking at the closed door trembling on its hinges, White Fawn fought her apprehension at Matt-Matthew Conway's anger. When the woman called Lupe faced her, she backed against the wall. Lupe's work-roughened hands settled on her hips, and she eyed White Fawn with . . . not anger. Curiosity, perhaps.

The lady smiled. "His bark is worse than his bite."

White Fawn knew better. "Kill my people." Not exactly true, but he was there.

"Ah. You do speak English." Lupe's gaze traveled White Fawn's length, then returned to her face. "Perhaps, but I'd bet he had reason. How many Texans did your people kill?"

Answering that question would gain her nothing. Instead, White Fawn reasoned, "No belong here. Let go."

"Probably should, but I won't. For some reason where sense doesn't enter, Matt says we'll keep you. That means you'll stay here on the Rocking C."

She means this ranch. C for Conway. White men put down roots wherever they went and named the land.

Eagle Feather had laughed at the practice. *"The earth belongs to no one. Would you catch the wind in your hands and name it?"*

"What will you wear?"

Lupe's words abruptly silenced Eagle Feather's voice in her head. Her buckskin dress had probably shrunk. The first garment she had tanned on her own, it was poorly done.

"Come, I won't hurt you," Lupe said.

She had heard that from Conway. Her bruises proved he lied. Not exactly lied. If she had not run . . . She backed toward the door. She was younger, more agile than the other woman; perhaps she could get to it and escape before Lupe caught her. Undecided, she glanced over her shoulder to measure the distance. A mistake.

Lupe lunged and clamped strong fingers around White Fawn's wrist. "You are to bathe, girl."

"No."

She pulled, but Lupe's grip was unyielding. With her other hand, the taller woman caught her fingers in the shirt's placket and yanked downward. Buttons flew as the shirt opened, revealing White Fawn's naked body.

"No!" She twisted her wrist but to no avail.

Lupe, as strong as any man White Fawn had faced, whipped her around as easily as a child, clasped the shirt's collar, and ripped it from her back. White Fawn dropped to her knees, arms around her body in an effort to cover herself.

Lupe sucked in a breath. "God have mercy!"

Crouched on the floor, White Fawn looked up. One hand covered Lupe's mouth, the other clutched the shirt to her breast. Her dark eyes rounded, her expression startled.

Lupe's mouth thinned. Fury sparked in her eyes. White Fawn turned her head, expecting a blow. It didn't come. Instead, Lupe stepped around her to the narrow bed, ripped off the quilt, and threw it at her.

"You won't go anywhere without clothes. Cover yourself while I bring water."

She left the room, turning the key in the lock, leaving White Fawn dazed and wondering. She sat still for several seconds, her arms wrapped protectively around her body, her fingers dug into her sides. Watching the closed door, she snatched up the quilt, threw it around her shoulders, and scooted back against the wall.

Legs raised, she wrapped her arms around her knees and hugged them close to her chest, making herself as small as possible.

She studied her surroundings. The only furnishings were a narrow bed, a waist-high bureau, and a ladder-backed chair. Craning her head, she saw a window high in the wall. Even if she could reach it by standing on the chair, she could go nowhere without clothes.

With her forehead on her knees, tears welled. She counted backward. Two days traveling with Conway, a day or two alone, two days at the rancher's cabin. And four days riding with the band. Nine days from the village.

She had to convince her captor that she must return to her people. If she could find them. If she could find them. The men outside . . . The blond giant was as tall as Conway but broader, his hands like buffalo haunches. Though the other man was short, from the way he had looked at her, White Fawn was more wary of him than of the giant or Conway.

Wiping her nose on the air-freshened, faded quilt, she chided herself. Eagle Feather would expect better of her.

"Matthew Ian Conway!"

Hearing Lupe's squall Matt muttered, "Oh, hell. What now?" He pulled out the knife he'd secreted in his boot and laid it on the bed. Weary beyond belief, he tugged off a snug-fitting boot, then dropped it to the floor just as she sailed into the bedroom, dark skirt swirling around her legs as if a strong wind pushed her.

"You didn't tell me she was injured!"

Wiping his hand over tired eyes, Matt inhaled a long breath. "Oh, yeah, I forgot. She took a bul—"

"You forgot?" Dark eyes shooting fire, Lupe advanced on him, his shirt clutched in her hand. "You forgot? What in God's name did you do to her?"

He frowned at her furious expression. "If you'll hold your horses a minute, I'll—"

"I would have never believed you could do something so cruel. A knife? Dear God—"

"What?" He rubbed his hand over his face again. "What are you talking about, woman? She took a bullet when—"

"So, it wasn't enough to carve her up? You shot her, too?"

Poleaxed by her accusation, Matt dropped his hands to the bed, his mouth agape. "Carve? Lupe, I didn't . . ." He lunged to his feet, clasped her shoulders. "She took a bullet in the arm. The same one that killed her man." He released her and shook his arm. "She clipped me with her knife." He pointed at it lying on the bed. "That little pig sticker could have done a helluva job had I not dodged it."

Lupe's gaze flicked to the knife, then back to him. "So, you decided to teach her a lesson? Give her a little of her own medicine?"

"Lupe . . . what in hell's name are you blathering about?"

"The knife marks on her arms, the back of her thigh."

It was his turn to be furious. The feeling swamped him so quickly he couldn't get a deep breath. "She's been tortured? Lupe, if someone took a knife to her it wasn't me. Dammit, you should know that without my telling you!" He whipped her around. "Show me."

"If not you, who?"

Lupe doubted his word? That hurt. She believed he could torture a woman? Hell, he wouldn't torture a warrior!

He plowed into her when she abruptly halted at the door to turn the key.

She lifted the shirt. "I just remembered. You can't go in there yet. She's naked."

"That's too damn bad. You accuse me of torture and now you think I'm not going to see for myself? Think again, woman."

He reached over her shoulder, rapped on the door. "White Fawn, I'm coming in. Cover yourself with something, or not. I'm coming anyway!" With that, he flung open the door and stepped around Lupe.

With the day about gone and only one window for illumination, the room was dark. His gaze swept over the furnishings, passed White Fawn crouched against the wall, then flicked back to her. Without a word, he crossed the floor, jerked her to her feet, turned her around, and ripped the quilt from her body.

She emitted an outraged squeak, then stood ramrod straight as his hands clasped her upper arms. Too bad if she was embarrassed. He held her too tightly but, dammit, he'd had enough.

"Matt . . ." Lupe cautioned behind him.

He paid no attention, allowing his hands to slip down to White Fawn's elbows. Breath stalled in his chest. She *had* been tortured. Though healed—which Lupe should have noticed—two long, jagged marks extended side by side from the shoulder to just above her elbow. On the other arm, half a dozen diagonal slashes had been inflicted. Holding her still, Matt knelt to look at the backs of her thighs. One had been slashed several times, the other was untouched.

His dark eyes narrowed. "Who did this to you?"

Only White Fawn's ragged breathing answered his terse question. She lowered her chin and shook her head as he rose behind her.

Damn her! Why couldn't she answer a simple question? Frustrated by her obstinate silence, he was within a whisker of turning her around to face him when Lupe stayed his hands.

"Matt, don't embarrass her."

Furious, he stared at her narrow back. Though small, White Fawn was perfectly proportioned. Without a doubt he could circle her trim waist with his hands. Her naked hips flared gently to shapely legs, surprisingly long for someone so short.

Visions of White Fawn beneath him filled his mind. Heat pooled in his groin, followed closely by disgust. She might be experienced, but he would never take a defenseless . . . He scooped up the quilt and flung it around her shoulders.

Pausing at the door, he glared at Lupe. "Take a closer look, woman. The *people* she's so anxious to return to did that to her. And she still needs a bath." He marched from the room, again slamming the door.

Stalking to his room, Matt plopped on the bed. She had suffered. Couldn't she remember? Why was she so determined to go back where someone had mutilated her?

He shook his head, pulled off his remaining boot and tossed it against the wall. Shucking his dirty pants, he grabbed a towel and a clean pair of jeans from the bureau, and headed for the river that snaked behind his house. He needed a bath, too. More than that, he needed the shock of cold water to cool his blood.

No matter how hard he tried to erase the image, no matter how disgusted with himself he became, White Fawn's sweet derriere was before him as plainly as if she stood at arm's length.

After bathing, seated cross-legged on the bank, Matt idly tossed dirt clods into the dark water. Night sounds, the swish of the river's flow, the *plop-plop* of the clods, and the half-moon's wavering reflection in the current should have calmed him. Not tonight.

Plunging into the river had served no purpose. His

nerves were drawn taut as a Comanche's bowstring, and his thoughts careened from one scene to the next, White Fawn commanding center stage. That first moment he'd realized she was white. Never before had he seen eyes the color of a twilight sky. Though tense, her breath labored, her body had been soft. Whether she realized it or not, she'd yielded to his hard frame. Twice. Sure, she fought like a cornered animal, but there had been that moment of . . . surrender.

"Yeah, right." Perhaps defeat better described it.

So tiny. How many times had she fought a warrior determined to have her? She insisted she was a woman. *Hell, maybe she enjoyed it.*

"No," he muttered. Though why should he care?

Because you want her.

No matter that she was young and doll-size. He was no better than other white men who would take advantage of women, or Indians who raped and maimed. He couldn't seem to help himself.

His chin dropped to his chest. He wanted her.

A soft step behind him brought his head around with a jerk. Lupe stood silhouetted in the lantern light coming from the house.

She paused, looking around. Wearing a black shirt and dark trousers, Matt was hard to see where he sat in deep shadow beneath an oak.

"Matt?"

"Here."

Lupe seemed to float toward him, her white shirt-waist illuminated by the moon's faint glow. She halted next to him, hands at the small of her back, and twisted one way and then the other, relieving an ache. Though her chores were different from the men's, she worked as hard as they, from sunup to sundown.

Her heavy, single braid swung forward to dangle in front of her bodice. "I'm sorry," she said quietly. "I know you wouldn't . . . It's just that I was shocked."

That helped.

"Hmm," he replied, unable to say more past the relief easing his heart. Matt thought of the Cruzes as family. Had she really believed he could be so cruel, well, it'd kill him. He'd shot his share of Indians, probably would again. But never, ever would he torture, scalp, or rape.

Lupe sat next to him, bent her knees, and wrapped her arms around them. "Why keep her, Matt? She wants to go back to her people."

Anger heated his blood. His hand shook when he scooped up another clod and chucked it into the water. "Right. Her *people* are the ones who cut her. Dammit, she's white. She belongs in this world."

"No longer, perhaps."

"Lupe—"

"She's frightened." Lupe shook her head. "Can't say that I blame her. I wonder how long she's been with the Indians."

He shrugged. "Wouldn't do a bit of good to ask. She won't even tell me her Christian name. I'll have to make inquiries." Though if he did, everyone within a hundred miles would know about her. Might be more dangerous than returning her to the Indians.

Lupe peered at him. "Maybe she's like you, Matt. The last of her white family."

"Maybe." He'd certainly thought of that possibility. If true, where could she live safely in the white man's world? *Here, with me,* a persistent, irrational voice said.

Lupe smiled. "Don't think I've ever seen such a tiny woman."

Lupe considered her a woman? That eased his guilt . . . a little.

"I had to move the button on one of my skirts three inches to fit her waist. And the hem . . ." She chuckled. "Turned it up a good five inches. My shirtwaist hangs like a sack on her, but it'll do for now." She bit her lip. "There's that length of muslin and another of calico in your trunk. I can sew something that'll fit better."

"You'd do that?"

She looked up. "Of course. She can't parade about naked or in clothes that practically fall off her."

He scowled. "She won't parade about, Lupe. But give her an inch and she'll be gone."

"Surely she wouldn't strike out alone. The Indians she rode with must live on the other side of nowhere. We haven't seen their like around here in two, maybe three years."

"Don't bet on it. She was already headed north when I found her, up into the *Llano Estacado.*"

"You can't lock her up like an animal."

No, but then again . . . He couldn't, wouldn't leave her to fend for herself, either. No telling whom she might encounter. Such easy prey for white men, and Indians, too. Of course, if found by Indians, she might talk them into taking her home . . . if they didn't kill her first and ask questions later.

Who was this Eagle Feather? She thought highly of him. Maybe he was the Indian who'd bedded her. That vision nearly strangled him. He swore she'd never slip between a damned Indian's blankets again! He'd take her . . .

Calm down. Getting riled would solve nothing. For that matter, maybe she didn't want to bed an Indian. Maybe it was simply a case of better the devil you know.

Lupe stood. "I've kept a plate warm for you. Better eat and call it a night. I expect Xavier back tomorrow."

Steady-as-a-rock Xavier. Maybe he could help sort out this mess.

Eagle Feather sat cross-legged, his faded eyes trained on the bright evening star. His heart lay heavy in his chest and he ached all over. Black Crow sat behind him to his left, Beaver Heart to his right. For three days they had traveled a zigzag pattern, looking for a sign. Yet he feared they were no closer to finding White Fawn than when they had started out.

They had come upon two old campfires made by *Nermernah*. They had been carefully obscured, so only another of their blood could have discovered them. A third had been obliterated by whites. He detected trampled grass. Four blankets had been spread.

Four shod mounts had churned the soil. A fifth showed the deeper prints of a pack horse. There was still another set of prints, unshod. Perhaps an Indian pony. He smiled faintly. If so, it had not willingly been led away.

His smile faded. The chances of finding One Bear and White Fawn in the vastness of *Comancheria* were slim. Eagle Feather knew this with certainty but quailed at telling his sons. He did not relish returning home, his mission unachieved.

A sharp stab in his belly signaled his aches might be more than the passing years and defeat's bitter taste. In more pain than he cared to admit, he slowly rose to his feet and picked up his bow and quiver. As he turned, his sons gained their feet as well, waiting for his orders.

"We return to our village. Our days of riding south toward the great water are over."

Black Crow blinked in surprise, but not Beaver Heart. His fierce young son's expression hardened. His black eyes narrowed.

"You would give up, my father? You would leave White Fawn to the fates?"

Eagle Feather nodded, defeat like bile in his mouth. Though reluctant, he said, "I do not believe we shall find her. Perhaps while we have traveled, One Bear and his party have already arrived at our village." He must convince Beaver Heart or the boy would search until the end of his days, if allowed.

Hope softened the boy's dark eyes. "You believe so?"

"Perhaps." He walked to his horse, hiding the fact that his stomach burned with every step. "Come, the sun will rise before long." When he heard nothing behind him, he looked back. Beaver Heart stared off to the south. Black Crow's attention swiveled uncertainly between his brother and his father.

Eagle Feather clasped the medicine bag, secured next to his most potent and magical organ. Drawing power from the deerskin through his breechclout, he peered at his sons, his expression implacable. "You would defy me?"

Black Crow shook his head, silent.

Beaver Heart sputtered, "No, no, my father. It is just that . . ." He clamped his mouth shut.

Though troubled by visions from the day White Fawn left, Eagle Feather harbored a greater fear. Both his sons could be lost. He could not allow that to happen. They *would* obey him!

He bit off each word. "We return to our village. If the Spirits smile, White Fawn will be there. If not . . ." He mounted and looked down at the boy. "I pray they find their way back to us."

The younger men mounted and followed. Eagle Feather sat as straight as his discomfort would allow, his back turned to a little cabin no more than a dozen miles to the south.

Scavenger birds still circled over scattered bodies. Two buzzards beat their wings in challenge when both landed to feast on the remaining flesh of one carcass. Only an occasional melancholy *caa* intruded upon the otherwise mute testimony to the carnage that had taken place there.

Chapter Six

Dim moonlight slanted through the small room's high window. White Fawn, still crouched on the floor, stared morosely at the long skirt billowing around her. She pulled at the constricting drawstring at her waist. Lupe had insisted she wear drawers. They would take getting used to. . . . *You will not be here that long.*

She pushed up the sleeves of the shirtwaist and *tsked* when they slid right back down to her wrists. Earlier, she had tried crossing the floor, and had tripped twice, nearly pitching onto her face when her feet tangled in the material.

She eyed the bed across the room, doubtful she could sleep there. Lying atop buffalo robes or between them was all she knew. The thin mattress had dipped when she sat on its edge to don her moccasins. If she lay on it, would it curl around her like a shroud or a box?

Her head snapped up when she heard a distant neigh. *Pepper.* She smiled. Like her, confinement discomfitted the mare.

Her gaze flicked to the door Lupe had locked. Conway's orders, no doubt. She would bide her time. One day Lupe would relax or forget.

She shivered, recalling the heat that crawled through her when he snatched the quilt from her, and clasped her arms. Despite his nearly painful grip, she had thought if she turned into his arms, she would be . . . safe. *Madness.*

He was a strong man. She bore bruises because of him, and he had tied her like an animal, had nearly drowned her. Still, the feel of his man part pressed against her lingered in her mind.

Vehemently, she shook her head. The first time Lupe lowered her guard, she would find her way to Pepper and escape.

"Boss?"

Matt moaned and pulled a pillow over his head. Damn, why couldn't they leave him in peace?

"Boss?" Hoby called again and rapped on the door.

Matt flung the pillow to the floor and cracked open an eye. Daylight . . . barely. "What?"

"We need you in the barn. That Indian pony is raisin' hell, breakin' slats out of the stall. She's gonna hurt herself if we don't get her settled. Sorry to wake ya, but Lars can't get her to cooperate."

And I can? He flopped to his back. Damn, he ached. And not from overwork. Muscles tensed for hours during the long night, Matt fought a rising need. *White Fawn's fault!*

"Give me a minute," he called, then heard Hoby's footsteps recede down the porch steps.

Matt swung his feet to the floor and braced his hands

on either side of his thighs, his head hanging. It took a moment to decide whether he was awake. Usually up before the chickens, today he could have slept till noon. Then again, maybe not.

He opened his eyes and grimaced at his cock. The thing stood at attention like a cobra, throbbing, swaying, looking for . . . He swiped a whiskered jaw and groaned again. Tonight, by God, he'd visit Widow Weatherly. Hadn't seen Stella in a coon's age, but he needed to bury this thing in a woman, and she was always willing.

She'd made it perfectly clear that she'd move in with him and warm his bed every night if he said the word; she'd be here in a flash. Only one problem: She insisted on marriage. Not on his life! He'd come damn close to making that mistake once and been thrown over for a man old enough to be Etta's father. Love? He snorted. Money, a lot of money, had won. His former fiancée had gone for the almighty buck, not a brawny, lusty twenty-year-old.

Nope, no woman would hog-tie him to her skirts, no matter how satisfying she might be in bed. Matthew Conway had learned his lesson. Besides, if he had a wife and ever returned to relive the carnage when his parents died, he'd never survive. He pushed away the remembrance of how his mother . . .

He picked up his trousers and drew them on. Untangling the black shirt from the rumpled quilt, he jammed his arms into the sleeves, then finger-combed his too-long hair and donned his boots and spurs. Buckling on his gun belt, he strode from the room.

With every step, rowels jingled, then clunked as they

punched the plank floor. Pausing on the porch, he rested a hand on an upright supporting the lean-to roof. Though still below the horizon, the sun's rays painted the sky a brilliant orange. A haze like cotton batting lay over the rolling prairie.

He scanned the outbuildings and fences he'd worked so hard to build. Nothing could bring back his family, but this was home. He was as proud of the place as he was pleased that he'd been able to provide a home for Xavier and Lupe. Burned out by *Comancheros,* they'd come south and found him working alone.

The sound of splintering wood and frantic neighing halted his musings. He leaped off the porch and started toward the barn. The mare had been as docile as a whipped pup when he'd tied White Fawn on the animal's back. No doubt about it, the horse belonged to her.

He stopped, hands propped on his hips. Swinging around, he headed back to the house. Rather than try to subdue the pony himself, he'd ask White Fawn to do it.

Ask? Yeah, right.

He turned the key and pushed open the door. White Fawn wasn't in the bed. His gaze swept the room. Slumped on the floor, head tilted at an uncomfortable angle, she was bundled in the quilt, her back resting against the wall. She slept.

Hair tumbled over the side of her face and onto the quilt. The urge to see those midnight tresses spread over his pillow, in his bed, tightened his whole body. Right on its heels, anger flared as he strode toward her, his hard steps vibrating the floor.

White Fawn's head snapped up. Hand against a stiff neck, she groaned. Her eyes rounded as she saw him, and she pressed herself against the wall. Her small hands clutched the quilt snugged around her shoulders.

He clasped both her arms through the quilt and lifted her to her feet. "What the hell are you doing on the floor?"

Mute as always, she simply stared.

He gave her a little shake and asked again, "Why are you on the floor?"

Her expression turned mutinous. Not surprising.

"Well?" he demanded, all too aware of her clean, womanly, arousing scent.

"No bed . . . box." After a second, she added, "Closed." She took a deep breath. "Buffalo robes on ground . . . open."

He understood too well. The girl was truly Comanche, comfortable only on robes with an Indian by her side, or on top of her. Anger laced with lust he couldn't deny pounded in his head and loins. He released her as if burned.

She staggered back, catching herself before she tripped over the trailing quilt.

Reining in both his anger and his lust, he reminded himself she'd been a captive. Whatever she'd endured, come to accept, even like, was history.

"Your horse is raising hell in my barn. She'll injure herself. Let's go."

"Do not . . ."

Matt shoved the blanket aside, clasped her upper arm, and yanked her right off her feet. His gaze raked her from head to toe while she steadied herself. He doubted White Fawn weighed more than a sack of grain. If he didn't stop hauling her around like one, he'd do some major damage.

Though he didn't release her, he drew her along at a reasonable pace. And sure as his gun held six bullets, she planted her feet and resisted.

"You want a lame horse?"

Her lovely eyes sparked as she huffed. "Pepper no my horse."

She'd named the black-on-white spotted horse Pepper? As Texan as "y'all." "I certainly won't be riding her," he said.

"Matt," Lupe called behind them.

"Later," he growled, continuing toward the barn. The recalcitrant horse was destroying his work, ruining lumber that had cost as much as forty head of prime cattle.

As he strode into the barn, Matt spied Lars halfway down the corridor, squatted at Pepper's stall, prying split, jagged timber away from the mare's hoof. If she kicked back again, the splinters would jab into her pastern.

"Easy," Lars coaxed, his voice eclipsed by the mare's frantic neighing.

White Fawn wrenched free of Matt's grip and plunged toward the stall. A string of Comanche sang in the air as she wiggled between the stall's slats.

Jesus, the horse was so spooked, it might bite the girl, or worse. She again spoke rapidly, then sprang to Pepper's head and laid a hand on her muzzle. Her steadying hand and words had the same effect on the mare as throwing the blanket over her face the other day.

Though her sides heaved, Pepper settled and ducked her face to nuzzle White Fawn's shirtwaist. She blew, acknowledging a trusted friend, then leaned forward. White Fawn stepped back to stay upright.

"I'll be damned," Lars said. He pulled on the splintered wood once more. The mare lowered her leg and stood as docile as a sheep, lapping up White Fawn's crooned words and gentle touch.

Squatted at Lars's side, Hoby stood and tipped back his hat, admiration lighting his face as he watched White Fawn soothing the mare. "I'll be damned," he parroted.

Lars rose and sighed. "That mare goes nuts if I get near her."

"Then don't," Matt said, watching White Fawn. She had a gift. At least, with this horse she did.

Matt stepped a bit closer and looked at the horse's leg. Blood oozed down the outside, a splinter lodged just below the hock. Damn, it would be as difficult to get that jagged sliver out as to pull an arrow from a man's body.

He blinked in surprise when White Fawn switched to English. "Easy, girl." She scratched the mare's jaw, then her throat latch. Turning her head against the mare's, she hugged the long face to her body. "Is okay," she murmured.

Matt envisioned his own face nestled between White Fawn's firm breasts. Gritting his teeth against sudden desire, he spoke more tersely than he intended. "She's hurt."

93

White Fawn backed away to assess the horse's hindquarter. Trailing a hand along the flank, she focused on the injured leg. Kneeling closer, she kept a gentle hand on Pepper's rear leg. Her gaze snapped to Matt. "Pepper no hurt outdoors."

Right. Unhurt and long gone. He glared right back. "You'll have to nurse her. Unless you prefer I use further restraint." He could certainly do that, but it would mean cross-tying, hobbling front and back, and maybe blindfolding again.

"Like me?" White Fawn challenged.

"You don't know the half of it." Such spunk! He stared down Hoby when he snickered.

"I'll get water and salve," Lars said.

The Swede strode away and Hoby followed, removing himself from Matt's proximity.

He had always prided himself on being slow to anger, but White Fawn pushed him to the flash point at every turn. *Not really,* a rational though irritating voice said in his head. If he were honest, he'd admit he did this to himself. His out-of-control desire was the culprit. Eyes narrowed on her, he snapped, "Well?"

She lowered her challenging gaze and rubbed the horse's leg. "I tend," she murmured.

She did so with an expertise that astounded Matt and gained Hoby's further admiration. Even Lars remained motionless, watching every move she made.

When she pulled out the splinter, Matt feared the mare might kick White Fawn right through the slats, but the pony only whinnied and lifted her leg. White Fawn stopped and spoke quietly until Pepper lowered her foot. When she picked slivers from the wound, the pony sidestepped and tossed her head. Again, the girl waited with a patience that Matt admired.

Finished, she tangled her fingers in the mare's mane and led her to the manger. "Eat."

She handed the supplies to Lars and edged back through the rails, then looked up at Matt. "Stable in corral, she no trouble. No like . . . pen."

Nor do I was the veiled message from troubled eyes.

Tough, Matt thought. She'd bolt as quickly as the horse. But the suggestion had merit. He'd relent and give her that much. "Fine."

He caught her surprised expression as he asked Lars, "Is that corral you were working on yesterday tight?"

"Aye." A half smile lifted his mouth. "But leading her out there might be tricky."

"I do it," White Fawn said.

Yeah, and I'll dog your steps, little lady.

Late that afternoon, the sun had begun to sink in the west when Matt heard a cow's bellow. He heel-tamped dirt around the last post on the second corral and looked southward. Dust billowed in the distance. Squinting, he made out four riders and several head of stock.

Four? Xavier must have hired another man while I was away.

Glancing toward the house, he found White Fawn on the porch in the same chair she'd occupied for the past hour. Her unrelenting perusal made him edgy. Doubtless biding her time, believing she could escape. After the midday meal, Lupe had talked him into allowing her to sit there rather than remain cooped up in the bedroom. Though a prisoner of sorts, she needed fresh air.

Matt was amazed at the change in the girl's appearance now that she wore a shirtwaist and skirt. Other than the moccasins that peeked from beneath her hem, one would never guess she was more Comanche than white. Actually, a few white women of his acquaintance wore moccasins. Besides, he reminded himself, she'd only adopted their ways.

Lupe appeared at her side with a small sack and a kettle. Good. She was putting her to work helping with supper. Snapping beans, perhaps. He grinned. At least Lupe had the wits not to put a knife in the girl's hands.

Still undecided what to do with her, he'd kept an eye on her while he worked. A good fifty yards away, she still might try to outrun him. But she couldn't get far without her horse, and he was working between them.

Retrieving his shirt from a post, Matt shrugged into it, then stepped on the shovel's bowl. The handle flipped up into his hand. As he put it away, Lars strode toward him in the barn's corridor.

"Riders coming," Matt said.

"I heard."

Lars balanced several lengths of lumber on his shoulder, carrying them as if they were featherweights. Next to Xavier, Lars was the most reliable man he knew. If he had a temper, Matt had never seen it. The big Swede paced himself like a swinging metronome, able to work for hours without rest. While others might consider him slow, Matt knew he accomplished a lot at his measured pace. Smart, actually, since Lars could toil the entire day even in midsummer's merciless sun.

Lars dropped the lumber next to the barn. Tomorrow they'd nail the boards as crossbars on the posts they had sunk today. And by evening, they'd see a second corral finished.

Matt looked back at the house. Lupe stood on the porch, a hand shading her eyes as she stared into the distance separating her from Xavier. More than once Matt had wondered if their hearts beat as one. They finished each other's sentences so often, he knew they thought alike. Like Matt's parents, they shared a closeness that he envied. But marriage wasn't for him; experiencing that rapport was not something he could look forward to.

He removed his hat, brushed sweat from his forehead with his sleeve, then clapped it on again. He could count the stock. Jim Foster and his brother, Bob, hazed two cows. A third was bawling, tethered behind the man Matt didn't recognize.

As she lumbered along in the horse's wake, Matt wondered how long it had taken to subdue her. Range cattle were wild as March hares. A calf draped across the saddle in front of Xavier also complained. Lars stepped up next to Matt.

"*Amigo!*" Xavier called and reined in a few yards out. "Found some, but know not how many we miss."

The cow bellowed again.

Suddenly, headed straight for Xavier, White Fawn sped past him. What the . . . ? The loose cattle bucked, spooked by her flurry of skirts. Matt charged after her, circled her waist, and drew her back hard against his frame. "What do you think you're doing?"

She craned her head around, a smile wreathing her face. His breath stalled in his chest. She should do that more often. What pleased her?

"No see calf many suns. I just . . ." The smile died. "May touch?"

Hell's fire. Of course! A calf was a calf, trouble more often than not. But he couldn't allow her to spook cattle this close to the house.

"Go ahead, but slowly," he said gruffly.

Xavier dismounted and pulled the protesting calf off the horse. When he set it down, the no-more-than-day-old heifer wobbled and collapsed. White Fawn went down on her knees and caressed the calf's neck.

"Who she is?" Xavier asked.

"White . . ." Suddenly, Matt wondered if he should run his mouth so readily. Though older men, Jim and Bob might gossip about her unless he made it clear they were to keep their traps shut. But that would only further pique their interest. He glanced at the new man. Slumped in the saddle, he was so skinny, if he turned sideways he'd disappear.

"Tell you later," he finally muttered.

"He hungry," White Fawn said.

The calf bawled and his mother echoed it. The cow's udder was distended fit to burst. Plenty of milk for her calf and some to spare. Matt's mouth watered at the thought of fresh milk for supper.

Bob Foster dismounted, his rawhide chaps flapping against his boots in the breeze. "That she is, ma'am. She's been bellerin' for the past hour."

He uncoiled his lariat, slipped the noose around one of the loose steers and tethered it to his saddle horn, then took the lead rope from the new man. "This here ol' gal'll fix 'er right up." He tugged the cow forward, then stopped and looked at Matt. "The barn?"

Matt nodded, though the cow would bear watching. She'd probably not take too kindly to being penned, but maybe if the calf was with her, she'd quiet some.

White Fawn's smile returned as she crooned lovingly to the calf. Such a simple pleasure, stroking a newborn animal. The girl was easy to please.

Suddenly, she scrambled to her feet, shoved her hands beneath the calf's belly, and lifted. Or tried to. The unwieldy, uncooperative animal bawled right in her face. Matt chuckled.

"Up," White Fawn commanded to no avail.

She laughed. A sound so genuine and astonishing, Matt stilled. Let it wash over him, through him, and warm his blood.

"You can no eat if mama in barn and you here," she chided.

Appearing from behind Matt, Hoby said, "I'll give ya a hand, ma'am."

Ma'am? Now there was a new wrinkle. The lustful glint was gone from Hoby's eyes. Seeing her handle the crisis with her horse must have mellowed him. The young man did love animals.

Well, thank God for that. One less randy man to worry about. Matt's rational mind still tried to convince him that she was a young girl, too young. But his body had other ideas. Deaf as a post . . . and *stiff* as new shoe leather.

She fell into step with Hoby as he braced himself against the calf's weight and headed for the barn.

"Wait!" Matt's command stirred the air.

She stopped, the smile melting from her face. "May I not—"

"Never mind." Why had he done that? She wasn't trying to run away. Escape hadn't even entered her mind.

Standing as still as a doe, White Fawn searched his eyes for what seemed like forever. Something flickered in hers. Sorrow?

Seconds later, her expression hardened to determination. *I will be gone before long. Wait and see!* He read that as clearly as if she'd spoken aloud.

Matt turned back to the remaining men, and the stranger's perplexed gaze. Her moccasins were in plain view with every step she took

Xavier swept off his hat. "How long you are back?"

While Lupe spoke flawless English, Xavier sometimes struggled. He knew all the words, just couldn't always correctly string them together.

"Yesterday," Matt said.

Xavier gestured to the new man. "This here Hank Gladstone, Stella's *hoosban.*"

Matt's brow creased. The only woman nearby with that name . . . "Stella who?"

"Weatherly," the man supplied as he swung down from his horse. "Gladstone as of last week." He extended his hand to Matt.

Holy hell! Stella Weatherly had remarried? He'd only been gone . . . Okay, six weeks. Still . . . "Bit sudden." Damn right. And there went his evening between Stella's sheets!

A sheepish grin lit the man's features. "I knowed Stella afore she married Daniel Weatherly. That ol' rooster got his hands on her afore I could." He shrugged amiably. " 'Course, Stella weren't interested in me a-tall. We had a small farm next to the Weatherlys' plantation. My paw worked for hers sometimes. When I heared she'd been widdered a while back, decided to try my luck again."

A *while back*? Daniel had died three years ago, trampled in a cattle stampede. Where had Gladstone been all that time? Before Matt could voice the question, Hank explained.

"Been workin' my way west for a spell. I knowed where to find Stella from her letters to kin in South Carolina."

Hank's buttery Southern drawl tickled Matt as he eyed him more closely. God-a-mighty! Stella had married this beanpole? Though not what you'd call fat, Stella was . . . fleshy, and nearly as tall as Matt. She'd crush this bag of bones if she lay atop him. And she would. Matt'd had his hands full with her sporting ways in bed. She could wear a man out in no time.

Gladstone might have been as tall as Matt if he stood straight, but his chest caved in beneath slumped shoulders. Looked as though he carried the weight of the world.

Still, the man offered a toothy grin and again extended the hand Matt had failed to clasp the first time. Hank's grip was firm. Stronger than he looked. He'd need to be, Matt thought wryly.

"Fine to meet ya, Conway. Stella told me all about ya."

He sure as hell hoped not. Hank Gladstone probably wouldn't be too pleased to know how much time Matt had spent in Stella's bed over the past couple of years. "Funny, I don't remember her mentioning you."

"Understandable," he drawled. "She didn't even re-co'nize me when I showed up on her doorstep."

It certainly hadn't taken her long to get reacquainted! Where did that leave him? In the cold, that's where. Frequenting whorehouses was not Matt's style, even had a sporting house been close by.

From the corner of his eye, Matt saw White Fawn leave the barn and start for the house. Her hips swayed provocatively; skirts swirled around her feet. Distracted, he turned abruptly when Gladstone spoke again.

"Y'all plannin' to round up more stock?"

"A few days," Xavier said. "You return, we happy you go along."

"Well, I best be gettin' on home." He squinted at Xavier. "Stella's been pinin' to come visit with your Lupe. She'll be right pleased to meet that purty little gal, too."

How did Gladstone know White Fawn was a new arrival? The minute the thought formed, he chided himself for seeing trouble where none existed. Hell, Xavier had just asked who she was. If Stella had told him about Matt, she'd undoubtedly said he was single. With no prospects or inclination to change.

"You plannin' to marry up with her, Conway?"

Startled, Matt mumbled, "Uh, no. She's . . . no." He left it at that. The less said about White Fawn, the better.

Matt didn't know this man, but he knew Stella. She'd shun White Fawn if she discovered the girl had been a Comanche captive. Confounding as the devil, white women held contempt for their sisters who'd survived Indian capture. Unsure how he'd prevent information from filtering out, he nevertheless needed to keep quiet right now about White Fawn.

"Well, see y'all in a few days." Hank mounted his sorrel. "Gonna be full dark afore I get home to my gal."

Chapter Seven

After supper, the two men sat on the porch. Matt enjoyed a cigar; Xavier puffed his pipe. A comfortable quiet reigned between them, as it had during supper. White Fawn had not joined them, choosing instead to retreat to her room.

Seated on the step, one leg bent, Matt leaned against the post. Xavier sat likewise on the other end of the step. Cicadas chirped. Out in the corral, Pepper shuffled, the sound muted.

They'd exhausted talk regarding the ranch, and Matt had told Xavier about the encounter with Cecil and Earl. His skin still chilled when he thought about what Earl would have done to White Fawn had he not come upon the grizzly scene in time.

She had played possum and fooled him, all right, but she wouldn't have been able to fool Earl had he set his knife to her scalp.

"Nice-lookin' horse," Xavier said.

"Um," Matt retorted noncommittally, uncertain about

discussing White Fawn. Though Lupe had taken the girl under her wing from the start, Xavier might not.

"I hope you no keep her locked in for long time?" Xavier asked, settling Matt's dilemma.

As long as it takes. "Who?" he asked vaguely.

"Come, Matt," he chided, tilting his head toward the breezeway. "Young woman in bedroom." The glow of lantern light spilling from the main room limned Xavier's face. He drew on his pipe, then blew a smoke ring. "You no think dangerous for she to be here? Comanches no like lose captives."

True enough. But as far as he knew, they didn't even know she was missing. For that matter, her band probably didn't know about the dead warriors. Undoubtedly, the crows and buzzards had continued to feast. After a fairly short time, bones were bones. He counted on Comanches not knowing the difference between male and female skeletons. There was the matter of clothing, though, and they'd find no buckskin dress there.

"Matt?"

"It could be dangerous," he allowed. "Though it's doubtful they'll look for her here."

"She be my woman, I no rest until I find her."

Matt glanced sharply at his friend. There it was again. Xavier saw White Fawn as a woman. Everyone sure played hell with his determination to think of her as a girl.

"How long she with them?"

Matt shrugged. "White Fawn's damn closemouthed. She hasn't even told me her Christian name, though she speaks English as well as you."

Xavier sat quietly for a time, puffing thoughtfully on his pipe. Matt inhaled an appreciative breath of the sweet tobacco. His more pungent cigar smoke mixed in a cloud that wafted above their heads.

"Lupe say White Fawn want go back."

"She's white!" Matt snapped.

"Is true." Xavier nodded. "She no think so now, maybe."

Irritated by the direction of the conversation, Matt said churlishly, "It doesn't matter what she thinks. She's white, and I intend to see that she's . . ." *What? Kept under lock and key? Forced to my bed?* He closed his eyes and breathed deeply, the cigar forgotten in his hand. No. He would never force a woman, and certainly not that tiny . . .

"Maybe you think careful on it."

Matt eyed the wise man he could depend on to defend his back. The man who had more sense than anyone Matt knew.

"She no want be here. What happen she run away and you no find her?"

That didn't bear thinking about.

When Matt failed to answer, Xavier smiled faintly. "Lupe like her spunk. She treat your White Fawn like daughter we no have."

My White Fawn? "I may take her to the orphanage."

Xavier shook his head, dark eyes troubled. "You know she pariah in Austin, Matt."

He did, dammit. But the more Xavier prodded, the more determined he was that White Fawn wouldn't return to the Comanche. If she stayed here, though, how long could he keep his hands off her? Did he even want to try?

He tossed away the cigar stub and refused to examine those questions. Hell's fire, he didn't need to. He already knew the answers . . . and they didn't bode well for the girl. "I'm going for a dip in the river, then turn in."

Xavier looked up as Matt stood. "Okay. But remember, you think on it."

That's all he'd done since he'd laid eyes on her. He couldn't get her *out* of his thoughts. Matt stomped to his room to get a clean shirt and trousers. Not only was she tantalizingly close during the day to feed his desire, her astonishing eyes accused him in his dreams.

Confined again. White Fawn took a shuddering breath, gazing at the four bare walls. She hated them. She hated the sound of the key turning in the lock. She hated Matt-Matthew Conway.

No longer truth. She feared him, yes, but the hate in her heart had subsided. Like the warriors she rode with, Conway killed only when he must. Her brow creased. Maybe not truth, either. Comanche warriors raided and killed with a purpose in mind. They wanted horses and captives. It was their way of life. Horses were proof of a man's superiority within a band. And all Comanche longed to drive the white man from their land. The land *Nermernuh* had settled first.

Seated on the floor, her back against the wall, she sighed, then rose and walked to the bed. She pulled the colorful quilt off the thin mattress and wrapped it around her shoulders. Returning, she slid down, her back supported against the wall again. She still could not bring herself to sleep in the bed.

She listened to the murmur of male voices. A faint smile curved her lips. Lupe's husband had, at least, spoken to her politely. Short and stocky, he had proved his strength by lifting the calf off his horse with ease.

Conway liked him very much. Though he was younger than Xavier by many seasons, she heard respect for the man in his voice, saw it in his face. He liked Lupe, too.

So did she, but she wished the woman would forget to lock the door. Until she did, White Fawn could not hope to return to her people.

Unable to fall asleep, she let her thoughts meander. Reluctantly, she examined the feelings that had risen within her this afternoon while she had watched Conway work. His broad, bare shoulders slicked by sweat as he set fence posts, his skin burnished as dark as a Comanche's.

She looked down at her fisted hands. The yearning to touch him, to caress his shoulders, was a living force within her. Her breathing slowed. Her eyes drifted closed as she recalled how his arms felt when he clasped her against his hard body.

His touch had scorched her back, and her buttocks nestled . . . Her eyes flew open when the same heat she had experienced then curled in her belly now. Had he turned her in his arms, had he kissed her . . .

Madness. She rested her head on bent knees and took slow breaths. She had never been kissed. It was not the way of the Comanche. A shiver shook her.

At the first opportunity, she *must* leave here. If the Spirits smiled on her, she would find her People and never see Conway again. Lifting her head, she stared into the dark room, seeing Conway's smiling face as clearly as if he stood before her. Though he rarely smiled, and certainly never at her, her heart knocked fit to batter her ribs from the inside.

Never see him again.

Sadness welled in her heart.

Eagle Feather gazed longingly at the clustered tipis; smoke curled skyward from each. Eyes dimmed by pain, he breathed a sigh of relief. Home. In a short time he could stretch out on his blankets and sleep. He hoped rest was all he needed. Every jolting step of the horse sent shards of pain slicing though his belly.

No longer able to hide his misery from Black Crow and Beaver Heart, he had slowed their progress. The ride south had taken three suns. The return had stretched to five since he could not sit the saddle until the sun dipped below the horizon. At least he had a saddle gifted by the black robe. His sons offered to carry him on a travois, but he had refused. Foolhardy, perhaps, but as chief he must ride into camp as he had left it.

Whoops of recognition wafted from the valley below as his People streamed from their lodges to greet him. Barking dogs added to the cacophony. He thrust back his shoulders and raised his head. Black Crow rode a step behind, but close enough to offer assistance if needed. It would not do for him to topple from the saddle.

He must alight from the horse without falling to the ground. Another pain pierced his weakened body. A hand clapped to his stomach, his smile strained, he greeted those cheerful faces watching him as he plodded toward his lodge. In times past, he would have ridden in fast, halting his steed on dancing legs before Bright Star and Willow Branch.

Willow Branch stepped forward, nodded at him respectfully, then looked at her son with a smile of welcome. Eagle Feather could not take his eyes off Bright Star. Very soon his first wife would brew a soothing tea to deaden his pain.

"My husband," she said, her eyes grave, assessing. "The Spirits smile upon us at your safe return."

Eagle Feather sensed that, though others might not, she had seen his distress. This woman knew him as well as he knew himself.

"Come. Rest." She came close, placed a hand on his thigh and spoke so others could not hear. "Do you need assistance to dismount?"

Black Crow and Beaver Heart rode up on either side of him, blocking his people's view. Slowly he lifted his leg over the pommel. As he slipped to the ground, Bright Star clasped his elbows, steadied him as he gulped air. Much shorter than he, she was strong from years of women's work.

"You can walk, my husband?"

"I will," he vowed, taking one tentative step, then another. Fortunately, his band had gathered around his sons, eager to hear of their adventures. No matter how he willed his body, once he leaned to enter the tipi, he could not straighten again. He fell headlong inside.

110

Shamed by his weakness, he crawled across the woven mats and collapsed on his blankets.

Suddenly Bright Star ducked into the tipi and rushed to his side. "You are ill, my husband?"

"A small pain in my belly." Weakly, he brushed a hand over her bent head. "I will recover." Sounding more confident than he felt, he smiled reassuringly.

By the time Bright Star had brewed his tea, his sons had entered and took their accustomed seats in his lodge.

His family sat quietly while she slid an arm under his head and raised him to sip the brew. Within minutes the pain eased, and he grew light-headed. Shortly, it was as though his body floated above the blankets; the pain faded away as if it had never been. He drifted into sleep.

As nightfall descended on the village, Straight Arrow returned from his hunt and spied his father's mount staked in the midst of the remuda. His brothers' mounts nibbled the scrub beneath their unshod hooves. He frowned. Where was White Fawn's pinto?

Women came to take the horses of the hunting party. He and the other two braves shrugged off the deer each had draped over his shoulders. Stands Tall Woman took his into her care. She would clean and skin the animal, then share the meat with at least three lodges.

One day, maybe soon, he intended to offer for Stands Tall Woman. Smiling at her welcome, he again admired the handsome, strong, and *silent* woman, so different from the chattering women he could not abide.

He strode through the village toward his father's tipi,

nodding to friends as he passed, accepting the admiring glances that were his due. Not once had he returned from a hunt without meat to share. He prided himself on his hunter's instincts and long-established abilities. Like his father, he knew his worth, as did every last soul in the band.

Pausing at the entrance to Eagle Feather's tipi, he waited for Bright Star's invitation to enter, then ducked inside. His gaze swept the occupants, settling on his father's pale face and still form lying on buffalo robes.

"He is ill, my son," Bright Star said quietly.

"What plagues him?" He sank to the skin-covered ground beside his mother.

"I know not. He said bad spirits have entered his stomach. He has much pain." She looked at her husband. "Eagle Feather is at rest now, but I know not how to cure him." She laid a gentle hand on his stomach. "It is swollen with bad medicine like a she-bear's in the winter."

Straight Arrow stared at the man he worshiped. Few chiefs were as wise and far-seeing as his father had proved himself to be time and again. A strong man, he would surely get well.

Though much admired and proud of his own worth, Straight Arrow knew his father's moccasins would be hard to fill when the spirit left Eagle Feather's body. Straight Arrow also knew that simply being Eagle Feather's oldest son did not assure he would be the band's next chief. A vote would be taken.

In agreement with his father, Straight Arrow had also counseled against war. Too many friends had died raiding against the white man. Be they farmers or soldiers, white men carried guns. The band's bows and arrows were no match for such deadly firepower. No warrior he knew owned a gun. Soon, perhaps, he would trade for one.

He shook his head, returning to the situation they faced. Dour musings would solve nothing. Rising, he spoke to his mother. "I would speak with my father when he wakes."

She nodded and drew her hand back into her lap. She and Willow Branch would keep vigil.

Straight Arrow pinned each brother with penetrating eyes much like his father's. "Come, we will go to my lodge and speak now."

In his tipi, gathered around the central fire Stands Tall Woman had kindled, Straight Arrow asked quietly, "When did Father take ill?"

"I know not for certain," Black Crow responded. "Four suns past, he became pale. By the time we made camp at nightfall, he no longer sat straight. He woke with the birds each day but mounted slowly."

"He has taken no nourishment for three days," Beaver Heart interjected.

"Very weak." Black Crow frowned "He broke off the search for White Fawn. He would not do that unless very ill."

"What news of White Fawn?"

Beaver Heart shook his head. "We saw no sign."

"None?"

Black Crow spoke before his brother could. "Signs of two camps made by the *Nermernuh*; a third made by white men. Nothing that would lead us to believe White Fawn was with them."

113

His father treasured White Fawn. He would not have abandoned the search lightly. Fear for Eagle Feather's life settled like a thorn in Straight Arrow's belly.

"I will return to look." Beaver Heart's tone was challenging.

A faint smile touched Straight Arrow's features. No surprise his young brother would say that. Before Beaver Heart's vision quest, he and White Fawn were inseparable. Even after Beaver Heart had surpassed her height, she treated him like her own child. Unless they played a game. Then she seemed a child herself. Her laughter painted the band's world brighter.

Had White Fawn not been claimed by his father as a daughter, Straight Arrow would have considered taking her to wife. Though tiny, she worked hard and, most important, rarely spoke unless spoken to. But what drew every young brave to consider her for wife was her extraordinary eyes, expressive and deep-hued as the evening sky. Stands Tall Woman was handsome in an austere way, but she did not begin to compare with White Fawn's beauty.

Beaver Heart jolted him from his reverie when he said, "I will ask Buffalo Hump and Snake Who Hisses to ride with me."

A seasoned warrior, Snake Who Hisses had accompanied Straight Arrow on many hunts. Two winters older than his young brother, Buffalo Hump had a heart as fierce as Beaver Heart's. Perhaps the three could succeed where Eagle Feather had failed, but Straight Arrow harbored doubt.

Black Crow's frown mirrored his. "You would leave while Father is so ill?"

"When Father wakes, I will promise to bring White Fawn to him. That will make him better."

Straight Arrow feared the maid's return would have no bearing on his father's well-being. Eagle Feather's world would gladden, but what ailed him had nothing to do with his heart's desire. If his youngest brother were lost, their father's grief would know no end until he, too, joined him in the Spirit World.

The boy would do as he wished, but Straight Arrow must try to dissuade him. "Counsel with our father before you do this, my brother. His heart is heavy because White Fawn is lost, but he will despair more if you do not succeed."

"Nothing will happen to me," the boy countered. He hesitated, then met Straight Arrow's eyes. "I will speak with Father. But I go. I will bring White Fawn back to our village where she belongs."

White Fawn sat in a ladder-back chair in the center corridor. A quilt frame secured by ropes to the ceiling and lowered to the proper height hung before her. She took pride that her stitches were even as she worked one side of the Lone Star pattern.

Lupe had not seemed very happy to see Mrs. Gladstone when she'd arrived with her husband this morning. Now the two women sat across from White Fawn.

"Land sakes, how long have you collected material scraps, Lupe? The colors make a right pretty pattern," Stella said.

Lupe shrugged as her needle pierced the layers of fabric. "Several years, I'd say."

Lupe glanced at White Fawn and smiled. She and

Lupe had settled into companionable silence as they worked side by side at their tasks. Apparently, Stella Gladstone did not know the meaning of the word silence. Ever since her arrival, she had talked about nothing in particular.

White Fawn thought she understood Stella's need to converse. She had heard white women who traveled west could be isolated upward of a year with no one to speak to but their men. If Conway was any gauge, white men were not prone to much talk. On the other hand, Lupe and Xavier shared a camaraderie that was a pleasure to watch.

"You certainly do a fine job," Stella said.

When White Fawn realized the compliment was directed at her, she glanced up and smiled. "Thank you." She lowered her head and continued to work.

Stella's curiosity about her had been evident from the moment she'd stepped down from her horse. Lupe had forestalled every question save one. White Fawn finally revealed the Christian name Father Anselmo had bestowed upon her. What did it matter if Conway learned it?

Stella had frowned when she spied White Fawn's moccasins, but Lupe had a story. "Actually, Matt brought them in from a raid a long time ago. Rebecca's shoes need repair from all her walking while traveling."

White Fawn had listened, as mesmerized as Stella was by Lupe's story regarding why and how White Fawn had come to be here. "Nothing short of a miracle that Matt came upon Rebecca's family when he did. Though too late to save the rest of her family, he rescued Rebecca. No telling what would have happened to her."

Lupe spun the fantasy with the effortlessness of a born storyteller, speaking of White Fawn as if she was not right there listening to every word. Her tale elicited Stella's sympathy. Who would not be appalled that every one of Rebecca's family had died?

"You poor dear, alone and defenseless." Stella spoke right on cue, her blue eyes sad. But her round face brightened when she said, "Matt will take good care of you, as will Lupe and Xavier."

Lupe and perhaps Xavier, but she doubted Conway would—or even wanted to. If his actions were a measure of his care, she would sooner face a bear in its den.

Expressing displeasure and pain from the branding, bawling cattle interrupted their conversation. White Fawn looked toward the corral. She had lost count of how many animals had been brought in off the range. Xavier and the Foster twins were out again today looking for still more, and were not expected to return for several days.

Conway, Lars, Hoby, and Mr. Gladstone worked in a cloud of dust, roping and bringing down the steers to singe the Rocking C on each one's rump, the tableau a new and fascinating experience to White Fawn. Other than a dozen or so calves, the steers and cows must weigh hundreds of pounds. Yet Conway and Lars roped and dragged the animals to the ground with astonishing ease.

"Ouch!" White Fawn's gaze snapped to a pricked finger.

Lupe chuckled and looked at the watch fob pinned

to her bodice. "I suspect the men are hungry. I'd better check the beans and tortillas and set out the nooning." She rose. "Rebecca, would you help set the table?"

Since it would appear odd if *Rebecca* did not help, she nodded. Though Lupe allowed her a measure of freedom to bathe in the river and take care of personal needs, not once had she failed to lock the door at night. Matt-Matthew Conway had ridden off for a couple of days, but his absence had done White Fawn no good.

She enjoyed the simple pleasure of being clean each night, as well as the modicum of privacy. Conway had shown her a spot ideal for bathing: not so deep she might drown, but deep enough to submerge her seated body to her shoulders in the cool water.

Lupe had fashioned two shirtwaists and skirts to fit White Fawn's slight figure. She also said Conway would purchase shoes for her on his next trip to the trading post five miles downriver. White Fawn did not look forward to them.

A half hour later, the men were washed and seated, along with Stella. Lupe set a large cast-iron kettle in the center of the table. White Fawn followed with the tortillas.

Not one to skimp on food for working men, Lupe told her to serve each man four tortillas. Judging from the other woman's robust size, White Fawn wasn't surprised when Lupe said Mrs. Gladstone ate as heartily as the men, so she placed four tortillas on her plate, too.

"Rebecca, would you get the coffeepot?"

Conway's head snapped up, his eyes locked on her. She stood rooted to the spot. His expression changed

118

from surprise to a grin, his eyes atwinkle. "Yeah, *Rebecca,* Lupe's coffee will hit the spot."

So, now he could call her by a white name. There had been no choice but to reveal it. Stella Gladstone was no different from countless whites—she hated Indians, no matter the tribe. And if she learned the truth . . .

White Fawn turned away from Conway's laughing eyes. Despite her attraction to him, she must find a way to escape.

Chapter Eight

"Stop that!" White Fawn admonished the determined pup romping at her feet as she walked toward the river. Undeterred, his head disappeared under her skirt's hem as he again bit at her moccasin. She scooped him up.

Only a few weeks old, he had a long way to go to reach his father's size and weight. His soft belly settled along the length of her forearm, legs dangling, chin resting on her palm. He latched onto her fingers.

"Teething you are?" She nuzzled his soft fur against her cheek.

He growled his version of ferocious, twisting his head back and forth. Needle-sharp teeth stabbed her flesh in his feigned tug-of-war.

"Ouch!" She dropped her clean garments, the soap and towel, and grasped the pup by the scruff of the neck. "You bite off my fingers!"

His rump resting in her other hand, he wiggled and growled again. Nose to nose, she laughed. The buff-colored pup looked like someone had splashed ashes across his face; a dark streak bisected his mouth, top to bottom. "A warrior, fine little fellow?"

"Crawling with fleas, I'd wager."

White Fawn whirled toward Conway's deep voice. He stood ten feet away, a shoulder resting against a tree. Mutt sat next to him, dark eyes on her and the pup. The other puppies milled around their papa, vying for attention but getting none.

"Fleas on all dogs," she said, her mouth suddenly dry.

As usual, Conway's presence unsettled her, though he appeared at ease.

"Mr. and Mrs. Gladstone gone?" she asked, but she knew they were.

He nodded. His gaze raked her length, then paused on the items she had dropped. She knew what he was thinking when he smiled. That endearing smile that did strange things to her insides.

"Lupe tells me you haven't missed a night bathing in the river."

He knew she bathed regularly, so she chose not to respond. When she'd balked the first time he insisted she bathe, it had not been the bath she feared. But he had not drowned her. Had not forced himself on her. Now, she was not certain she would fight his advances if he did. Her body responded to his desire in ways she did not understand. And he did desire her. She knew it.

She shook her head to break the mesmerizing contact of his dark eyes and looked at the pup. He still growled, squirming for release. She set him on the ground, gave his rump a pat, and sent him on his way. "Practice warrior skills with brothers and sisters."

The pup tripped over his own feet as he tumbled his roly-poly self into the midst of his siblings. Yips and barks erupted as the pups nipped at each other and scrambled toward the house.

As she knelt to pick up her things, Conway spoke again. "Rebecca."

Her gaze snapped to his.

"Pretty name. Why you wouldn't tell me is a puzzle."

Because she did not know what her real name had been. And, as plain as the nose on his face, her life as a white person was long over.

Ignoring him as best she could, she moved to the riverbank. Would he allow her to bathe in private? She jumped when he spoke again.

"White Fawn is a pretty name, too, but your name is Rebecca."

No. It made no difference what he said. No difference that in the dim recesses of her mind she might wish to be the white person she no longer remembered. Fate had willed otherwise.

She paused at the outcrop of rocks to deposit her clothes and the soap.

At the same time Mutt barked, Conway yelled, "Rebecca, stand still!"

Defying his command, she turned to face him. "I White Fa . . ." The words stuck in her throat as she stared down the barrel of his gun. She raised her hand as if to deflect the bullet from the enormous bore.

Time seemed to stand still. Mutt's incessant barking, Conway's warning faded into the distance, as did the gun's report.

Bone and soft matter splatted her hand. No more

122

than a foot from her hem, rattles buzzing, a snake's body undulated in the throes of sudden death. She looked at her hand as if it did not belong on her body.

In the next instant, Conway scooped her into his arms and fairly bellowed, "Did it bite you?"

Crushed against his hard chest, she could not breathe. His belt buckle dug into her belly. Dimly, she realized his hand cupped the side of her face, then slid behind her head, fingers tangled in her hair.

"White Fawn," he coaxed, "did it *bite* you?" Concern and something else she did not understand colored his voice, shone in his eyes.

She began to shake as the enormity of what had nearly happened sank in. Had the rattler struck her, she would surely . . . Not everyone died from snakebite, though one might wish for death during the agony of recovery.

Woman Who Sees Far had not seen far enough. Bitten by a water moccasin, her foot had blackened. The shaman had cut it off to stop the slow shriveling of flesh that inched up her ankle. Four moons later, she was found where she had crawled away to die. She had slit her wrists and bled to death rather than survive as a cripple. Few mourned Woman Who Sees Far, for she had done the right thing. The *Nermernuh* must be strong and whole to survive.

"Answer me," Conway demanded.

Unable to stop shaking, she shook her head. What she saw in his eyes gave her scant warning.

"Rebecca," he murmured before claiming her lips.

Searing heat slashed into her body. One moment she shook with chilled fear; the next she burned. When she gasped, he took advantage of her parted lips.

His tongue darted into her mouth, claiming, exploring, imploring. White Fawn responded as innocently as a lamb led to slaughter. She moaned, savoring the sheer pleasure never before experienced. Of their own volition, her hands slid over his broad shoulders. Unerringly, her fingers tangled in his long hair. So soft. She had known it would be.

He echoed her moan, and oddly, a thrill zinged through her that she could elicit that response simply by twining her fingers in his thick hair. Tentatively, she met his tongue with her own.

He actually growled and held her even tighter. A bulge pressed against the juncture of her thighs. Desire for her had turned to need.

"Matt?" He jerked back when Xavier's voice sounded nearby. "Where you be?"

Staring at her as if he'd lost his mind, he stepped away. "That shouldn't have happened," he muttered, then raised his voice. "Over here."

She blinked at his terse, accusing words. *It was her fault he had kissed her?*

Xavier pounded into view, a rifle in his hand. "I hear gunshot!"

She watched Conway calmly turn to his foreman, then nod toward the snake. Mutt's inquisitive nose snuffled the fascinatingly beautiful diamondback's length.

"Santa Maria!" He inspected both of them. "No bite?"

"Fortunately." Matt looked at her as if she had committed an unpardonable sin. "Watch your step while

124

taking your bath." Turning on his heel, he strode toward the house, Xavier beside him.

She watched him walk away. How could he do that? Not by voice or backward glance did he show the kiss had affected him. She still shook, her breath merely short pants. She touched her lips. Still hot, still burning. Wanting more.

"No!"

Conway had just shown her what she had feared all along. The man had little or no feelings for her, for any Comanche. His mouth might insist she was white, but his actions proved otherwise.

Perhaps, in the end, he was no different from other men, white or Comanche. Men used women and threw them away without regard for their feelings. White Fawn had seen it time and again in the tribe. And only rarely did Indian women divorce their men.

She shook her head. She must not be swayed by these new feelings Conway had awakened. He did not really want *her*. To slake his lust, perhaps, but that would not happen.

Though I wish he would kiss me again.

Matt sat on the side of the bed, grateful there wasn't a madhouse nearby. Anyone with a grain of sense would surely commit him. Hands fisted on his knees, he battled the heat raging through him. Closing his eyes, he relived that moment when White Fawn's delicate fingers feathered the back of his neck, then tangled in his hair. The sensation had been so, so . . . erotic.

He snorted. Now there was a swell-headed, silver-dollar word if there ever was one. But it nailed exactly how he'd felt. Still felt! "Jesus."

He jumped up to pace the length of the small room. He stopped to stare at a knothole as if it could answer the question he'd asked himself time and again. What in the hell should he do with her?

He plunked down on the bed again, the springs creaking fit to collapse under his weight. He was a hard man. He'd had to be to survive in Texas. He'd lusted after women and bedded more than his share. But what he felt for White Fawn went beyond lust.

To what? Love? Eyes narrowed, he snorted again. Not likely. He'd fancied himself in love once and learned his lesson. When Etta had thrown him over, Matt had gone on a drinking, whoring rampage. The first and last of his life.

Only later did he realize it wasn't rejected love that fueled his binge. His pride had been hurt. Hurt, hell! She'd trampled it into the dust under her not-so-dainty feet.

Fortunately, not long thereafter, his folks had pulled up stakes and moved to Texas. He'd gladly joined them.

He sighed, released his gun belt, and hung it on the bedpost. Unbuckling his spurs, he let them clank to the floor, then nudged them under the bed with his boot heel.

A shudder shook him when he remembered the snake so close. White Fawn had stepped within a foot of the damn thing. She'd been distracted by him, perhaps, but that was still no excuse for her to walk around without her eyes alert. Not this time of year. Snakes were everywhere, basking in the warm sun.

What would have happened had she been bitten

didn't bear thinking about. He didn't want her to suffer more. The healed knife marks were proof she had at some point.

"Goodnight, Rebecca." Lupe's voice filtered through the closed door.

"I am White Fawn."

"Here, you are Rebecca." Lupe's voice rang with exasperation.

"No."

Hell's fire, the girl was stubborn!

"I *Nermernuh*. Claim long ago."

"Rebecca—"

"Would not Mrs. Gladstone sh . . . shun me if she knew?"

"She needn't know. No one here will reveal where you've been for . . . How long were you with the Comanche?"

Silence. Matt waited, wondering how far back he'd have to begin his search.

"Many seasons, Lupe."

Which told him not a damn thing! Neither woman spoke again. He heard the key turn in the lock.

As he undressed, he thought it time to reconsider his original plan. As soon as they finished the branding, he'd take White Fawn to Steven Voight's orphanage. Though Matt suspected she might be older than he knew, she was so tiny, she could fit in with the children. She might even be of help to Steven.

Lying back on the quilt, naked as a newborn, he stacked his hands under his head. Heaviness settled in his loins. How could he travel with her for four days and three nights and not touch her? Earlier, had Xavier not called out, Matt knew as sure as God made him that he'd have lowered White Fawn to the ground and sunk into her right there.

Would she have fought him? He heard her soft moan again as if she were there in the room. Her response told him she wasn't experienced. Not with kissing, anyway. But she probably wouldn't have denied him.

No excuse, Matt Conway.

He rolled to his side and drew up his knees, a futile attempt to relieve his tumescence. A longing for White Fawn he couldn't deny battered its way into his body and mind. His groan of frustration echoed in the small room.

As the weeks passed, White Fawn remained uppermost in Matt's thoughts. He continually reminded himself to think of her as Rebecca. But dammit all, White Fawn was a pretty name.

Around Gladstone, he too often came close to addressing her by the Comanche name. If he slipped up, Lupe's elaborate story of how he'd found *Rebecca* would be shot to hell as fast as a wildfire raced across the prairie.

With one booted foot hooked on the bottom rail, his arms crossed on the top board, he watched the girl ride Pepper in the corral. It had become more or less routine for White . . . for *Rebecca* to exercise Pepper after the noon meal. Though Matt had yet to allow her out of the corral, she rode very well. Too well.

And that fed Hank Gladstone's curiosity. "Ain't a thing wrong with how that little gal rides. Wonder why she don't ride nowheres else?"

If Hank expected Lupe or Xavier to give him more information, he was shinning up the wrong tree. A crowbar wouldn't loosen their tongues. Lars and Hoby remained closemouthed, too. Matt was grateful that everyone ignored Hank's proddings.

Over the weeks, he'd watched his men's admiration grow. Yeah, she rode well, but he figured her doctoring abilities were probably the deciding factor.

Pepper's leg had healed in just a few days. Lars had thought a feverish cow would dry up, but White Fawn stayed with that critter for two nights running, and when the fever broke, Lars was able to milk her to nourish her calf.

Matt believed she had a gift. People, too, benefitted from her healing potions and poultices. Her arm healed completely, leaving little evidence a bullet had taken out a chunk of her skin.

Her quiet manner also appealed to his men. Though stilted, her English was getting better. Would her speech ever take on a Texas drawl?

Focused on her as she rode by, he shook his head in a futile effort to dispel his thoughts. He scowled at the moccasins peeking from beneath her skirt. Nothing was ever easy with this girl. He figured he had a royal battle ahead of him this evening.

After supper Matt went to his bedroom and pulled White Fawn's gift from beneath his bed. Gift, hell! He grinned and rubbed his fingers over the smooth leather of one of the little boots.

Unsure of White Fawn's size, he'd measured with a spread hand several pairs of boys' boots for close-to-proper length if not a snug width. He hoped she could lace them tight enough so she would not get blisters.

Reasonable or not, he was determined to destroy the moccasins. Not that it would change much. Comanche tripped off her tongue if she were agitated. She was careful, though, to speak English in the neighbors' hearing—unless provoked. Which he was about to do.

"Lupe." He rounded the door into the parlor.

The odor of fatback and greens lingered from supper. An oil lamp in the middle of the table shone brightly on her and Xavier's dark hair. She looked up from her mending.

"I need your help." He scowled. "Not help. I need a pair of your socks and garters."

"For Rebecca?" Lupe never failed to use her white name.

Would that he could remember to do the same. He was coming to the realization that he'd always think of her as White Fawn. "Yeah. I bought these boots at Goodlight's but forgot socks."

"You think she wear them?" Xavier asked, busily oiling his own boots.

"She'll wear them," he assured them, "though she'll probably balk at first."

Lupe rested the shirt in her lap and eyed the footware with a frown. "Determined is your middle name, Matthew Conway. Why is it so important she give up moccasins that are probably far and away more comfortable than those stiff boots?"

"If we are to pull off your story of how I found her—"

"Carolyn Parks wears moccasins. So does Prudence

Caldwell. Not all the time, I grant you, but no one questions where *they* came from."

True, Matt thought. The *why* to which Lupe wanted an answer was mixed up with his equally jangled feelings about White Fawn—Rebecca. He wanted the evidence of the Comanche erased. *What will that accomplish?* his pesky little inner voice asked.

Rebecca had lived with the Comanche. As White Fawn, she'd probably lain with a warrior. Would removing those moccasins from view allay his thoughts to the point of convincing himself she had remained untouched? Why was that important? Because he wouldn't follow where an Indian had taken his fill.

But you don't intend to. Right, Matt?

"Dammit, are you going to let me have a pair of your stockings or not?"

Lupe and Xavier jumped at his outburst. She laid her mending aside and rose. "Of course. I was just . . . curious."

Curious, my eye. Lupe knew him so well. Too well. She sensed that he waged internal battles. Battles he feared he was losing as each day and night passed with White Fawn tantalizingly close.

He wanted her as he'd never wanted another woman. Desire for her had exploded in him almost from the moment he'd seen her.

Disgusted with himself, he pivoted and followed Lupe to her room. Moments later he listened at White Fawn's door, then wondered why he bothered. She was as quiet locked up as she was in company.

* * *

131

During the time White Fawn had been on Conway's ranch, she had moved from the floor to the ladder-back chair. Still, she could not sleep in the bed. It would be dark before long. And here she sat with nothing to do.

She must admit, though, the isolation was partly her own doing. Many times Lupe had asked her to join them after the evening meal. So had Conway. She had refused, uneasy in the same room with him, and confused by her interest in the man.

More than once, she had been jolted from a trance-like perusal of him. Despite her better judgment, he attracted her. His hands . . . Big, like the rest of him, his hands had hurt her. But they had soothed her, too.

He would bring pleasure if he stroked her body. Though not sure how such pleasure would feel, she longed to find out.

His kiss . . . She closed her eyes, reliving that moment when he had taken her lips as if they were his possession. Perhaps his kiss would have led to mating. She frowned. Not mating. Father Anselmo had said that if a man and woman loved each other, their coupling was a natural part of that love.

Eyes dim, she stared at her limp hands in her lap. She wanted to experience that . . . with Matt-Matthew.

No!

Leaping to her feet, she took several turns around the room, her arms wrapped protectively around her waist. She must not think of him that way. She must return to her people as soon as possible.

This idleness was driving her mad. From earliest memory, there had always been enough to do to keep herself busy. Sometimes the work was drudgery. Other times, a pleasure.

She liked to cook, delighted in discovering wild prairie plants to season buffalo, bear, deer, or rabbit stews. But she refused to prepare or eat horse as the Comanche were wont to do when wild game was scarce. Perhaps what she enjoyed most was seeing Eagle Feather and Beaver Heart's pleasure when they ate one of her dishes.

What she disliked most was striking and setting up the tipi. Woman's work, heavy work—too heavy. She had wondered how she would manage alone once she mated with One Bear. One day in the future, Eagle Feather would send her to another's lodge.

She sank onto the chair and leaned back. Useless to fret about those things now. She enjoyed quilting with Lupe. One more pleasant afternoon should see them finished with the lovely bedcover.

Mrs. Gladstone was nice, but the woman's incessant talk frayed her nerves. That she had not been back since that one visit pleased White Fawn. More often than not, she and Lupe worked in companionable silence.

Lupe worked hard and would not tolerate slapdash performance from others. Just this morning, while White Fawn ironed sheets with the flatiron, Lupe said, "If a job is worth doing, it's worth doing well."

Apparently a belief of all people. Recently, Bright Star had uttered different words meaning the same thing. "My heart is glad when Eagle Feather is pleased."

Conway's voice broke the silence. He sounded vexed.

Massaging her temples, she sighed. She must stop thinking about the man. He was her enemy, was he not?

"White Fa . . . Rebecca?" The door swung open. His tall frame filled the space.

Chiding herself was useless. Upon seeing him, she remembered too clearly his broad chest when he bathed in the river and worked in the sun. Her mouth went dry; unbidden heat boiled in her belly like molten rock. She clenched her fists in her lap.

"So, you've decided to sit in a chair like the rest of us."

Hat in hand, he walked into the room. When she failed to answer, his smile faltered. "I have a gift for you." From behind the hat, he produced a pair of boots.

Her glance snapped to his smiling face, to her moccasined feet, then back to the boots. "I think no, Conway."

"You've been cooped up night after night. Thought you might like to take a walk."

"I would." Anything to get out of this room. She lifted a foot. "Waste money. I have shoes."

He wagged his head, laughter dancing in his dark eyes. He waved the boots. "These have good soles, and the leather is better protection against . . . snakes."

He was using the near-bite incident to his advantage. Snake fangs could penetrate moccasins. But she did not want his gift, more of this white man's life. She was Comanche.

"No."

His smile vanished. "Do you know how often you

134

say that? Is it the only way you can react to my wishes?"

"Yes." She smiled. The irony of the reversal tickled her funny bone. Not his.

"Look, Rebecca—"

"White Fawn."

"Now that you are here, you must accept how we address you. In case you haven't figured it out, Lupe is rare. Other women would ostracize you in a heartbeat if they knew your background."

A frisson of fear lanced through her.

He tossed the boots at her feet. "Put them on. We can discuss this while we walk. Lupe stuffed socks and garters in one boot."

She remained still as stone. Maybe he would go away.

"Look." Exasperation laced his voice. "We've been here before. If you persist, I can and *will* take those moccasins off you."

So true. Visions filled her mind of their fight when he insisted she bathe the first time. No question, he could overpower her and have his way.

"All right," she mumbled.

He spun on his heel. "I'll wait on the porch."

Chapter Nine

Frustrated, White Fawn tugged at the lace. Not easy to tie these white man's boots. Then, she tried to walk. That presented a challenge. The heels, about a half-inch high, tilted her forward when she stood. Rather than lift her feet, she gave up and shuffled to the doorway, clamping a hand on the jamb. "I know not how walk in these."

Matt stared, then grinned.

The skunk.

"Slow and easy, then." He beckoned.

She had not realized how foreign boots would feel. The leather was so stiff, her toes could not flex.

"One step at a time, Rebecca."

She glared at him. "I White Fawn!"

He glared right back. After a moment, he conceded. "All right. When we're alone, I'll call you White Fawn. But don't blame me if I slip up. If I forget to address you as Rebecca when I should, it'll bring calamity down on your head."

Pleased at gaining one concession from him, she nevertheless realized he spoke truth. Few knew of her existence. Lupe would say nothing, nor would Xavier. After that first encounter with Mr. Varner, he and the rest of the men, though polite enough, never called her by name. But if Mr. or Mrs. Gladstone found out . . .

"Are you going to stand there all night holding up the house?"

Forgetful of her awkwardness, she moved forward too quickly. Two steps and the toe of one boot snagged her skirt's hem. Another and both feet tangled in the material. Pitching forward, arms cartwheeling, she wailed, "Conway!"

Reacting to her dilemma, he lunged. His left spur's rowel caught the lip of the step and wrenched him off balance. He went down on his back like a felled bear. In the next instant, she landed across his chest.

"Oof!"

Breathless, her body felt nailed to his broad chest. Struggling to rise, her hand slipped on the plank floor. She finally levered herself up enough to look into his face. The astonishment there surely mirrored her own. "I sorry!"

Laughter exploded from him at the same time Lupe asked, "What's going on out here?" She stood in the doorway, the ever-present mending in her hands.

White Fawn stared at the man beneath her who was guffawing like one demented. His white teeth glimmered in dusk's light.

"Are you all right?" Lupe's voice came closer.

Conway's laughter was infectious and White Fawn joined him, sounding as crazy as he. "I . . . fell. Skirt . . . tangled."

Lupe helped her sit up on the floor beside Conway. Legs straight in front of her, toes pointed skyward, she glared at the offending boots. Then laughter overtook her again when she realized how ridiculous they looked sprawled on the floor.

"Trip on hem." Shaking her head, she gave up. Conway's chortles had subsided, but he still grinned like an idiot. So pleasing, his laughter, his smile, his devilish eyes.

He brushed a hand down his face. With the other, he clasped hers and squeezed ever so gently. "You okay?"

She took a steadying breath and nodded. So easily she could get used to his gentle touch, which sent fire flashing through her veins. Did he have to be so appealing? Must he awaken feelings better left alone? Disquieted by her thoughts and his warm hand, she snatched hers away and started to rise.

Lupe clasped her elbow and guided her up. "What in the world were you doing?"

Conway rolled to his feet in one graceful motion. "Attempting to walk."

"Attempting?"

"Well, yeah." His grin returned. "You tell her."

White Fawn looked at the square-toed leather peeking from beneath her skirt. "Hard soles no bend."

Lupe joined the merriment. "Well, Matt, perhaps you'd better take the lady's hand and lead her for a while."

Not a good idea. A light in the depths of his dark eyes made White Fawn aware of her own body's need. "I think—"

"That's a good idea." He extended his hand.

Touching his palm, allowing him to touch her, would lead her to disaster. Lying atop him, her body had become aroused of its own accord. Though she did not know what surrendering herself to the feelings would be like, more and more she longed to find out.

"White Fawn?"

The compelling light still in his eyes told her that he would welcome her with open arms.

Hesitant, she laid her hand in his. His fingers closed around hers like a warm cocoon. Though expected, she bit her lip when heat raced through her body and settled at the apex of her thighs.

"You'd better not go far. Snakes are everywhere."

White Fawn shuddered, the thought of snakes bringing back that horrible encounter at the river.

"We won't. Just out to Pepper's corral," Conway said.

White Fawn had taken no more than two steps when Lupe called, "Wait." She walked up behind her, clasped her shoulder, and splayed her other hand on her back and pushed. "Stand up straight or you'll be head over teakettle in no time."

Conway's lips lifted in a smile. She ducked her head, warmth flooding her cheeks.

"How long has it been since you donned boots?" Lupe asked.

Lupe and Conway never missed a chance to pry information from her. She could not seem to make them understand that she did not know. Could not remember her life as a white child. If not for Father Anselmo, she would not have known the English tongue. "Many seasons," she finally answered.

"A chatterbox," Conway quipped and started off.

With her hand firmly held in his, White Fawn discovered that though she might stumble, he would not allow her to fall. A surprisingly companionable silence settled between them. The quarter moon had set, leaving the heavens studded with diamond stars.

Pepper's corral stood between them and the bunkhouse. Faint light glowed from two small windows on either side of the closed door. She had never been inside, but the structure looked as though more than the few men housed there could live comfortably in it.

She occasionally came upon the men eating Lupe's breakfast or noon meal. But never the evening meal.

"Where men eat supper?"

Conway pointed at the bunkhouse. "Lars is a good cook, and Bob Foster can rustle up a mean batch of fried rabbit or chicken."

Startled, White Fawn halted. "Men cook?" Not once had she ever seen a brave near a cookfire. "Woman no cook, Eagle Feather starve."

Conway's fingers squeezed her hand to near pain for a second; then he eased his grip. "Who is Eagle Feather?"

She had brought it on herself, she supposed. Mentioning anyone in the band by name was not wise, and she had done so several times. But what could it hurt to tell him? He would never know Eagle Feather.

She stopped at the corral rail and looked through the slats. Pepper stood on the far side, one leg hip-shot while she dozed.

White Fawn clicked her tongue. "Pepper."

The mare's head bobbed up and around in recognition. She blew a welcome, then ambled over. White Fawn extended her hand between the slats to brush Pepper's face and scratch her jaw.

Without warning, Conway lifted her to sit atop the fence. Pepper stuck her head in front of White Fawn's legs.

"Easier to reach her," he said.

She stroked and petted and scratched between Pepper's ears, speaking softly in Comanche.

Pepper nodded and snuffled as if answering.

"Content outside, she is." White Fawn frowned. That had not come out right. She still could not speak the white man's tongue very well. But Conway did not seem to notice.

Arms crossed on the top rail inches from her knees, he shrugged. "Most horses prefer the outdoors. Trooper sure does. But we usually bed the stock in the barn. Safer that way."

Pepper shied and backed away. She trotted off, stopped, and looked back, as if she expected White Fawn to follow.

"Safer?"

"Indians."

Of course. Though her people would not think twice about entering a barn. It made stealing horses a bit more challenging.

"Who is Eagle Feather?" Conway asked again.

Stubborn man. She saw his dark eyes search hers with unsettling intensity.

"Father."

Had relief flitted across his features? If so, it was so

quick, she thought she had dreamed it when his lips thinned.

"No, he's not."

"You ask, Conway. He father I know."

"You speak English too well not to remember your family."

He knew not that Father Anselmo had taught her, and she did not tell him. The less he knew about her, the better.

"How many?"

"How many?"

"In your family." Irritation etched his voice.

"Seven."

"So many?"

"Eagle Feather, Bright Star, Willow Branch . . ."

He jerked her off the fence and crushed her against his chest. "Dammit! I meant your white family and you know it!" The Spirits knew she had tried in vain to remember her life as a white child. After a while, it mattered not. Conway might not ever accept that, but it was truth.

She kicked and pushed against Conway's chest. Pressed against him, she found it difficult to breathe and impossible to ignore his heart beating strongly beneath her hands.

Looking up, she forgot what she wanted. With his lips only a breath away, she went still. The desire for him to kiss her again stole her resistance. Her limbs turned to mush.

Perhaps he divined her wish. He lowered his head, and just before his lips closed over hers, he muttered, "Damn you."

Doubtless, she was. Damned to live the rest of her life as a Comanche squaw. Damned to live without the love of this man. *Only this man,* her heart cried.

Conway tilted his head, his lips slanting over hers. Hot, moist, heady. Delicious. Wrapping her arms around his neck, she burned and gave herself up to the heat coursing through her. She moaned.

He answered with one of his own and darted his tongue over her lips, across the seam, asking . . . *what?* She gasped for breath and found out. His tongue delved into her mouth. Soft, searching, tasting her as if she were a sweetmeat.

His arm slipped under her legs and he lifted her in his arms. Then he walked. She knew not where and did not care. Her whole being was centered on his mouth, his tongue giving her pleasure. Then she floated down. Her back rested on his forearm, her body on a pile of hay. In the barn, she thought, and cared only that he go on kissing her.

He pulled back. In the darkness, his eyes glittered as brightly as the stars in the heavens. "Damn you," he repeated. "Damn me," he added, and reclaimed her lips.

Confused, she simply gave herself up to sensation. Sank her fingers in his long hair, as silky as a newborn calf's hide. She drew her hand along the side of his face. Smooth skin, beard stubble. And his lips . . . Spirits of the People, was there another man gifted with his firm yet soft lips?

As she rested her hands on his shoulders, hard muscles shifted beneath her touch. Oh, to feel his bare skin! She groaned her frustration.

He loomed fully over her and bent his leg across her

lower body, securing her in the hay. Breath ragged and hot, cheek resting on hers, he gasped as if he had been running. "I want you, White Fawn. I shouldn't, but I do."

Her heart fluttered anew when he lifted his head and stared directly into her eyes. "I want to pleasure you. I want . . . I *need* to be inside you, your beautiful legs wrapped around me."

Thrilled by his words, she brushed the back of his head in a soothing motion. Not only unwise, it was madness for her to desire the same thing. Somehow she knew Conway would bring her the pleasure of which he spoke. For her first time, he would give her what she suspected Eagle Feather and Bright Star shared. Lovemaking. Not simply the coupling she dreaded.

She had seen more than one maiden go once to a warrior's tipi to couple, then leave, never to return. It was not forbidden. But once a bride price was set, once a maiden accepted a warrior, she was mated for life. If she slept with another, she risked mutilation, the shame of having her nose cut off, even death. Only a woman widowed could lie with another warrior, usually a brother or cousin of her dead mate. One who would protect her.

Unable to say the words, but driven by building desire, White Fawn cupped the back of his head and pulled his lips to hers. His body as taut as a ceremonial drum, he moaned his understanding of her agreement. Her heart soared.

He had given her a choice.

Moments later, she got another of her wishes. He removed his shirt, and her shirtwaist as well. Not only was she free to explore the planes of his muscled torso, she felt the hair on his chest coax her nipples to buds. Another bolt of heat scorched through her when his lips settled over one. His tongue swirled; then his teeth bit ever so gently.

Unsure of her role, she hesitantly found his flat nipple with her tongue.

"God! Don't, or it will be over before we start."

She smiled, wrapped her arms around his broad chest, and feathered her fingers down his spine. Another curse erupted from him. He pulled away to remove his trousers and boots.

She wished for more light. The desire to see his naked body warred with a little fear. Willow Branch had told her some men were quite large . . . there. If the rest of him was a gauge, Conway must be immense. Willow Branch said it hurt the first time, but then pleasure followed if the man was gentle and caring.

She searched what she could see of his shadowed face as he released the button on her skirt and began to tug it over her hips. Knees bent, she lifted her buttocks to help him. *Please let him be gentle.*

Pleasure, more pleasure than she ever could have imagined followed. For a while, not a word passed between them. He coaxed and teased, caressed and kissed every part of her body. If she had been hot before, now she flamed.

As his warm tongue flicked over her belly, she pressed her knees together, the heat and moisture between her legs provoking a need she could barely suppress. Kneeling, Conway spread her thighs. She gasped when his lips touched her most intimate place.

"Oh!" Her eyes flew open when his tongue swirled. Shock coursed through her. Her hips bucked in his hands.

"Easy, darlin'." He slid up and over her and rested his weight on bent arms.

His face came into focus. "Conway, I—"

"Don't you think Matt is more appropriate now?" A white-toothed grin curved his lips.

It captured her heart and her wits. She felt the size of his hot, hard length against her belly and forgot what she intended to say. He lifted his hips and entered her slowly. Though he gave her time, her body protested the stretching.

"Ah, God, you're so tight." He pulled out, then plunged in quickly, more quickly than she expected.

"Ahh!" Again she bucked, but from pain this time.

Conway stilled. Arms trembling, he slowly raised his head, disbelief coloring his gaze. Her eyes rounded in apprehension.

"Jesus! Why didn't you tell me?"

Panting, she realized the pain had eased, but he *was* enormous inside her. "What?"

"What? *What?*" he repeated louder. "God-a-mighty, you've never been with a man. I thought . . ." He scowled.

"Does matter?"

"Of course it matters!"

"Why?"

He had not moved. His arms stopped trembling, but

sweat beaded his brow. When he gave every indication of pulling back, she clasped his torso and held on tight.

"Why you . . . No leave."

He rested his forehead against hers. "Look, sweetheart, had I known you were a virgin, I wouldn't have started . . . this."

"Why?"

"Stop asking why!"

"I want know."

He sighed. "Because I've never taken a virgin before. I don't intend to marry. So—"

"You marry virgin?"

"Yeah." Though clearly stricken by his actions, he looked thoughtful. "I think you're younger than I wanted to believe."

"Twenty, maybe." The words were out before she thought.

"Then why haven't you—"

"Be with warrior?"

"Well, yeah."

Because I wanted more than to couple. I wanted to know what lovemaking is like. Because you are the man . . . "My choice." She moved her hips. "You ready, Conway?"

His laugh sounded strangled. "I'm a man, sweetheart. And you're . . . hot and tight."

"Pain, she gone."

"God, I'm sorry," he said fervently, and cupped the side of her face. "It must have hurt like hell. Had I known—"

"You no take virgin. You have. We continue?"

"Dammit, White Fawn."

"It what I want."

Soon I shall be gone. Never to see you again. She would take these moments, his lovemaking, tucked away to remember. The smell of him, the feel of his big body, his touch. Someday she would have to take a warrior to her blankets, but it would not be the same. Down deep in her heart and against her better judgment, she had fallen in love with this impossible man.

"Please," she whispered, and drew his head down for a kiss.

Though he hesitated, she felt his member pulse inside her. She had won. He might be reluctant, but Conway could no longer resist. She knew it and smiled when he groaned . . . in frustrated surrender.

His frustration turned to flames, then frenzy as he took her to the heavens.

Just this once to feel the power of his big body, his hands, his lips, his tongue.

There's a fool born every day, Matt thought. At the moment, he damn well led the pack. In the age-old stance of every rancher who stood beside a fence, he hooked his boot heel over the bottom slat and crossed his arms on the top.

Trooper dozed in the far corner of the stall. Eat and sleep. Wouldn't it be wonderful if his life were as simple? He grimaced. He'd forego the gelding part, thank you.

Blessed with the night vision of a cat, he glanced sidelong at White Fawn, still seated in the fragrant hay. Now dressed, she braided her glorious hair. Yeah, he could see her just fine. A virgin, for God's sake. Well, no more. What was the old-fashioned word? Oh, yeah, deflowered.

He swung his head back to stare straight ahead. It certainly described what he'd done, how she'd responded. He swiped an unsteady hand over his face. It didn't erase her image one bit.

For someone who'd lived on the plains, exposed to the sun and a hard life, her skin was surprisingly soft. Like rose petals. And he'd plucked each petal, caressing her cheek, laving her throat, her ears, her shoulders with an eager tongue. Her inner thighs were even softer than a rose petal, by God.

"You'll experiment just like all men have since time began, Matthew. I'm not wasting my breath telling you otherwise. But, by God, keep your pants buttoned around a virgin!" Ian Conway's words echoed in his mind.

Gentlemen did not bed virgins before the wedding. There were whores aplenty upon whom randy young men could appease their appetites. His father could not have made it more clear. And Matt had heeded his words. Sort of. If it came right down to the truth, Stella Weatherly wasn't a whore, but she was experienced. She'd needed his attention as much as he'd needed hers.

And, dammit, how was he to know White Fawn had remained a virgin? She hadn't said a word. She'd welcomed him. Hell's fire, she'd *asked* him to make love to her. Fool that he was, he'd complied. And enjoyed every moment. He sighed, ducked his head, and rested his forehead on his arms.

No justification. Doomed to remember her soft skin, her breathy gasps, her lovely eyes staring at him in wonder as sensations pulsed through her body. At least he'd given her pleasure.

No matter whom he'd slept with, be it Stella or the few whores he'd bedded over the years, he always found as much pleasure in giving as taking. No way could he simply rut like a boar, needy or not. He made love, dammit!

Night sounds seeped into his consciousness. Trooper shuffled restlessly; a newborn calf gave a half-bawl, then silenced abruptly. From the henhouse behind the barn, chickens made that quiet, throaty noise, as if disturbed or resettling on a nest.

"Conway?"

Matt straightened. "Yeah?" *What the hell should he do now?*

"Is late." She fingered her long braid.

Marshaling his courage, he walked toward her. "I'm sure you're tired." *And probably sore as the devil.*

White Fawn peered up at him; a smile trembled on her lips. "Angry with me?"

"No." *Only with myself.*

"Thank you. I want . . . I hope you gentle and you were."

Matt anchored his thumbs over his belt. "Not as gentle as I should have been. I wish you'd told me, White Fawn. I wouldn't have taken it so far."

She frowned, tipping her head. "I no understand why important I no been with man. Maidens lie with warriors before take one mate."

He gritted his teeth, clenched his hands. "Stop it! You're white. You're back where you belong. And now . . ."

When she married, her husband would know. How would he treat her? With contempt? Anger? Would he hurt her? Matt quelled the thought. White Fawn in another man's arms didn't bear thinking about.

"You never understand." She huffed and tossed a boot at him. "Forevermore I Indian. Long ago white world lost. Must return to Eagle Feather. The *Llano Esta*—"

Her eyes rounded. She'd said too much, told him what he'd suspected. The band she'd traveled with had gone far south to raid. In a way, he breathed a little easier for it. The farther away the Comanches were, the better for him and all the white settlers in these parts.

"*Llano Estacado*. You're not going back to the Staked Planes, White Fawn. You might as well get that through your head."

Her full lips, still swollen from his kisses, firmed. Lips he wanted to kiss again. Now, tomorrow, the day after.

His expression resolute, he was as unshakable as she. She intended to escape, but he wouldn't let her. He'd take her to Austin tomorrow. If she remained near him, sure as shootin' he'd take her again. And that was wrong, wrong, wrong.

Matt clasped her arm and turned her toward the house. No point telling her his plans. Why stir up more trouble?

An hour later Matt lay in bed, his head resting on stacked hands. A thought had lodged in his mind and he couldn't let it go.

What if he'd planted a child in her belly?

Chapter Ten

Matt woke to the sound of hoofbeats. Diving for his pants, he dressed in record time and headed out the door as he buckled on his gun belt. Xavier and Lupe met him in the corridor, and together they walked out on the porch.

Bettencourt and Cecil dismounted, faces grim.

"Mornin'," Isaac said.

Cecil nodded as Matt returned the greeting.

"What's up?"

"Nothin' good," Isaac said. "Buster Caldwell rode out to find me yesterday. Said he saw Indians. Wanted the Rangers to warn ranchers in the area."

"Oh, shit. Where?"

"Strangest thing," Cecil said. "They stood 'bout a quarter-mile from his cabin but didn't go no closer. Just watched."

Isaac nodded agreement, and Matt frowned.

"Three of 'em, accordin' to Prudence. She herded her little ones inside. Odder still, a day or so earlier, Andrew Perkins saw one lurkin' 'round his place, too. Think we'd better take a look-see?"

"Right." Matt turned to Xavier. "Were you riding out today for more strays?"

"*Sí.* Not now. Gladstone coming. He go with Fosters. Send Lars and Hoby, maybe?"

"No. Just Gladstone and the Fosters. You may need Lars and Hoby."

Lupe stood behind Xavier, a rifle resting in the crook of her arm. Braver than some men, Lupe could shoot to kill as well as anyone he knew. His gaze flicked to the door behind which White Fawn was locked. He nodded. Lupe got the message. The girl would bear watching until the danger passed.

The few Indians could be a scouting party for a larger band. Though why they'd show themselves, Matt didn't know.

As he gathered his bedroll, canteen, and extra ammunition, he recalled what he'd planned for today. Shot to hell. But as soon as he returned, he'd take White Fawn to Austin. He'd already disobeyed his father's admonitions once. If she remained here . . .

He could pay her a visit every few weeks. If she showed signs of being with child . . . *Don't borrow trouble. Leap over that gully if or when the time comes.*

In the bedroom, White Fawn held her breath in an effort to hear the conversation outside. Indians close by? Looking for her? Perhaps not, but if she could find them . . . Members of Eagle Feather's band or not, Comanches would help her find the way home.

153

Weeks ago, Lupe had spirited away her buckskin dress. Her moccasins were missing, too. She stared morosely at her attire, the uncomfortable footwear. But she must wear the white woman's clothes until she returned to her village.

Surely when she spoke, Indians would know she was one of them. One look at how she rode Pepper would tell them as well. Somehow she must find a way to get out of the house and spirit Pepper from the corral.

Over the past week or so, Lupe's vigilance had eased. But with Conway gone, she might be more careful. For how long, was the question. Long enough for her to fool Lupe into thinking she had resigned herself to living in the white world?

She stared at the offending door. If only Lupe would forget to lock it.

She must make Lupe think she was asleep and had not heard the conversation. If the woman thought her unaware that Conway had left, that Indians were close, maybe she would not intensify her vigil.

Tears pooled in her eyes when she heard hoofbeats. *He is gone.* She had not been able to see him once more. . . . Wrapping her arms around her waist, she keened softly to herself. Matt-Matthew was dead to her now. It hurt more to lose him after they had made love.

Despite her resolve to return to her village, she had fallen in love with the rugged rancher. Most unwise. She pressed her hand against her chest. Could a heart break?

Never to see him again. Never to feel his lips, his hands. His infrequent smiles, his dark eyes, his strong body would live in her dreams. Forever.

The drumming hoofbeats had long since died away

when she said softly, "Good-bye, Matt-Matthew Conway."

Shaking herself from the sad thoughts, she concentrated on what she must do. She needed Lupe to forget to lock the door one night.

Though she fought them, she still couldn't completely erase her thoughts. Her anguish.

Matt-Matthew, you never know my heart go with you.

Beaver Heart stared morosely at the flames of the tiny, almost smokeless fire. For days he and his companions had crisscrossed the prairie, stopping at each white man's cabin. The sight of Buffalo Hump or Snake Who Hisses had sent the whites into fearful flight. He smiled without humor.

Buffalo Hump intruded on his thoughts. "We should return to our village. The Spirits have not smiled on our search for your sister, Beaver Heart."

Beaver Heart squinted, unable to see Buffalo Hump. Foolhardy. Looking into a fire blinded a man long enough to court death if he was attacked. He blinked away the blindness.

"I am not ready to give up the search."

"Eat." Running Mouth Woman shoved a wooden bowl into Beaver Heart's hands. "I do not cook for pleasure."

Older than Beaver Heart by four summers, Running Mouth Woman had warmed his blankets since the season of falling leaves. She had taught him much about the pleasures of the body, and she was a good cook. But she never shut up. Her father had named her well.

As he dipped his fingers into the hot mixture and brought out pieces of deer meat, he resolved to discard the woman when they returned to the village. He had his eye on a younger maiden.

"Is good," he mumbled around the mouthful.

She presented him with a gap-toothed smile. "I looked most of the morning for herbs and wild onions. You like it?"

Beaver Heart sighed. What did he care how she found the food she cooked for him? It was her duty. "I said so, did I not?"

"Yes, but—"

"I am hungry as well," Snake Who Hisses interrupted.

"Bring my bowl, woman. My patience is at an end," Buffalo Hump said. "This journey has been too long with no results. We could have captured countless horses and slaves by now."

Though his friend spoke truth, Beaver Heart found it difficult to abandon the search. For some indefinable reason, he felt White Fawn was near. Had they not traveled farther south by several suns than with his father?

He held up his hand and counted off fingers. "Three suns, Buffalo Hump. If I have not seen my sister by then, I shall do as you wish."

"Maybe White Fawn wants to remain with the white people if that is where she is," Running Mouth Woman said. When no response came, she continued, "We have seen nothing of One Bear's raiding party. How do you know she still lives?"

Beaver Heart narrowed his eyes. He did not know. He sensed . . . He was not ready to admit defeat. If his father still lived, he longed to take his sister back to Eagle Feather. Perhaps his father would not rise from his blankets again, but his heart would gladden in his last days with White Fawn by his side.

"Three suns, Buffalo Hump. My heart will be heavy if we have not found my sister, but I will turn my face north on the fourth morning as you wish."

Ugh! Wash day. By the time White Fawn finished the breakfast dishes, Lupe was already at work on the backbreaking chore. White Fawn joined her and took over the scrub board. The lye soap ate at her hands; the rippled tin scraped her knuckles as she rubbed the clothes. But she was not adept at wringing water from the garments, especially the large sheets.

"Matt-Matthew's shirt has tear under arm, Lupe."

Lupe turned from the line stretched between two trees, a perplexed expression on her face. "Who?"

Looking up from the tub, White Fawn brushed sweat from her forehead with the back of her forearm. "Matt-Matthew. He wore last night when we fall."

When he made love to me. Her heart constricted, but she kept her face passive, and wondered at Lupe's puzzled expression.

"Why do you call him Matt-Matthew?"

"That his name, is it not? He say—"

"His name is Matthew Ian Conway." Lupe grinned. "Where did you get the idea—"

"No, he yell when I say 'Mr. Ranger.' Say name Matt-Matthew Conway."

"Mr. Ranger? I understand now. He *was* a Ranger,

Rebecca, but that was a time he doesn't remember
with . . . pride."

Her expression turned serious. "He joined the
Rangers after Comanches massacred his entire family."

"Killed? All them?"

Lupe nodded. "Mother, father, brother."

"Oh," she said softly.

"Knowing him, I suspect he was irritated with you."
She feigned a stern expression and bellowed, "My
name is Matt . . . Matthew Conway!" She chuckled.
"Is that what he said?"

White Fawn stared at her, openmouthed. She
sounded so much like the man. "Uh, yes. He say, 'Use
it!'"

"And have you?"

White Fawn looked down at the garment in her
hand. Her cheeks warmed. She'd avoided that name because it sounded too intimate. "No. I say Conway."

Lupe shook her head and picked up a pair of wet
trousers, flung them over the line. "Matt is short for
Matthew." She chuckled. "You needn't call him by
both."

"I . . . see." She did not, but Lupe certainly knew his
name. She had misunderstood and was glad she had not
addressed him as Matt-Matthew. He would have
laughed at her.

On the heels of that thought, sorrow swept through
her. Now she could understand his hatred of her people.

"Don't worry about it, Rebecca. He can be an exas-
perating man, but his heart is in the right place." Still
smiling, Lupe returned to her chore.

What did that mean? Where would a heart be but in one's chest? She sloshed the shirt against the board. The one he'd removed before they made love. The one he had donned again, covering muscled shoulders and arms.

Even now she could feel his taut skin, feel the strength beneath her hands. Hands which had eagerly caressed him. She wished there had been more light in the barn so she could have seen him clearly. Perhaps it was well she could not. It was enough to remember his hands on her body, his mouth, his tongue. Memories of his face and man's body would only add to her longing as the days, the years, dragged by.

"Almost finished."

Lupe's words ended her reverie. She resumed the brisk scrubbing that had slowed while her mind wandered, then added the shirt to the pile. Lupe dropped a petticoat over the wet laundry and picked up the basket.

"At least it's a sunny day. The clothes will dry quickly."

Lupe walked toward the middle of the line. As one pup trotted close to her feet, he snagged her skirt hem in his teeth.

"Git!" she snapped, but the puppy clung to the material.

Another step and the pup danced in front of her, tangling her feet in the skirt. Instead of dropping the basket as she fell, she held on. Her leg wrenched sideways, and the weight crashed onto her knee. Then the basket rolled away, strewing wet clothes for several feet.

White Fawn raced toward her friend and slid to her knees. "You hurt, Lupe?"

159

"Oh," she moaned, lying on her side. Her hands clasped her knee.

The boisterous pup jumped at Lupe, licked her face.

White Fawn slapped him aside. "Cause enough mischief, you!"

He yipped and scuttled away, only to rush right back. Splaying sturdy front legs, he bowed, rump high in the air, tail whipping back and forth, ready to play. His bark brought his siblings on the run. They distracted him as they growled and tumbled into rough-housing balls of fur.

In obvious pain, Lupe tried to sit up. "Oh," she gasped again.

"Xavier help maybe."

Lupe pushed herself to a sitting position and shook her head. She took a deep breath. "No. I'm . . . all right." Biting her lower lip, ever so slowly she extended the leg, but it wouldn't straighten completely.

"Broken?" White Fawn hoped not. She had splinted many broken arms and legs for children in the tribe. They usually healed straight and true, but once a bone had protruded through the skin. Not only did the bone mend wrong, but bad Spirits nearly took the child's arm before the shaman cauterized the putrid flesh.

Carefully poking and prodding her knee, Lupe grimaced. "I don't think so. Sprained, probably." With a rueful smile, she glanced at the wet, dirt-smeared clothes. "Oh, dear. We have to wash those again."

White Fawn shook her head. "No *we*, Lupe. You go inside, rest." She scrambled around to Lupe's side. "I help you."

Legs shaky, Lupe couldn't put weight on the knee.

She gave White Fawn a pained smile. "I can hop if I use you as a crutch."

As Lupe draped an arm over her shoulder, White Fawn circled her waist. Two hops, rest. Two hops, rest. At last they reached the back stoop. Lupe sat and levered herself backward up the steps. White Fawn helped her scoot to the wall without getting a rump full of splinters, then steadied her to stand again.

Determined that Lupe lie down, White Fawn guided her toward the bedroom.

"No. I can rest in the parlor for a bit, then get back to work."

White Fawn did not argue; she simply guided her friend to her bed. When Lupe did not object again, White Fawn knew she must be in much pain.

Lupe eased onto the bed. "Ask Xavier to help clean up the muddy clothes."

"I do it. Xavier do own chores."

"But—"

"Rest."

"The midday meal—"

"Leftover roast beef. I fix sandwich."

Lupe was strong and worked hard. White Fawn expected she would be up in a couple of days, pain or no.

As she went outside to pick up the soiled clothes, she paused on the step. Realization dawned that perhaps her opportunity to escape was upon her. But not until dark.

She squeezed her eyes shut on the next thoughts. Never again would she see Conway. Never again would his dark-eyed gaze send blood pumping through her so swiftly that her breath left her. Her fingertips touched her mouth. Never again would she feel his kiss, the enchantment of his lips.

Sudden heat sluiced through her body and pooled at the apex of her thighs. She collapsed on the step. Clamping her legs together, she rested her forehead on her knees. Tears pricked her eyes. The taste of him, the feel of his man part buried deep within was so real, she did not think she could bear the remembrance. But remember she would. Time and time again . . . with despair.

Yet, she must leave. She stared with unseeing eyes at the river, shivering at the thought of the degradation she would bear if her life with the Comanche were ever discovered.

Dragging herself from the steps, she began picking up clothes. Escape would not come till nightfall, if then. She took the soiled garments to the river and let the gentle current wash away most of the mud, then scrubbed them twice to return the whites to white.

A litany played over and over in her mind. *Forget to lock the door, Lupe. Forget. Forget . . .*

Later, after checking on a sleeping Lupe, she carved the beef, thoughts ajumble. The knife slipped and sliced her finger.

"Ow!" She stuck the digit in her mouth and sucked welling blood. "Think what you do," she muttered.

Xavier arrived promptly at noon and was immediately distressed about Lupe's injury. Assuring himself she slept peacefully, he sat at the table and took a huge bite from a sandwich. He chewed with relish.

"Is good. Lupe, she sleep. Be okay, I think."

162

White Fawn nodded.

"Dogs." Xavier shook his head. "Trouble all time. Sometime I shoot them all, I think."

Appalled, White Fawn exclaimed, "Oh, no! They only puppies. Outgrow mischief."

Xavier grinned. "I tease you. Mutt, he good. Warn of danger." He drained his coffee cup and stood. "You need help, you call."

She nodded, intending to do no such thing. Time was her enemy, but she would iron sheets for Lupe this afternoon. Even now, the flatiron heated on the back of the stove.

Exhausted by the time the supper dishes were finished, White Fawn sought her room. Thoughts tumbling, she swung from yes, she would leave, to how could she while Lupe needed her? She almost howled with frustration.

Lying atop the quilt on the bed she had just learned to sleep on two nights before, she listened. All was quiet.

Lupe had not locked the door. Neither had Xavier.

She sat up and stared into the darkness. And had second thoughts . . . and third! It would not be right to leave when Lupe could not attend to her man or herself. Perhaps in a day or two . . .

But how long would Conway be gone? She did not know the distance of the ranches where Indians had been seen.

She shuddered at the memory of her companions' deaths. Would Conway kill . . . *He* might die. No! Her heart rebelled at the thought. Though she must disappear from his life, she wanted him to live and prosper. Hard in some respects, he was gentle, too. Matthew Conway's lovemaking would remain in her heart all the days of her life.

One day he would find a white woman and marry. She would bear his children. White Fawn squeezed her eyes closed and held her breath against the pain that thought caused.

Her fate had been written on the wind by the war whoops of long ago. Why torture herself? She was not destined to feel Conway's touch again, the ecstasy of release he had given her.

If only . . .

By the next morning, White Fawn had decided she'd finish the ironing, then cook a big pot of beans in the afternoon. Though she could not prepare delicious tortillas like Lupe's, she would bake two batches of biscuits. Wrapped in a towel, they would store nicely in the bread safe. She would stuff as many as she could carry in her coat pockets for the trail.

With enough food prepared to last a couple of days, Lupe could stay off her feet. Xavier knew nothing about cooking, but Lars did. He could help out once the beans were gone. The rest of the household chores could wait for Lupe's sprain to heal.

Tonight, after everyone bedded down, and if the door was left unlocked, she would take Pepper and be gone before she was missed. With luck, her absence would not be discovered until long after dawn.

Her mind settled, White Fawn went to Lupe's bedroom. The door stood open. Lupe half-sat, propped against the pillows.

Relief flitted over Lupe's features when White Fawn smiled. Good. Since she had not slipped away last night, perhaps Lupe believed she was resigned to staying on the Rocking C.

Spirits of the People, hear my prayer. May the door be left unlocked this night.

"Good morning." Lupe pushed herself farther up against the pillows and winced, then put on a brave face. "I believe I can get up today."

White Fawn advanced into the room, shaking her head. "One more day, Lupe. I do chores. Knee swollen?"

"A little." Lupe slid her leg from beneath the quilt and pulled up her nightgown.

White Fawn grimaced. Lupe's knee was twice its normal size. "Hear me: Stay bed. I wrap knee and fix breakfast. Eggs from yesterday. Like food now?"

"I am hungry this morning."

As the day wore on, White Fawn looked in on Lupe and listened to her grouse about staying in bed. Twice, White Fawn found her preparing to rise.

"Lupe, please. You rest, heal better."

"But you'll work yourself to exhaustion without my help."

"No, no. I do fine." She grinned at her friend. "I no here, you work by self. I cook beans."

"Beans? We need tortillas."

Again, White Fawn shook her head. "Biscuits do well, no? Make plenty."

She was satisfied the next time she stopped at Lupe's door and found her asleep. The pinched lines around her mouth had eased. Sleep would soon restore her.

White Fawn hoped Lupe's nap would not spoil her plan. If Lupe slept much of the day, she might be restless and awake tonight. Her escape depended on everyone sleeping soundly.

Xavier spent an hour in the bedroom with Lupe. Though she could not hear their words, White Fawn envied their companionable conversation.

After supper, he insisted on helping her clear the table and even brought hot water to wash the dishes. Then he retired to the bedroom once more.

Seated in the parlor, White Fawn busied herself with the basket of mending Lupe kept near her chair. She bit off the thread and lifted the shirt to inspect her handiwork, then checked to see there were no more frayed seams or loose buttons.

She sighed, folded the shirt and laid it aside. For years to come, as surely as night followed day, she would envision Conway wearing that shirt. His powerful body filling the material, wide shoulders flexing with every move.

"I call it a night."

She jumped so violently, she jabbed herself with the needle. Her head snapped around, eyes wide. For the second time in as many days, she sucked blood off her finger. Nerves. Hers were so taut, she found it hard to breathe.

"Sorry." Xavier gave her a lame smile. "Go to bed now. Lupe, she sleeps already."

White Fawn had intended to speak with Lupe once

more, but now . . . She gazed at this kind man, lamp-light dancing on his swarthy face. She had come to like Xavier. Like Conway, he was strongly built. Perhaps many men just like them would one day swarm over Texas. Though she could not help wishing them well, she feared what their coming would mean to her Indian People.

"She need sleep," White Fawn finally managed.

He shrugged. "My Lupe be up with chickens. One day her limit in bed."

White Fawn smiled and stuck the needle in the pin-cushion.

"Day long for me, too. I sleep now."

When Xavier started to step into the room. She fore-stalled him. "You go. I douse lamp."

If he went to bed before her, he would not lock the door. Fortunately, he left. She turned down the wick and sat, waiting, hardly breathing until she heard his door shut.

Air whooshed from her. Rising on unsteady legs, she went to her room. She shut the door, and put her ear to the wood and listened. Mutt's nails clicked on the floor as he trotted off the porch.

She eased down on the bed, sitting still for some time and listening to every night sound imaginable. An owl hooted. She shivered at a mourning dove's lonely cry. Somewhere in the distance coyotes yipped. From the pups under the porch came an occasional whimper and a rhythmic beat as they scratched, paws hitting the dirt.

She blinked back sudden tears. The sound conjured Conway's words so many weeks ago: "*Infested with fleas, I'd wager.*"

In despair she lay back on the coverlet. "God of the white man, capture my memories and hold them here." A futile prayer, she knew. Nothing would erase her memories of the man she had come to love.

At last she rose, moved carefully to the chair, and donned her stolen coat. She glanced around the dark room that had been her prison for many weeks, but now felt like . . . home. If her life had been different, perhaps a house like this would have been her home forever. "No can be," she whispered.

She tiptoed to the door and reached for the knob.

A light knock sounded.

Snatching her hand back to clamp over her mouth, she stifled a cry. Her heart hammered behind her ribs.

"Miss Rebecca?" Hoby whispered.

Chapter Eleven

Thunder sounded in her ears. White Fawn clutched her chest, barely able to breathe. One more second . . .

Another rap, and Hoby Varner's faint whisper came again. "Miss Rebecca?"

Catching her breath, she murmured, "Yes?"

"Could you give me a hand?"

White Fawn looked down at her fully clothed body. She could not let him see her like this, yet she must open the door before Xavier heard him, if he had not already. She moved close, opened the door a crack, hiding her body behind it.

"What?"

"Lars ain't here. I got a calf scourin' somethin' awful. Can't get no eggs down his gullet."

"Scouring?" Then she remembered what the word meant. "Oh, yes, just a moment."

She shut the door, stood motionless for the time she figured it would take her to dress, then reached for the knob. She put her hand in one of the coat pockets, bulging with biscuits. Would he notice? Taking a deep breath, she opened the door and stepped outside, sticking her hand in the other pocket. Maybe he would think she was cold.

"Come. No talk here. Wake Lupe and Xavier."

Hoby nodded and tiptoed behind her until they gained the outside. Halfway across the clearing, he explained. "The little varmint's a mess. Gonna die if'n I don't get him to bind up."

As White Fawn entered the barn, she glanced at the bridles lined up on pegs, Pepper's rope bridle among them. If the Spirits smiled on her, later she would take it and Pepper and steal away into the night.

As she moved deeper into the barn, the stench of the diarrhea-weakened calf assailed her. Hoby stepped inside a stall, and she followed. Lantern light fell on the black calf curled on soiled hay, his hindquarters smeared with excrement, so weak he could not raise his head.

White Fawn dropped to her knees, unmindful of soiling her garments. She rubbed the animal's ears. "How long he this way?"

"Started squirtin' this afternoon. Lars said to pump eggs down him, but I ain't got but one into him all this time. I'll hold up his head if'n you'll pour eggs down 'im."

"Where Mr. Gunnerson?"

"He's, uh . . ." Hoby's cheeks flushed. "He's gone . . . visitin'. "

She understood, grew jubilant at the news. Lars Gunnerson was no different from other men when it came to appeasing his needs. The Fosters and Mr. Gladstone had ridden out this morning. That left only three besides herself on the ranch.

Hiding her smile, she said, "Get eggs. We try."

Hoby scooted to the fence and pulled a pail filled with raw eggs toward him. Rather than soil the too-large coat's sleeves, White Fawn removed it. Praying the biscuits would not fall out, she carefully folded it and laid it aside.

She dipped her hand into the eggs and brought up a yolk, the white slipping through her fingers to plop back in the pail. She frowned. "A glass. No hold in hand."

Hoby nodded and ran to the bunkhouse, returning shortly with a cup. She dipped in and caught two yolks along with the transparent whites. He lifted the calf's head, angling his mouth up.

"Come, little one," she crooned. "Drink."

The poor animal's tongue pushed out more of the eggs than he swallowed. She tried again, massaging his throat to encourage swallowing. When he did, she smiled and patted his back. "Good boy."

"Take time, Hoby, make eat. More now. More later."

"Sure."

She patiently poured, massaged, and poured some more. Slowly the bucket emptied. As the minutes passed into an hour, the secretion from the calf's hind end slowed. After nearly two hours, the animal appeared to rest rather than droop from weakness.

Hoby lowered the calf's head, then rubbed his arms. He trembled with fatigue. "Maybe he'll live."

171

White Fawn passed her hand over the calf's soft head. "Perhaps. He sides no bunch from pain. Where mama is?"

"In the end stall. If'n he stops scourin', I'll milk her and feed him a bit after daylight." He grimaced. "Somethin' besides them raw eggs."

White Fawn chuckled. "Medicine no pleasant, but if work—"

"Yeah," Hoby agreed. He sighed and stood. "You must be tuckered. Thank ya for your help."

He was dismissing her. She did not move. "I stay." Again she petted the calf. "Go find bed. You more tired."

His eyes widened. "Oh, no, Miss Rebecca. Lars'll have my hide as it is for wakin' ya. I didn't tell ya what else he said."

Alarm shuddered down her spine. "What?" she asked, her voice small.

He rubbed the back of his neck. "If'n I couldn't stop the scourin', I was to shoot him, but I hate like billy-heck to kill young critters. You was so good tendin' your horse, I thought . . ." He shrugged.

She smiled . . . with relief. How difficult could Hoby Varner be if he possessed a soft heart for animals? "Kill animals hard if sick. I stay, make sure he rest." She waited a beat. "You go bed. I fine."

Clearly undecided, Hoby scowled, staring. He was tired. A need for rest warred with what Lars would say if she were found here after daylight. But she would not be . . .

"Rest, Hoby. I go bed later."

Still, he hesitated. "If'n you're sure."

She nodded as he stretched. Exhausted, he stumbled away.

After he left, White Fawn turned the lantern's wick to a faint glimmer, donned her coat and sat down again. She would wait until she was sure Hoby had gone to sleep.

Just as she laid her hand on the calf's head, Hoby reappeared. She jumped.

"It's gettin' a mite chilly, Miss Rebecca. I brought you a cover." He handed her a folded wool blanket.

"Thank you. I have coat. I no be here long to get cold."

He could not know she meant she would be gone from the ranch, but he left the blanket. She was grateful. She would need something to bed down with at night while traveling north. Hoby was right: The nights were cool, especially the hour or so before dawn.

In the next few minutes, the calf roused twice. She petted and crooned to him. With luck, he would be all right. By morning, Hoby could give him a small amount of his mother's milk.

Tense herself, White Fawn's stomach rolled as she listened to night sounds. Inside the barn, horses and cows shuffled, snorted, leaned against the protesting fence. A pig snorted, then rooted around to get more comfortable. When she heard the chickens begin to make low sounds, she knew she must be gone before a rooster crowed.

She gave the calf one last pat, kissed the top of his head, then crept from the stall. Closing the gate ever so carefully, she remembered the lantern and went back to douse the wick, plunging the barn into blackness.

173

After a moment, her eyes adjusted enough that she could find her way to the open door. Pausing, she fingered several bridles before finding the right one. Outside, she looked first toward the house, then the bunkhouse. Quiet. Blessed quiet.

When she arrived at the corral, Pepper nickered and trotted toward her. She quickly squeezed between the rails and put her hand against the horse's soft muzzle. "Shh."

Pepper stood docilely while she slipped on the bridle. The corral was so new, the latch did not squeal when she lifted it and led Pepper out. Closing the gate, she led the mare toward the trees that bordered the north of the ranch.

Though unshod, Pepper's hooves sounded like gunshots. As she gained the trees, she heard a faint noise and something brushed against her leg. She jumped like a startled deer and clamped a hand over her mouth to stifle a scream. Whipping her head from side to side, she could see nothing. The noise came again, and then she saw him.

One of the pups sat on his haunches, his head cocked to the side, and repeated the sound that had frightened the liver out of her. Tongue lolling to one side, it sounded as if he cleared his throat.

White Fawn inhaled a shaky breath, knelt, and snapped her fingers. The little guy bounded toward her, his tail wagging his whole body. Head down, he whined when she touched him.

White Fawn moistened her dry mouth before she could speak. "Stay, little pest."

She walked Pepper deeper into the tree cover, not

surprised that the pup ignored her command. He was right on her heels when she tethered the horse, so she scooped him up.

"Even if want to, no can take, pest." She smiled as the puppy turned up his face, listening to her whispers. "That you name if mine: Pest. Where I go you end in cookpot. No like!"

Walking back the way she had come, she set down the dog and gave him a push toward the house. He turned around, splayed his feet, and prepared to play, yip-bark and all.

If she'd thought Pepper's hooves sounded like pistol shots, the bark resembled cannon fire. "Shh!" She slapped the pup on the nose. Undeterred, he came back for more. He yipped again and danced on his hind legs.

No! She was reluctant to hurt him, but she had to make him leave. If he kept this up, everyone within miles would be awake in minutes. Finding a thin branch on the ground, she whacked him on the rump—hard. He yelped in pain, scuttled away, and disappeared beneath the front porch.

A light flared in the house.

She dropped the branch, spun toward Pepper, and in a leap that would have made Eagle Feather proud, landed atop the horse. She wrenched the reins from around the tree limb and kicked the mare's flanks. Noise or not, she galloped away, a wraith among the trees.

"What is it?" Lupe squinted in the sudden lantern light flare.

"Know not. Noise. I check."

Lupe sat up and flipped back the covers. He smiled and shook his head as he pulled on his trousers. The nightgown buttoned to her throat was at odds with the passionate woman beneath the cloth. Such a proper picture. Even with her knee painful, his caresses of the night before had awakened the fire in her blood. What he had intended as a simple kiss good night, the wish to hold her until she slept, had escalated into satisfying lovemaking.

"Is early. No leave bed, Lupe."

"Maybe it's trouble."

He shook his head again and stomped bare feet into his boots. "Just noise. I look around."

He kissed her, then picked up the rifle propped beside the door. Glancing down the corridor, he saw the door to the little lady's room was closed. He nodded with satisfaction. She had gone undisturbed. He hurried down the back steps.

Mutt crawled from under the house and looked up at him. Absently, Xavier scratched his ears. The pups whimpered and moved around but remained under the house with their mama.

He scanned the cleared area down to the river. Nothing moved. No noise other than the faint rustle of leaves. Cocking his head, he listened. Hoofbeats? Surely not. Not the least bit agitated, Mutt followed him to the front of the house. The big dog looked to the north and wagged his tail in a slow arc.

Xavier inspected the clearing as the strident crow of a rooster heralded dawn. He started to turn back to the house, then arrested his motion when he caught movement to the east. He raised his rifle. Not until the shadowed rider was partway across the clearing headed toward the barn did Xavier recognize him: Lars.

Where he be? Loco question, he thought wryly. Where else but visiting a willing woman? He frowned. Lars should have told him that he was leaving the ranch. It was unwise for Lars to wander away. Every gun hand might be needed.

With Mutt padding behind, Xavier walked toward the barn. He had passed the corral before he realized something was amiss. His gaze swept the two corrals, one finished, the other nearly so. Why had the mare been moved?

His boots crunched on the rocky ground as he entered the barn. A faint noise prompted Lars to pull his rifle from the scabbard even as he spun around.

"Is me." Xavier stared uncomfortably down the bore of Lars's firearm.

The big man lowered the barrel and leaned the rifle against the stall's rail. Lars looked relaxed and said nothing as he began untacking his mount. As sexually sated as himself, Xavier thought. Still, he had a bone to pick with the man. As foreman, Xavier was responsible for Matt.

"You think wise to leave and no tell me?"

Lars tossed his saddle atop the stall fence. "You'd turned in before I decided to take a ride."

"Mornin'." Hoby strode in and went directly to a stall beyond Lars. "Hey! He's on his feet! Looks like this guy's gonna make it. He ain't scoured since I left him earlier."

"Is good." Xavier remained focused on Lars. What could he do? Lars was one of the best damn hands in these parts. If he let loose, Lars didn't have to take it. Hell, he'd saddle up and be gone before Xavier finished the dressing-down.

"Next time, tell me. *Comprende?*"

"Yeah. No sign of Indians, though." Lars led his dun gelding into the stall and had the grace to apologize. "Sorry, Xavier. I had . . . other things on my mind."

Xavier could understand that. Nodding once, he turned to go back to the house. Then he remembered. He looked the length of the seven stalls that lined both sides of the barn.

"Where girl's horse?" he asked, though he had a sinking sensation in his stomach that he already knew the answer.

Lars frowned, his perusal taking the same path Xavier's had.

"What?" Alarm painted Hoby's features.

"Indian pony. Where she is?"

"In the corral." He ran past Xavier, then halted and hung his head. "She-it!"

Xavier sprinted toward the house, leaped onto the porch, then skidded to a halt; Lupe stood next to the girl's door. The *open* door.

Her alarmed expression matched his own trepidation.

"There's going to be hell to pay," she said.

In the trackless wilderness, White Fawn sat where she had bedded down the prior evening. Absently, she braided her hair, then tied the end with the piece of leather Matthew had given her long ago. Oh, how she wished for a bath.

Four days she had traveled north. Last night she had

found wild berries, but no water. Fishing the last biscuit from her pocket, she eyed the hard-as-stone bread, wondering if she could choke it down her parched throat. She stuffed it back in her pocket. Before she tried to eat, she must find water, for herself and Pepper.

Yesterday when the sun was mid-heaven, she had crossed a stream. They drank their fill, but she had no container in which to carry water. Finding the stream had buoyed her spirits for a time. The farther she traveled into *Comancheria* the less chance she would find water. She further chastised herself for not bringing twine or gut to make a snare. Of course, she had no knife to skin a rabbit even if she caught one.

At least the horse would not go hungry. Though drying as autumn approached, grass was plentiful. Morning dew was brief. She hoped it was enough to satisfy Pepper.

Gazing back the way she had come, White Fawn wondered if she had made a bad choice. Which would be worse? To be shunned, even spit upon, degraded by white men, or to die alone on the prairie?

She envisioned Conway astride his horse, then immediately prayed her visions of him would dim with time. The heat that swept through her just thinking about him took her breath.

She grimaced. He would never ride out without supplies. A knife, a canteen, a rifle, a handgun buckled to his trim waist, and a bedroll. She was thankful for the blanket Hoby had given her, but it was little comfort.

Sitting here bemoaning her plight would accomplish nothing. Pepper snorted and blew as she cropped grass. White Fawn stood and folded the blanket.

By the time the sun peeked over the horizon, she had walked or ridden maybe three or four miles. Thirsty, lips near to cracking, she sensed water ahead. A good sign—Pepper had picked up her pace without prodding.

Midmorning and ten miles north, directly in the path White Fawn would travel before the day was done, Matt, Isaac, and Cecil weaved along a dry gully following signs. Matt had lost them for over an hour, but now, faint though they were, he'd spotted hoofprints where Indian ponies had misstepped in soft sand—half a print once and whole prints twice.

"There!" Isaac pointed at newly sheared rock that had tumbled down onto the flat.

Matt dismounted and examined the ground. "Unshod," he said.

Indians had been this way, not too long ago. Yesterday, maybe. No more than two days.

"Not many," he said as he stood. "We'll continue on a while."

The Indians traveled north, away from the Perkins and Caldwell ranches. These Indians had ridden near white people. Maybe a threat, maybe not. Scouting for a larger band? Hell, he didn't know, but he for damn sure didn't intend to lead men into an ambush. If the trail continued north, he'd quit and head home.

The farther he rode from his own ranch, the more anxious he became, although *anxious* didn't quite describe it. Every time he left home, he'd always champed at the bit to get back; this time the reason was entirely different.

Horny nailed it. Prize jackass that he was, Matt's

every thought was of White Fawn. He had wanted her, and right or wrong, he'd acted on his desire. He still wanted her. More than ever.

He remounted, leaned forward, and gave Trooper his head to scramble up the bank. Isaac and Cecil followed. All three reined in on level ground. Matt wagged his head, determined to center his thoughts on the moment at hand.

Hill country. A heat mirage shimmered in the distance, but it didn't blot out the hills, gullies, swales, and rock outcrops aplenty that provided dandy places from which Indians could mount an ambush. Still, he had a job to do. For a couple more days, anyway.

Though it was beautiful and largely untouched up this way, Matt preferred the flatter terrain down by his place. Sure, a stand of trees blocked the view here and there; land rose and fell a little, too, but a man could see for miles in any direction. Damn few Indians could sneak up on a man in brush country.

Flash tossed his head, his bridle clinking in the stillness. Trooper shied away, and Matt let him. Cecil, who hadn't bothered to settle his mount either, glanced at Matt.

Surrounded by sun-burnished skin, Cecil's startlingly light blue eyes held little humor, though his mouth lifted in a half-grin. "Guess we have no choice."

Matt nudged Trooper. "Well, let's see what we can see." From force of habit, he warned his two companions, "Stay alert."

As all three men rode forward, Isaac and Cecil hung back on either side of him in a staggered line of sorts. Better to keep side vision unobstructed.

* * *

Someone followed. Though whoever trailed them had gone unseen for the past couple of days, Beaver Heart had discussed the matter with Buffalo Hump and Snake Who Hisses. All of them sensed it. This morning, rather than continue on, they dug in behind a rock outcrop. Lying flat on the hard ground, they peered around large boulders that provided good cover if a horseman happened into the gully below.

An hour or so after sunrise, three men rode into view. They reined their mounts and looked in the direction in which Beaver Heart lay, hatchet in hand. As accurate as any warrior with his bow, he preferred his war ax in close-quarter combat.

It rankled, but he had agreed to head home as promised. Until now, he and his companions had honored his father's command that they not engage white men. But now that these men followed, he smiled with grim satisfaction. Three against three, and they had the upper hand, surprise on their side.

"We lie here until the sun crosses the sky and again sleeps?" Running Mouth Woman grumbled behind him.

"Ssst!" Snake Who Hisses made the sound that had given him his name many seasons past. He slammed her head against the ground.

"Ouch!"

"Silence!" he whispered. "White men are within bow range."

Running Mouth Woman glared at him, then turned her narrow-eyed gaze on Beaver Heart.

He ignored her. She now bored him. Her demands to

permanently mate with him had begun to grate on his nerves. Summer Moon, who had seen thirteen summers and begun her monthly flow, was now a woman. His mother had told him the maiden would be pleased to accept him.

"Look!" Buffalo Hump whispered.

Beaver Heart let the pleasant thought die and focused on the riders again. First one horseman, then a second turned his mount and started back the way they had come. The last man, on the handsome gelding, sat a moment longer, looking directly toward Beaver Heart. Still as a prairie dog sensing danger, Beaver Heart took in a deep breath, the dirt smell filling his nostrils. The white man had not seen him or he would not have finally wheeled about and left.

Many times his people had faced men like these. From their appearance, they must be Texas Rangers, men who had taken the lives of many of his Comanche brethren. Now they had decided to stop hunting him and his companions. He shrugged. Perhaps he would one day face them again.

Running Bear, a fierce *Kwerhar-rehnuh* warrior of the *Llano Estacado*, as was Eagle Feather, was returning along the Comanche Trace from a raid deep in Mexico. A dozen warriors followed him, glad to be within four or five days of their village. Trailing behind, three naked Mexican women staggered, wrists bound and tethered to ropes held by warriors.

The captives were a fine prize, but of greater worth were twelve horses herded by four braves. Running

Bear was pleased. In a few days, he would see his sons, seven sturdy boys who would grow into warriors like himself. The Spirits had smiled upon him.

White Bear, the youngest, only three, needed a few years to prove himself. But he could already let fly an arrow from his small bow and hit the mark more often than not.

Running Bear had claimed one of the Mexican women as his slave. Quiet Spring, his second wife, would be pleased. Though he had three mates, he always thought of her first, for she was his favorite. That did not sit well with his first wife, Wailing Woman. Had he realized what a nagging mouth she had, he would never have taken her to his blanket. Singing Water, his youngest mate, was great with her first child.

He blinked, his reverie shattered. He raised his lance to signal a halt.

Wildcat, his brother, rode up next to him. "A horse?"

With deliberate care, Running Bear searched the prairie east, north, west. Other than brush waving in the wind, nothing moved on the empty plain. "Remain here. I will look."

He approached warily. As he neared, he saw a body lying on the ground. The mare loomed protectively over the prone figure. She shook her head, snorted, and lunged as if to run him off.

"Peace," he murmured, and reached out to snag her headstall with the ease of long years' experience. A rope bridle. Comanche. Eagle feathers decorated the headstall on either side of the mare's ears.

GET UP TO 4 FREE BOOKS!

You can have the best romance delivered to your door for less than what you'd pay in a bookstore or online. Sign up for one of our book clubs today, and we'll send you **FREE* BOOKS** just for trying it out...with no obligation to buy, ever!

HISTORICAL ROMANCE BOOK CLUB

Travel from the Scottish Highlands to the American West, the decadent ballrooms of Regency England to Viking ships. Your shipments will include authors such as CONNIE MASON, SANDRA HILL, CASSIE EDWARDS, JENNIFER ASHLEY, LEIGH GREENWOOD, and many, many more.

LOVE SPELL BOOK CLUB

Bring a little magic into your life with the romances of Love Spell—fun contemporaries, paranormals, time-travels, futuristics, and more. Your shipments will include authors such as LYNSAY SANDS, CJ BARRY, COLLEEN THOMPSON, NINA BANGS, MARJORIE LIU and more.

As a book club member you also receive the following special benefits:

- **30% OFF all orders through our website & telecenter!**
- **Exclusive access to special discounts!**
- **Convenient home delivery and 10 day examination period to return any books you don't want to keep.**

There is **no minimum number of books to buy**, and you may cancel membership at any time. See back to sign up!

*Please include $2.00 for shipping and handling.

YES! ☐

Sign me up for the **Historical Romance Book Club** and send my TWO FREE BOOKS! If I choose to stay in the club, I will pay only $8.50* each month, a savings of $5.48!

YES! ☐

Sign me up for the **Love Spell Book Club** and send my TWO FREE BOOKS! If I choose to stay in the club, I will pay only $8.50* each month, a savings of $5.48!

NAME: _____

ADDRESS: _____

_____

TELEPHONE: _____

E-MAIL: _____

☐ **I WANT TO PAY BY CREDIT CARD.**

☐ VISA   ☐ MasterCard   ☐ DISCOVER

ACCOUNT #: _____

EXPIRATION DATE: _____

SIGNATURE: _____

Send this card along with $2.00 shipping & handling for each club you wish to join, to:

**Romance Book Clubs
20 Academy Street
Norwalk, CT 06850-4032**

Or fax (must include credit card information!) to: 610.995.9274. You can also sign up online at www.dorchesterpub.com.

*Plus $2.00 for shipping. Offer open to residents of the U.S. and Canada only. Canadian residents please call 1.800.481.9191 for pricing information.

If under 18, a parent or guardian must sign. Terms, prices and conditions subject to change. Subscription subject to acceptance. Dorchester Publishing reserves the right to reject any order or cancel any subscription.

JOIN NOW!

As he dismounted, he dropped his hand from the rope near her jowl. Had she intended to bolt, she would have done so already. His own mount ground-tied wherever Running Bear dropped the reins. Had he not quickly learned to stay, the gelding would have been stew long ago.

A woman. Wearing white woman's clothing. She looked too small for a full-grown woman. She lay on her stomach, her face turned away. A few loops of her braid held, but the rest of her black hair blew every which way.

He frowned at her and then the horse. Riding a Comanche pony? He knelt and flipped her over none too gently.

She groaned. "Conway."

Con . . . way, Running Bear mouthed to himself. Though he was not fluent in English, he could speak many words and understood more. The woman had uttered a white man's name. He grabbed her shoulder and shook hard.

"Wake!"

"Water," the girl croaked in Comanche.

Surprised, Running Bear sat back on his heels. He studied her face. One cheek was scraped raw, dirt imbedded in the flesh. Rivulets of blood beaded down her cheek to her mouth. The eye above the torn flesh was bruised and blackened.

She muttered, "Water," as her lashes fluttered. Blinking several times, she fingered her bruised cheek and moaned. Then her eyes focused on him and widened. *"Nerm?"* She sat bolt upright.

185

The girl was either out of her head or not who she appeared to be. Her violet eyes and clothing warred with her reaction to him. Upon seeing a Comanche warrior, white women screamed loud enough to wake every Spirit in the Great Beyond. And he was painted for war. Confused, he stood and jerked her to her feet.

"Come."

Without waiting, he tugged her along. Stumbling, she caught herself, then appeared to go willingly.

"I have no water for two days. Neither has Pepper."

Running Bear halted so quickly, she crashed into him, then hastily stepped back.

"What is pepper?"

She pointed to the mare that had dogged her skirts. "My horse."

My horse. Ah, yes. White people named their animals. She was obviously white. Yet she spoke his tongue well. Perhaps she had been a captive for many years. But if she was a slave, why did she not fear him?

Chapter Twelve

White Fawn stumbled behind the Indian warrior. *Keep your wits about you.* Though he appeared confused, he could turn on her in an instant, raise his war ax, and she would be dead.

She had wakened to his face looming close, painted black on one side, red on the other. The warriors of her band preferred black and white as war colors. If she could but remember to which band this brave belonged. But thirst consumed her! Coherent thought was beyond her at the moment.

Again, she stumbled into him when he halted. He glared at her. Though far from Conway's height, this Indian still had the advantage over her. Most men did. But she had to say her piece. She must make him help her.

White Fawn glanced at the silent warriors and the whimpering girls ranged around her. She did not intend to wind up at the end of one of those lariats. Pity for the Mexicans fluttered in her heart, but she could spare no more than that if she was to convince these men she was truly Comanche.

Squaring her shoulders, she looked at the Indian still staring at her; confusion and curiosity lit his black eyes. "I am White Fawn, daughter of Eagle Feather."

"Bah!" several warriors scoffed.

She ignored them, her haughty expression reserved for the man who held her life in his hands. "I am thirsty. I and my horse need water and food. I demand you take me to Eagle Feather."

"Demand?" His lips curled in what she surmised passed for a smile.

"I was abducted by white men. My father is doubtless worried."

Standing tall and proud before this band might be her only salvation, though doing so became more difficult by the minute. First one, than a second and a third warrior dismounted and approached. They circled, dark eyes raking her up and down. One lifted a strand of her hair, then gave it a yank. She stifled a gasp. Another inserted grimy fingers inside her shirtwaist at her collarbone. He tested the fabric between his fingers and leered at her. Her skin crawled.

The third warrior did not touch her, but he seemed more menacing than the others. He stood to one side and spoke to the man who had found her. "She speaks our tongue, but that means nothing, my brother."

Brother? Eagle Feather's sons enjoyed a camaraderie that included real affection for each other. But some brothers nurtured envy in their hearts if one rose to be chief while the others had to accept subordinate standing. Such jealousy often led to cruel and sly behavior. She could only pray this brother was not that sort.

"Um," the first Indian muttered noncommittally.

188

Lance planted in the hard soil, his left hand clasped the shaft. The other arm held akimbo, his fist rested at his waist above his war ax.

"Eagle Feather?" His brow knit. "Chief in a band of *Kwerhar-rehnuh?* I have met him. Tell me of his family," he ordered.

"Eagle Feather has two wives, Willow Branch and Bright Star. My brothers are Straight Arrow, Black Crow, and Beaver Heart."

The brother swung so quickly, White Fawn had no time to move. His open hand crashed against the side of her head. She flew sideways and sprawled on the ground.

"A slave would know that. It proves nothing," he sneered.

White Fawn's ears rang as she shook her head, fighting nausea. She swallowed hard and cupped her cheek, sure that side of her face now sported a bruise nearly as painful as the other. She doubtless had a black eye, too, from the way the bone ached. Lifting her head, she glared at the warrior, then remembered the one thing that might convince these men she was indeed Eagle Feather's daughter.

She reached inside her dirty shirtwaist and drew out the amulet. "I am Eagle Feather's daughter!" she repeated forcefully. "He will not take kindly to your cuffing me."

The brother narrowed his eyes, jerked her to her feet, and reached for the talisman. Fearing he would break the leather, White Fawn reacted with foolish, even fatal bravado. She slapped his hand away.

Silence. Total stillness descended on the men and

189

captives. Eyes rounded to saucers, the women stared at her as if she had lost her mind. Perhaps so. But if she had learned one thing over the years, courage was the single attribute a Comanche warrior admired. Though she had lashed out without thought, perhaps these men would view her action as courageous.

Leaning into her face, the warrior bellowed, "Stupid woman!"

Not to be denied, the first Indian inspected the amulet, careful of the leather.

She watched his eyes as he turned over the gift of protection. She glanced down as his thumb rubbed the spent bullet. Her gaze flitted back to his face when he spoke.

"Captured by white men, you say?"

She nodded, hope thick in her throat.

The chief turned to his brother and the other men. "She wears a talisman of possession. Comanche possession, Wildcat. Whether she is Eagle Feather's daughter remains to be seen. For now, she is a guest." He made eye contact with each warrior, his brother last. Then his voice thundered with authority. "Running Bear has spoken!"

Her heart seized when an older brave spoke. "Guest? For how long? How do you know the truth of her words?"

Another stepped forward, disdain lacing his comments. "She is a stupid white woman who cannot find her way in our land. If she were truly Comanche, she would not be lost and thirsty." He swept his arm west and looked at her as he might a child. "The Colorado flows not more than a league from here."

White Fawn's heart sank. She had been traveling parallel to the mighty Colorado River. Only three miles had separated her from needed water. But how could she know? True, Comanche chiefs knew this wilderness. There was not a warrior alive who could not find his way. But she, a woman, followed, never led. A day or so ago, Pepper had smelled water. Why not this time?

"I am not stupid!" Frustrated, the words slipped out before she could call them back. She tilted her chin with mock defiance. "I am a woman but not stupid. It is not my place to lead Eagle Feather's band. I need not know the way."

Running Bear actually laughed. What was more astounding, his brother did, too. Perhaps these men were of a kind, like the warriors she called brothers.

Wildcat spoke again. "Bring water for the horse. The woman will share with the slaves."

Well, at least these men allowed the captives to drink. Most did not. Captive women, forced to walk mile upon mile, were beaten if they fell. Male captives were usually dragged until incoherent or dead. If they survived, they met the knife or died staked spread-eagle in the broiling sun.

Only once had she seen the aftermath of such treatment. She had vomited and retched, unable to eat for several days. She shivered and put the gruesome memory from her mind.

Pepper received enough water to revive her without foundering. Allowed but two meager mouthfuls herself, White Fawn mounted Pepper. *Thank the Spirits*. She could not walk far in the boots. Though hunger gnawed at her belly, she vowed to show no weakness to these men.

Running Bear had named her a guest, but she rode surrounded by warriors. Who stank to high heaven. She had lived apart from her brethren long enough to learn the simple pleasure of a daily bath. Though now filthy herself, she had forgotten in that short time the odious stench of unwashed bodies.

The evening meal consisted of pemmican. Though it eased her hunger, her thoughts lingered on the pot of beans she had cooked at Conway's ranch. She could almost smell the seasoned pork, taste the rich broth, feel soft but firm beans on her tongue.

Lying wrapped in her blanket after dark, White Fawn savored the quiet, the view of crystal-bright stars. A scream brought her upright. Laughter and male yips followed. Another scream rent the air. She scrambled from her bed and peered into the darkness. A few of the warriors had bedded down close to the fire, including Running Bear and the girl he claimed as his. But the others . . .

A third scream sent shivers down her spine. At her first step, Running Bear loomed before her, a shadow backed by the low fire.

"Return to your blankets."

"What are they doing to those girls?" she asked, but she knew. As she grew older, slaves in her own band enlightened her. But these captives were little more than children, and at the mercy of several warriors.

"It is none of your affair," Running Bear said, his voice glacial.

"I was not treated thusly."

His teeth bared. "You may be if you persist."

She recoiled from his menacing threat. A maniacal laugh pierced the darkness. A slap followed. The girl's scream silenced abruptly.

"Well?" Running Bear, bare feet planted wide, appeared to relish the thought that she might continue to argue.

Pure folly to challenge him. She could do nothing for those girls. If she did not want to suffer their fate, she must do as he ordered. Eyes sparking with contempt, she returned to her blanket. But sleep eluded her. Her heart bled for these abused captives.

When she finally dropped off, sleep was fitful. Like a phantom, Conway crept into her dreams. She moaned and started awake, peering at the lumpy forms around her. She had no idea of the time.

Another moan rose in her throat when the vision of Conway lingered. She clamped her teeth on the side of her hand to stifle the noise.

Rolling to her side, she pulled her knees close to her chest. His member deep inside had pleasured her beyond belief; his tongue, his hands . . . Unlike the women captives, her experience had been pure ecstasy. Sucking in a breath, she squeezed her eyes closed.

Would the man forever stalk her dreams?

Dawn was barely upon them when White Fawn heard noise; the warriors were preparing to depart. She had no more than sat up when Running Bear spoke, his voice harsh.

"Take care of your needs. There is fresh cactus and water. Drink little. We ride through dry land this day."

He pulled the young girl who had occupied his bed to her feet. "You may ride."

The girl darted a beseeching look at White Fawn. Her own position precarious at best, White Fawn shook her head. She must do nothing to anger Running Bear or she would never see safety with Eagle Feather.

Obviously, the girl did not understand Comanche, and pity for her and her friends struggled with fear for her own well-being. Though unwise, White Fawn opened her mouth when it would have been better closed. "The women will be sunburned, unable to walk by nightfall if their bodies are not covered, Running Bear."

He halted his long strides toward his horse. The girl stumbled against him. Running Bear was not the only one staring at White Fawn. Were she not quaking like leaves shimmering on an Aspen tree, she would have laughed at the astonishment on every brave's face. A woman questioned their actions?

Then, Running Bear's eyes narrowed to slits. "You do not gain wisdom, do you, woman? Once more, heed my words: These women are none of your affair." He made a chopping motion with his hand. "Do not question me again. Mount your horse and ride when you are told to ride. Speak only when I tell you to speak."

She met stony glares from a dozen pairs of eyes. To challenge them again would get her killed. Glancing quickly at the captive, she shrugged. The girl seemed to realize she had been the subject of the conversation. Her nod was as infinitesimal as White Fawn's shrug.

Though it galled her, White Fawn heeded Running Bear's warning. Patience was not a warrior virtue. In fact, she believed they had none. She picked up her blanket and obeyed.

By midmorning, White Fawn noticed two of the women draped with blankets. Like Running Bear's slave, another rode before a warrior, her head drooped so low, her forehead almost touched the horse's withers.

White Fawn searched in vain for the third girl and fought back tears. It would not do for these warriors to see her weakness. Bile in her throat surged thick and bitter.

The young woman had not survived the night. These warriors had raped her one after the other . . . unto death.

Almost home, Matt thought. It had been two weeks since he'd ridden away from the ranch. He always looked forward to his first glimpse of the place, but this time the feeling was . . . joyous. Though he'd fought it, his anticipation had more to do with a pair of violet eyes than his pride in the sturdy structures.

You've slipped over the edge into insanity. He smiled wryly, his eyes trained on Trooper's nodding head as the gelding plodded through brush and between trees.

White Fawn probably wished he'd never return. Maybe by now, though, she was resigned to living in his world again. Maybe he could stop locking her in at night. *Uh-huh. Maybe Trooper will sprout wings and fly.*

The thought of keeping her a prisoner lodged like a boulder in his chest. *But you won't do that anymore, Matt. You're taking her to Austin as soon as you rest up a bit. Right?*

Could he do that? Cart her off to the orphanage and dump her in the midst of people she didn't know, then ride off and leave her to fend for herself? He shifted. Hell, maybe someone would recognize her. Maybe she had kin as close as Austin. If he was ever to hook her up with family, he needed her surname, for starters. Rebecca was as common as dirt.

Matt lifted his head at the smell of onions frying. His mouth watered. Supper. He nudged Trooper to a trot, sat straighter as he broke from the trees. The ranch spread before him, his haven in a harsh land. Home.

Almost a ritual by now, he drew up and scanned the place, enjoying the moment. Smoke curled skyward from Lupe's fire and the bunkhouse chimney. The second corral was completed and filled with a half-dozen steers. Although he didn't raise alfalfa or oats, there was a large stand of corn. In good years, they squeezed in two plantings. He traded hides and beeves with Goodlight for supplemental grain and the staples Lupe needed.

Today, the corral Pepper had been penned in was occupied by a lone Durham bull. He intended to breed the bull with wild longhorns. Blood from the Durham would strengthen his stock and result in beefier cattle.

He should have been happy to see the Durham, for which he'd paid a whacking big price. Instead of quiet satisfaction, he frowned. Likely, White Fawn's mare was in the barn. As Trooper started forward, the dogs set up a ruckus. Mutt and Susy loped toward him, the pups behind, a ragtag parade. Seconds later, Xavier stepped out to the porch.

He lifted his hand in greeting, as did Matt, who rode straight to the barn. He'd put Trooper away before facing White Fawn. Loco maybe, but he'd relish the anticipation a little longer.

He'd lost the battle. He wanted to see her. To hold her.

He simply wanted her.

When he leaped up the porch steps twenty minutes later, he immediately noticed the door to White Fawn's room was closed. He dropped his saddlebags in his room and headed for the parlor.

Pausing in the doorway, he found Lupe and Xavier at the table, but no White Fawn. His hope of her acceptance blew away like a puff of smoke.

At the same time Xavier said, "*Buenos días,*" Lupe said, "You're back." Neither smiled.

Befuddled by the lack of enthusiasm, Matt's own smile died.

Lupe rose, brought a plate and cup, and poured him coffee. She returned to her chair and motioned to the platter laden with two steaks swimming in the onions he'd smelled.

"Help yourself."

Something was wrong, but he didn't know what.

"How you fare?" Xavier asked. "Comanches you see?"

Matt shook his head. He forked a rare steak and onions onto his plate, then added a heap of fried potatoes from the bowl Lupe pushed toward him.

"Saw signs aplenty. Trailed four or five days into *Comancheria* but didn't see a one."

Around a mouthful, Xavier asked, "How many?"

"Three, maybe four." Matt cut his steak and glanced apprehensively at Xavier and Lupe.

"Why you think they act funny?"

It was a puzzle for Indians to show themselves and not attack in some way. He shrugged an I-don't-know and chewed. Lupe made whatever she cooked tasty, but range beef was tough. He assessed his two friends as he swallowed another bite, then put down his fork and sat back.

"So, what's happening around here?"

He wanted to ask about White Fawn. He wanted to ask, "What's wrong?" but the anxiety that niggled at him was enough to handle at the moment.

"We count four-thousand-one-hundred-sixty head on range, and no finish. Find sixty-five calves."

"That's good," Matt said, but those details interested him not at all.

Lupe and Xavier concentrated on their food for a few minutes while Matt picked at his. Apparently, White Fawn remained as stubborn as ever. Sighing, he laid the fork and knife on the oilcloth, no longer hungry. He was determined to see her.

"Our guest is making herself scarce. You still locking her in at night?"

From the troubled look in Lupe's eyes, he should have seen it coming. But he didn't.

"She gone, Matt," Xavier said.

Matt had never felt the impact of a bullet, but at that moment he sure as hell knew how it felt to have his chest blown away. He stared at Lupe and Xavier, unable to speak.

"Two nights after you left, she ran away," Lupe said.

He heard her over the single word *gone* screaming in his ears. "No! She can't be." He lurched up, driven like a man possessed. He wouldn't believe it!

He stalked to White Fawn's door—unlocked—and threw it wide to bang against the wall. One sweep of the room left him fighting for breath. He ran to the barn, searched each stall for the mare. He hadn't even looked earlier. He'd assumed Pepper was there. *You're an arrogant fool, Matt Conway.*

He stopped at the last stall and laid his forehead on the fence atop crossed arms. Only once in his life could he remember crying: the day he'd found his family massacred, the house burned to the ground. But he was damn close to doing so now.

"Goddamn you, you're mine."

She was. He believed it right down to his soul. Making love to her had sealed the bond . . . for him. He had pleasured her. He knew it! Why couldn't she understand that he would protect her? No one need know that she'd lived with the Comanche.

Raising his head, Matt glared at the wall as if it offended him. *I'll go after her. If I have to drag her back to the Rocking C kicking and screaming, I will.* She was not going to be claimed by a damned Indian. By *any* man but him.

Trooper needed rest. He'd give him this night. Brow furrowed, Matt thought of what he'd need. A couple of shirts and trousers, along with a bit of food. Plenty of jerky for the trail. Coffee makings, string. His knife, of course, strapped inside his boot as always.

No white man with a lick of sense ventured into Comanche country alone. Except him. He wouldn't put his friends' lives in jeopardy. Solo, he'd take all the ammunition he could carry . . . all the way into the godforsaken *Llano Estacado*.

No matter how long it took, he'd find her. And when he did . . .

The plan set in his mind, Matt swung about to return to the house. Funny thing about plans, he thought. They could be thwarted. That thwarting stood directly in his path in the forms of Xavier and Lupe.

Before they could open their mouths, he said, "I'm leaving at dawn to go after her."

Neither argued. Instead, Xavier said, "Lars and Hoby go, too."

Matt looked from one to the other. "No. I go alone."

Lupe's words gave him a jab in the solar plexus. "They quit. Xavier talked them into bunking at Gladstone's until you returned."

Holy smoke! Xavier and he would have one helluva time doing all the work on the ranch. "Why?"

"Because each one thinks Rebecca's disappearance is his fault."

More befuddled than ever, Matt ran an agitated hand through his hair. "Why in hell's name would they think that?"

"The night she ran away, Lars had gone. Thinks if he'd been here, he'd have heard her. Could have stopped her."

So much for relying on Lars Gunnerson, Matt thought. No, that wasn't fair. The man worked like a team of horses. He was entitled to a little pleasure once in a while.

Matt shook his head. "Not his fault. White Fawn was determined." God knew, he'd seen her defiance often enough. "What about Hoby?"

"She helped him in the barn with a sick calf. He didn't know we locked her in. And I . . . forgot to lock the door that night."

"No!" Xavier snapped. "Me. I forget. Lupe, she laid up. No can do chores for couple days."

Though not surprised at Xavier's defense of Lupe, Matt admitted it was no one's fault. Except his own.

He scowled. "Laid up?" She looked perfectly healthy to him.

"I sprained my knee. White Fawn did all my chores and hers, too." Lupe gave him a forlorn look. "We tried to tell them, but they wouldn't listen, Matt. You have to talk to them."

"*Sí.* I no run Rocking C alone when you gone. Bob and Jim, they okay. But no good as Lars and Hoby." He glanced at his wife. "More cattle roam. I no leave Lupe alone to look."

Of course not. Matt wouldn't expect him to. But hell's fire . . . He shoved his hands in his pockets and hunched his shoulders. No help for it.

"Okay. I'll head over to Weatherly's . . . Gladstone's tomorrow."

Matt gazed north. Was she safe, one small woman finding her way in the vast plains?

Where are you, White Fawn?

Six days she had traveled with Running Bear's party. Six seemingly endless days of eating dust, drinking little water, and feeling sorry for the Mexican women.

They had endured countless indignities and cruelties, but they had survived.

White Fawn suspected they had been pampered girls. When Running Bear ordered his slave to cook a squirrel over the fire, she spieled a string of indignant Spanish. It gained her a cuffing that left her almost senseless. He then picked her up and literally threw her near the fire. She bent to the task with a head that surely spun. That night, Running Bear gave her to two warriors.

For the first time, White Fawn witnessed how captive women were treated. Other females had been brought into camp as bedraggled as these two, but until now she had not known what had befallen them.

Though White Fawn's garments were tattered and dirty, her skin grimy, her filth did not compare. Still naked, with only threadbare blankets over their heads, they had not been allowed to wash. Dried semen and black, dried blood smeared their legs. Their faces were a mass of bruises. Running Bear's slave had burned her hand, but no attempt had been made to clean the wound or ease the pain.

White Fawn discovered something about herself that made her sick to her stomach. She was a *coward*. The word was bitter in her soul. Her one show of bravado had gained the women blankets, perhaps, but Running Bear's threat had served its purpose. Not once had she again spoken in the women's defense. She only answered in a rusty voice when Running Bear or Wildcat spoke to her.

Bitter indeed, she thought, her gaze skipping over the slave riding with the warrior she thought of as *Pig*. The woman had called herself Juana until she'd stopped speaking at all.

White Fawn's perusal slid over *Snake,* then to *Badger*. She had no desire to learn their real names. Pig ate like one. Snake's eyes were beady and cold as death. Badger was just plain vicious, as the animal could be if cornered. He slapped Juana around until she passed out, just for the hell of it.

White Fawn grimaced. It was childish and cowardly of her, but thinking disparagingly about these men was the only way she had been able to endure these past days.

She was deeply concerned. They still traveled directly north, had surely left behind the meadow where her band had camped when she'd last seen them. Where was Running Bear taking her? To his camp? She shuddered at the thought.

She swiped sweat from her chest where her shirtwaist gaped open, then rubbed the moisture on her dusty skirt. Inside her boots, her cotton socks were threadbare at the heels from sweat and dirt. Blisters rubbed against the leather.

Looking longingly at Wildcat's moccasins, she vowed that when she saw her people again, she would bathe, change into a buckskin tunic, and wear nothing but moccasins again. Ever!

Her gaze traveled from Wildcat to Running Bear. Though she feared both men, they seemed honorable compared to the others. After taking the Mexican women to their blankets once, they now ignored them.

Suddenly, Running Bear lifted his lance. As one, the men reined in their mounts. The captured horses milled behind, sending dust billowing over her. Smoke hazed the air directly ahead. And hundreds of birds circled over unseen prey.

She blinked as bushes rustled. Then, astonished, she saw warriors stand, brush anchored to headbands and draped over shoulders, ranged in a line ahead of them. Lookouts!

Running Bear's voice boomed. "My brothers, I have returned."

With no more greeting than that, the party rode forward at an easy pace. The lookouts dropped to the ground, melting into the chapparal.

White Fawn suddenly realized where she was. They rode toward the great slash in the earth known as Palo Duro Canyon. It had been two full circles of seasons since White Fawn had seen this natural wonder.

A quarter-mile farther, Pepper halted at the lip of a cliff that dropped hundreds of feet, straight down. Below, the immense valley sheltered hundreds of tipis. Caught by the breeze at the top of the cliffs, smoke from campfires dissipated into the crystalline air. Like a silver ribbon, the river coiled and flowed through the depths of the canyon.

She cut a glance at Running Bear. "My father is not camped here."

"Eagle Feather led his band here one moon past, woman."

Her brow furrowed. "But—"

"Bad spirits plague him." Callously, he shrugged. "Maybe he has passed to the Spirit World by now."

"No!" It could not be. Her father was a strong war-

204

rior. Old, perhaps, but straight and tall. "Why did you not tell me?"

"You did not ask how your people fared."

Because it never occurred to her that Eagle Feather might be ill. She had ridden for days swallowing the bile of fear. Now a new fear rose, this time in her heart.

She could not bear it if Eagle Feather had slipped into the next world while she'd been gone. He was the only father she knew.

If he no longer led the band, a number of warriors qualified for the position. White Fawn and Bright Star hoped that Straight Arrow would become chief.

Though many muttered displeasure about not raiding, like his father, Straight Arrow counseled against it. But Eagle Feather was revered by their people. His firstborn son, though a fierce, respected warrior, had not lived so many seasons that the mantle of wisdom cloaked his shoulders.

White Fawn fell in behind Running Bear. A narrow trail switchbacked like a sidewinder down the rock canyon's sheer face. She dismounted along with the warriors and began the slow descent, Pepper in tow.

Her heart lay heavy in her breast. If the soul of her Indian father had flown . . .

Spirits of the People, hear my prayer. Do not have taken Eagle Feather.

205

Chapter Thirteen

"Have you lost your mind?"

Lupe planted her hands on her hips and glared at Matt, who continued to jam supplies into saddlebags on the dining table. The bottoms of both pouches were lined with ammunition, clothes folded on top.

"I told you night before last I was going after her." He sounded as if he discussed nothing more important than the weather.

"I put that down to insanity."

"Well, now you know different."

"Sure. You head into *Comancheria*—alone, mind you—and that doesn't scream madness? Matt, you can't do this!"

"I can. I am!"

"Is loco, Matt." Xavier sat at the table, dark eyes troubled. "You know not where she is. She be dead now, maybe."

"No!"

Matt buckled the pouches, then hefted them over his arm. His muscles bulged from the weight, tautening his shirtsleeve. When he started to leave, Lupe stepped in front of him.

"You'll get yourself killed. And for what? Rebecca didn't want to be here. She doesn't want to be found."

"That's too damn bad. I will find her and bring her back where she belongs." He cast a lame smile at them. "By the way, if I don't return, the ranch is yours."

"Listen to yourself!"

He could make light of the danger? She had never been so exasperated with him. Matt had done some foolhardy things in his life, but this far surpassed credibility. Fear gnawing at her, she tried another tack.

"You say she belongs here. Does that mean you plan to marry her?"

That got his attention in a hurry. He jerked back as if she'd slapped him.

"You know my thoughts about that."

"So, you'll bring her here, an unmarried, unprotected woman, and expose her to ridicule?" She shrugged. "Or maybe you plan to send her to that house close by Goodlight's Trading Post."

Fury built in his eyes, but she ignored it. "I'm sure Rebecca will gladly spread her legs for any *vaquero* with the money."

Face thunderous, Matt stepped toward her. Xavier lunged from his chair. Though her man's protectiveness was no surprise, it was unwarranted.

Matthew Conway was a strong, fearless man. He rode like a demon from hell, fought with his fists like a champion if need-be, and had killed Indians by the score. But it wasn't in him to strike or knowingly hurt

207

a woman. Matt wouldn't raise a hand to her if she pummeled his head.

Bringing Rebecca back here to pose as a white-reared woman could be as dangerous for her as being captured by the Comanches. She had survived, even prospered with the Indians, but reentering white society might well be beyond her capability.

"That's enough, Lupe," Matt warned.

"Is it?" she shot back. Then her expression melted into worry. For him, for Rebecca. "Please, Matt, think this through. Now, before it's too late."

"I have. She's mine."

"Your lightskirt?" The words slipped out before she could call them back. But if Matt wanted Rebecca, and Lupe suspected he'd already taken her in the most intimate way, then he must marry her.

Quietly and with conviction, she said, "Matthew, if you don't die out there someplace, if you manage to bring that young woman back here, you'd better be prepared to make her your wife. I will *not* stay here and watch her become your . . . soiled dove."

His brows slammed together. "I intend to take her to Austin."

" 'She's mine,' you said. Remember that while you're riding into hell. If by some miracle you find her, ask yourself if you can leave her in Austin and walk away." She searched his face. "I think not."

Matt had barely disappeared into the trees before Lupe, madder than a wet hen, barged into the bunkhouse without knocking. She caught Hoby with his trousers down around his ankles.

Not one to bother with underwear, he glanced up the instant before he yanked up his pants. "Miz Lupe," he croaked, feeling flames lick his cheeks.

"Hoby, saddle up and ride to Isaac Bettencourt's place. Matt has gone after Rebecca. He needs help, whether he wants it or not."

Lars swung away from the cookstove, a cup of black, walk-to-your-mouth coffee in hand. The hot brew sloshed over his fingers and down his pant leg. "Holy sh . . ."

Bob Foster turned over in his bunk and looked bleary-eyed at Lupe.

Though she hadn't appeared to notice his privates, it was a beat or two before Hoby overcame his embarrassment. "Ma'am, what . . ." He fumbled with his belt buckle. "Ride to Isaac's?"

"*Now,* Hoby. If Matt gets very far, Isaac won't be able to find him."

He dropped his hands to his sides and glanced at Lars, who appeared as bewildered as he. "The boss has . . ."

Xavier stormed into the room. "*Sí.* He loco like he drink much *mescal.* But no can stop him." He glowered at his wife. "You no should be here, woman."

That was a fact, Hoby thought, but Lupe paid Xavier no mind. Hoby still felt guilty, and he knew Lars did, too, for letting Miss Rebecca get away. But the boss had yammered a blue streak yesterday morning, making them feel more guilty if they didn't come back.

"How would you feel if Indians or no-accounts attacked Lupe with no men on the ranch to protect her?" Matt had asked.

Lupe was a strong woman, but she couldn't fight like a man. Hoby'd had little truck with Mexicans until he'd met Xavier and Lupe. The Cruzes was good folks.

He and Lars couldn't argue the boss's point, so they'd come back. Glad to, really. Matthew Conway was most near the best man he'd ever worked for. And he'd been kickin' 'round on his own since he was ten years old. He'd learned from more than a few missteps how to judge a man. His boss stood tall. Hoby would just as soon see a lot of fellers six feet under.

"Stop standing there like a lump of cow dung and ride, Hoby," Lupe fumed.

He scratched his head, looking to Lars and Xavier for guidance. Finally, he asked, "Ma'am, you think that's a good idea?"

Lupe looked ready to flatten him. Before she could erupt in a shout, Hoby asked, "What do I tell Isaac? Ain't nobody but us and the Gladstones knows that Miss Rebecca was on the ranch. You think he'd want folks to know she lived with the Comanches?"

Lupe's anger deflated to a frown of confusion, and he knew he was right. Just like he'd thought at first that she was soiled goods, most other white folks would think so, too. If'n the boss hadn't put him straight, he'd 'a gone at the little gal with glee.

Maybe she *was* soiled goods, he didn't know, but he'd come to like her. She was handy at takin' care of sick critters. He liked animals more than some people.

Lupe interrupted his musings. "You're right." Her chest lifted in a huge sigh. "We can't do a thing to help

210

him. He'd never forgive me if . . ." She started out the door.

Xavier clasped her hand. "You no can help him this time, Lupe."

"There's no one better than Matt at tracking." Lars sipped his coffee.

"None better," Jim Foster chimed in. Another in-the-raw sleeper like his brother and Hoby, Jim remained huddled beneath his blanket. "If she's to be found, he'll find her."

"He be okay," Xavier said as he and Lupe left the bunkhouse.

Hoby pulled on a shirt, his brow knitted. Maybe the boss would be okay; maybe not. Maybe he'd find Miss Rebecca; maybe not. Too many maybes. But Hoby couldn't see what else they could do except hope Xavier was right: The boss would return in one piece.

Maybe.

Surrounded by his family, save Straight Arrow and White Fawn, Eagle Feather sat cross-legged in his lodge, a cup of Bright Star's pain-killing brew beside his knee. Each day he persisted in showing himself to his People, but walking tired him.

He was dying, but he could not fly to the afterworld just yet. Last night, a vision had disturbed his dreams. Danger stalked his People. He was unsure when chaos would befall them, but it approached as sure as Father Sun rose in the morning sky.

In his dreams, many bluecoats swept into Palo Duro Canyon. The thunder of gunfire still echoed in his head. He must convince Straight Arrow to flee north with his People. The season of the long summer was upon them. Not too many moons distant, the season of falling leaves would come. By then, Eagle Feather hoped his People would be many leagues from harm.

Straight Arrow entered and dipped his head respectfully. "You wished to speak with me, my father?" Crossing his ankles, he sank to the buffalo robe across from Eagle Feather.

"I am not long for this world, my son. Soon the Spirits will take me, and you shall be left to lead our People."

Denial flamed in Straight Arrow's eyes. "You must not speak so. The tea—"

Eagle Feather lifted his hand. "Little time remains before I die. You must convince our People to travel north. They will be safe for a time."

Straight Arrow scowled and glanced at the somber faces around him. "Safe? From what?"

"Bluecoats. Many will die."

His son shook his head. "How can you be certain? Few white men have ventured into our land. Few know where we camp."

"A vision, Straight Arrow. Death stalks this canyon. You must make haste."

As still and quiet as frightened rabbits, Bright Star and Willow Branch huddled against the slanted tipi wall. Eagle Feather regretted their fright, but perhaps it would save them. If he could not convince his three sons of the danger, all would be lost.

"You cannot travel," Black Crow said.

"It matters not how far I travel." He shrugged. "Per-

212

haps the Spirits will smile on me until snow blankets the earth."

"We cannot leave you," Beaver Heart cried.

Beaver Heart's failure to bring White Fawn home still smarted in his breast, and he had been sullen and silent since his return. Eagle Feather was now glad that White Fawn had not been found. If she lived and had been reclaimed into the white man's world, her life would be far better than with him.

"My father, not one chief camped here has sounded an alarm. Bluecoats cannot enter the canyon without being seen by the lookouts. We would be warned before an attack."

"When they come, it will matter not. They will number more than leaves on a tree."

Straight Arrow shook his head as if he scoffed at his father's words. Perhaps he did. His son spoke truth. Other than his own unease, there was no sign of danger.

He sighed. It would have been helpful if his vision had foretold *when* calamity would strike. He had only seen countless men on horseback lining the rim of the canyon. More men swept up the canyon from the south, guns blazing. In his vision, his People and the Kiowa dropped like felled buffalo calves.

A commotion outside the lodge halted his next words. Just as well. The tea deadened the pain, but still his belly was unsettled. He must sleep for a while, and take up his argument later.

A scratch on the tipi brought Bright Star to her feet. Every head turned when she lifted the flap, gasped, and staggered back a step.

Joy blossomed in Eagle Feather's heart, quickly followed by alarm. "White Fawn!"

She had lost track of the weeks, but surely she had not been gone so long that her father should have aged so. Face drawn and thin, he must suffer much pain.

Dismay rose in White Fawn as expressions chased over Eagle Feather's countenance. Disbelief, joy. Anger?

"You should not have come," he said.

Each word of censure dropped into her belly like a stone. Not welcome here?

No one spoke, no one moved. Sober-faced, her brothers simply stared at her. Expressions softer though grave, Bright Star and Willow Branch came toward her, hands seeking hers.

After the initial surprise, only Beaver Heart leaped up and spread his arms wide. Then, suddenly he stopped. "My father does not welcome you, but I do."

That helped, but before White Fawn could speak, Running Bear and Wildcat sought entrance, stepping past her as if she were an apparition.

"Greetings, Eagle Feather. I am Running Bear, and this"—he gestured—"is my brother, Wildcat. The woman claims to be your daughter."

Alarm flared anew when her father sat mute. Finally, he said, "She speaks truth. We thought her dead."

"You say you don't want her here. I will take her as my slave."

A chill froze her heart. No! Had she escaped Conway's locked room only to serve in bondage to a cruel man? She had learned a hard truth while traveling with

214

these warriors. Conway had spoken true when he said Comanches could be vicious.

Silence lengthened while her nerves tautened like a drawn bow. She stepped sideways so she could see her father and spoke with her eyes, hoping he understood. *I will kill myself rather than be slave to this man.*

"My daughter is slave to no man."

Her knees almost buckled with relief. Running Bear's head jerked back.

Eagle Feather nodded regally, then spoke to Straight Arrow. "Cut two horses from my remuda. Gifts of thanks to Running Bear and his brother for returning White Fawn to my lodge."

As the two men left, Running Bear flicked her a deadly glare.

Nevertheless, White Fawn breathed a sigh. Running Bear had not taken kindly to her father's rebuke, but she cared not. If she never saw either man again, she would be happy.

Quiet reigned in the lodge. White Fawn stood, feeling apart from the family. Her insides churned as she searched for something to say.

In the past she had always addressed her father as Eagle Feather. Now, in an effort to change the subject and break through the invisible barrier between them, she said, "My father, you are ill?" Her solicitous question served only to put a scowl on his face.

He repeated, "You should not have come."

Why? Where else could she go? Why had he gifted two horses for her safe return if he truly believed his words?

Before she could ask, he spoke. "What has become of One Bear and the warriors who rode with him?"

Gruesome images played in White Fawn's mind, but she chose not to dwell on them or specifically enlighten Eagle Feather. "All are now in the Spirit World. Cut down while raiding."

Sadness colored his features. "As we suspected. You escaped without injury?"

"A bullet grazed my arm." She drew the amulet from beneath her shirtwaist. "Your charm saved me, my father." She looked down at the pendant, marveling anew at how close she had come to death, then returned her gaze to him. "Your strong medicine caught and held the bullet, sparing my life."

For an instant, but only an instant, Eagle Feather's countenance softened.

White Fawn swallowed her sorrow at his distant manner. She must explain. . . . "My father, One Bear died bravely; so did all the warriors. Little Elk . . ." Tears pricked her eyes. "I must speak with She of Small Voice. She must know her man was brave."

"No." Eagle Feather's eyes dimmed, as if looking into eternity. "When you did not return, She of Small Voice mourned. She walks the Spirit World with her man."

"Oh, no." White Fawn's heart constricted. She of Small Voice had gone to Little Elk's lodge having seen only thirteen summers. A mere child.

Her father waved his hand. Sounding exceedingly weary, he said, "Leave me to my rest."

After reveling in a much-needed bath, White Fawn donned a floor-length, fringed doeskin tunic. Willow Branch gave her strips of leather, and Bright Star provided a bone needle. She set about making a new pair of moccasins.

Women worked over cookfires preparing the evening meal. Children played with hoops or ran wild for the sheer joy of it. Dogs barked or yipped when kicked from underfoot. Warriors strode about importantly . . . whether they were important or not. She smiled. The old ones tended the very young, taking them into their laps to spin tales the children listened to with rapt attention.

White Fawn worked on one moccasin while her two mothers served the men inside the tipi. Then, the women filled bowls and joined her near the fire. Startled, she found herself wrinkling her nose at the odor wafting from the two women. After dark, they would bathe. Odd, how the short time on Conway's ranch had changed her.

When Bright Star scooped up venison stew with work-worn fingers and popped the dripping mixture into her mouth, White Fawn swallowed to settle her stomach. It was wrong for her to think disparagingly of a woman who had been nothing but kind to her all the years she had lived with the band.

"You are troubled, daughter," Bright Star murmured. "Eagle Feather is pleased you are home."

White Fawn conjured her father's stern visage and shook her head. "That is not what he said."

"His heart is heavy, and he is in pain. The *puhakut*'s chants and potions have done naught to chase bad Spirits from his belly. He fears for our People as well."

White Fawn tied a knot at the heel of the moccasin and bit off the sinew. Anxiety rippled through her. "Fears for the People?"

217

"My husband saw bluecoats in a vision. They come, he says." She gazed into the distance, her features as troubled as White Fawn's.

Pulling on the first moccasin to check the fit, she paused and looked up. "Here? To Palo Duro Canyon? White men dare not venture this far into our land."

The moment the words were out, Conway's image rose. He would ride into hell if he chose, and damn the consequences. The sounds of booming guns echoed in her mind. In the next instant, she remembered his lips on her breasts. Her nipples beaded with wanting. So real!

"He says it is so," Willow Branch said. "When has Eagle Feather erred?"

White Fawn thrust away the feelings. Her mothers spoke truth. Eagle Feather had the gift of sight.

Time and again the chief had led the band to abundant hunting grounds. He'd counseled against war these many seasons past. While Comanches in other bands had perished, not a single one in his band had died—until One Bear and his men defied Eagle Feather's counsel.

"This fear is why he said you should not be here." Bright Star cast a smile at her. "Since your return, you are different, daughter. Your thoughts roam many leagues. Perhaps you found a warrior to your liking?"

White Fawn ducked her head and doggedly pushed the needle through heavy leather, avoiding Bright Star's curiosity. How could she know?

Conway was not to her liking! *And pigs fly in the sky,* an inner voice taunted. No. He had locked her in that room for days, weeks. She would not think about Conway. She would not long for something that could never be.

The annoying voice persisted. *His lovemaking awakened your body to exquisite ecstasy.* And she wanted him. Now.

She scrambled to her feet; the leather, needle, and sinew tumbled to the ground. "I will eat," she said, and walked away wearing one moccasin.

Chapter Fourteen

As days and then weeks passed, bouts of melancholy claimed White Fawn. While the canyon simmered under the summer sun, she went about her chores without complaint, but her heart was troubled. Images, feelings, longings plagued her during restless nights. She tried to forget them during the day. It wasn't that she was unhappy, exactly; she just felt . . . out of place somehow.

When Beaver Heart presented her with two doeskins and a beaver pelt, she made a second tunic. She persisted in bathing each night. Her daily ablutions garnered more than a few snickers from some of the women, but White Fawn cared not. She washed one tunic every few days and wore the other.

A Mexican trader came through the camp. She bartered the beaver pelt for a cake of sweet-smelling soap and a pair of scissors.

White Fawn threatened to cut her long hair if Bright Star would not. Relenting, her Indian mother cut the hip-length tresses to her waist. White Fawn had never adopted the practice of greasing her hair. Instead, she braided the mass to tame its tendency to curl.

Among the People, time had no meaning. White Fawn thought about three weeks had passed after her return when Eagle Feather sank into a melancholy more debilitating than her own. He rarely spoke. When he did, he urged Straight Arrow to heed his words and lead the band north.

Though his illness did not worsen, he lost more weight. Only when Bright Star sat next to his blankets and coaxed every bite would he eat more than a mouthful or two.

It was a measure of Eagle Feather's stout heart that he walked through the camp every day. He hid his pain from others, but his family knew he suffered greatly. Then he seemed to overcome the pain, walk straighter, and smile more.

Taking advantage of the night breeze, White Fawn decided to sleep beside the river. Staring at stars glittering on high, she felt small and unimportant in the Great Spirit's world.

Soothed by the river's song, she heard an owl's hoot, the rustle of small animals, then drifted into sleep. Sometime in the night, she jolted awake and sat up. A second sob like the one that had awakened her erupted. Her own. She brushed tears from her cheeks.

Powerless to stop the ghostly image that danced before her eyes, she raised her knees and clasped her arms around them. What did the vision mean?

Tied and slumped against a tree, Conway appeared unconscious. His dust-covered hair dipped over his brow and obscured his face. Large tears in his dirty shirt revealed abraded skin. Blood oozed.

She reached out as if to touch him. Her fingers curled into a fist. "Only a dream," she assured herself. But why would she have such an unsettling vision? She must be daft.

Her brow crinkled as the vision came again. Braves walked about, ignoring Conway. He raised his head. His lips curved in a wry smile. He spoke. But she could not hear.

Impossible. Conway lived far to the south. Safe, secure. Still, the image of his battered body lingered.

Matt slumped forward, forearm resting on the saddle horn, and stared morosely at the barrier before him. It was as if the Comanche had set a war shield against invasion by white men. Only this twenty-five-foot shield was a rocky cliff that jutted skyward.

He scanned both directions. Didn't see a break anywhere close. How the hell could he traverse this abutment? Somehow he would, dammit. He'd come this far; he wasn't about to turn back.

In the five weeks since he'd started north, he figured he'd traveled about four hundred miles as birds fly. Since he wasn't flying, rather zigging a few miles one way, then zagging the other, always pressing north, he suspected he'd seen more of *Comancheria* than any other white man alive.

He'd come across lots of signs, but nothing that assured him he was actually following White Fawn. This was Comanche and Kiowa country, uncharted and vast.

Grass. My God, there was enough in these millions

of acres to graze twenty million steers. No wonder buffalo roamed here; the land was a plentiful breadbasket for the shaggy beasts.

He patted Trooper. "Well, old son, we gotta find a way up this cliff." Trooper nodded and mouthed the bit. Matt chuckled and nudged him forward.

It was slow going. Time and again, he leaned up in the saddle, urging the gelding up a few feet, then traveling sideways a bit before attempting a further climb. Rock and soil broke away and tumbled down behind them.

The sun, a ball of fire, beat down on them. Sweat ran down his face, trickled beneath his arms to soak his shirt. He persisted. Trooper was game and strong.

Midday, they finally crested a plateau. Matt reined in, lifted his hat, and wiped his brow with his sleeve. The horse had done the work, but he, too, was bone tired.

Matt's chest tightened, his eyes wide when he saw what lay before him. Mile upon mile of tableland covered in high grass stretched forever, north, east, and west, to meet a sweep of cerulean sky at the horizon.

Suddenly, he knew where he was. The southern boundary of the fabled *Llano Estacado*. Overwhelming in its loneliness.

"Holy shit!" He jumped at the sound of his own voice. The horse's breathing whispered in his ears; wind moaned ever so softly. Somewhere in this vast no-man's land, he hoped to find White Fawn.

He licked his parched lips, shook his canteen. "Not good." With luck, it was half full, and Trooper needed water right now.

Matt dismounted and checked the oilskin pouch that

held extra water. Lifting it from the bottom, water gurgled, but the bag collapsed around his fist. He'd filled it two days ago from a narrow creek. Now the skin was almost empty. Maybe a couple quarts left.

A meager offering, but it would wet Trooper's mouth and throat. Matt poured a scant two cups in his hat and stuck it under the gelding's nose. He slurped it up in no time and nuzzled the crown for more.

"Sorry, boy. That's all for now."

Matt clapped his hat back on his head to Trooper's snuffled protest. Rivulets of warm water slithered down his forehead and neck. He flicked out his tongue to capture minute amounts that trickled by his mouth. Thirsty as hell, he vowed to wait as long as he could for a drink. One mouthful at a time, he cautioned himself.

The devil only knew where water holes might be scattered in this dry land. And the devil would probably keep that information to himself. Or loose hell on Matt in the form of screaming Comanches.

His lips lifted. Hell's fire, he'd just arrived in this lonely place and his thoughts were as addled as a madman's. He remounted and pointed Trooper's head due north. Though instinct pointed him that way, Matt was unsure if it was the right direction. Good as any, he supposed.

As the hours passed, he spied black birds overhead, flying north, then angling slightly to the west. He drew Trooper to a halt and watched the wedge. They'd know where to find water. He turned in their direction. In the cloudless sky, it was easy to keep the west-tracking sun over his left shoulder.

He rode at a walk to conserve Trooper's energy.

Stopping once, he portioned out another snoutful of water to the valiant horse. Matt chewed hardtack as they moseyed along, then allowed Trooper to graze. The horse could eat from now 'til time's end and not make a dent in the belly-high forage.

The blood-red sun hovered at the horizon when Matt unexpectedly broke from the tall grass onto a trail. He looked both ways, northwest to southeast. Horses. Many horses had passed this way not long ago. The grass lay churned and flattened with no regard to hiding tracks. Indisputably Indian domain. Safe from white men.

Matt dismounted and knelt to inspect the ground. "Hmm," he muttered, comforted by his own voice. Unshod horses mixed with shod had walked, not run this way. He suspected the unshod stock's deeper prints carried warriors, though he couldn't tell how many. Ten, fifteen of them, perhaps. To his left, the trail bent out of sight. Headed to their village?

White Fawn's village?

His pulse quickened. It was the first sign he'd seen on the Staked Plains that humans—Indians—inhabited the area.

Rising, he squinted at the sun. It would be dark before long. And he had no idea how far ahead this band was. Sure didn't want to stumble upon Comanches in the dark. He'd make camp. Come morning, he would follow the well-defined trail with ease.

He was bone tired, and Trooper could use a rest. His heart thumped an erratic tattoo. He sensed White Fawn's nearness. Tomorrow, maybe the next day, he'd see her again.

Her specter rose before him. His gaze raced over deep violet eyes, her small, naked body. His own quickened in remembrance of her response to his hands, his mouth. Loins heavy, he shifted uncomfortably.

There had to be a way to steal her from the Indians. Fighting his way in and out of a Comanche village bordered on madness, but if he had to face the damn savages, he would. White Fawn would never bed an Indian.

Not as long as I draw breath.

White Fawn gazed at the new tipi with mixed emotions. Though small, it was hers, a gift from Bright Star and Willow Branch. The two women were convinced she had her eye on a brave, that he would offer for her before long.

Bright Star giggled when she caught White Fawn lost in reverie. "Perhaps he will come today," her Indian mother had said moments ago. "Now you have your own lodge to begin a new life."

If she wanted a new life. But the man she desired was not of her world. Now she was banished from Eagle Feather's tipi. It was not meant to be an unkind gesture, but was simply the way of the People, when a maiden was grown and ready to take a warrior to her blankets. Many of her acquaintances as young as twelve summers accepted offers.

Her own tipi also ensured Eagle Feather's band would survive. With so few braves left to hunt game, the one White Fawn chose would live with them. Help provide meat for hungry bellies.

"I do not wish to mate, Bright Star."

"Your words speak not for your heart. You envision a man in your dreams." Bright Star's lips curved in a sly smile. "Running Bear is a fierce warrior. Perhaps Wildcat?"

Though most Indian women would consider either an excellent mate, White Fawn shuddered. "They are brutal men, Bright Star. I will mate only with a man I love."

"Love comes when you choose wisely." Willow Branch's smile reflected Bright Star's. "I am fortunate my father insisted I accept Eagle Feather. Now my heart overflows when I am with him."

"Eagle Feather says Running Bear and Wildcat have many coup between them," Bright Star added.

Undoubtedly true, but they captured women, abused them, and made them slaves. Slavery was a tradition the People had followed for centuries, but White Fawn had seen its degradation firsthand. She wanted no part of men who took pride in mutilation and rape. Since any attempt to make her Indian mothers understand her feelings would be futile, she did not try.

"I love not either man. I will not wed."

She wondered, though, if she would be given a choice. Though women were never forced to a man's blankets, maidens were advised by their parents to accept a warrior considered able and worthy. She prayed Eagle Feather would allow her, his adopted daughter, to make her own decision.

She would miss the evenings spent beside his fire. He was surely considered uncivilized by white men, but she had found the old warrior compassionate and wise, even gentle. Her Indian father's visions had taught her much about his dreams for the future.

He wished to live free, to hunt, to move with the seasons on the vast plains. Now sad, even alarmed, he prodded his sons daily to heed his warnings to leave this place and distance themselves from white men. Though Eagle Feather's health seemed better, his time as leader of his People grew short.

Perhaps her Indian father was right. Though not a bluecoat, Matthew Conway would slaughter Indians to protect his land. She had seen his determination.

And she loved him.

Matt spent a restless night figuratively kicking his own sorry ass. Every time he wakened, White Fawn's eyes mirrored the stars in the vast sky. "Dammit." He turned over—again—to relieve his engorged member. Nothing but lust, he assured himself. *Uh-huh*, a little voice taunted.

He sat up, rested his elbows on bent knees, and scrubbed his stubbled face with both hands. He still saw the wonder in her eyes as her body awakened to his touch. When her release came, she might as well have shot an arrow into his heart. He scowled. That meant his heart was involved.

"Nope," he said aloud. He'd never love any woman, and for damn sure he'd never marry. Women. Fickle as the wind.

That settled, he stood and fished for his pocket watch. Right at 4:30. Might as well gather his gear. It'd be light enough to travel before long.

As he rode, the stars winked out. Tall grass gave way to mesquite. Rich soil yielded to hard ground and scattered rocks, then slabs of limestone that echoed like metal when struck by Trooper's hooves.

Midmorning, through narrowed eyes, he saw vultures ahead, and damn close to the ground. Vultures circled for a reason.

Dismounting, he dropped the reins to ground-tie Trooper and cautiously walked forward. His attention on the birds, he missed the rocky ground's sudden slant. His boots slipped.

When he glanced down, his eyes widened in shock. He scuffled backward as best he could. Unable to gain purchase with the leather soles, he threw himself back and landed hard.

What was left of his breath whooshed from him, but he lay on solid rock. Thank God. He closed his eyes with relief. Sitting up ever so slowly, he scooted back, then rose on unsteady legs.

High atop caprock, he stared down into a canyon several miles wide and longer than he could see as it disappeared around a bend. Had he and Trooper reached this precipice in the dark, they'd have plunged hundreds of feet straight down.

"Jesus!"

Suddenly, his wits returned and he dropped to his belly. No need to sky-light himself. Countless tipis dotted the valley floor. Through smoke holes, wisps curled into crystal air, whisked to nothing on the slight breeze.

His glance flicked to the vultures. They soared on updrafts and circled, but nowhere near the ground as he'd thought. Not by a long shot. Though the tipis were far below, the birds would undoubtedly swoop in to make a meal of the Indians' scattered debris.

"Jesus, Mary, and Joseph," Matt whispered his mother's favored oath.

How many redskins were there? Thousands? Remembered conversation pricked his memory. Was this the fabled Palo Duro Canyon Father Anselmo and Father Sebastian had spoken of with such awe? Had to be. It was immense and beautiful, with walls of red, russet, and gold; even yellow layers darted through the strata. A river spilled through sandy soil; stands of oak and cottonwood lined the banks. Their silvery green leaves flickered in early light or in deep shadow, untouched by the sun.

Along the outskirts of what must be several villages, perhaps a thousand horses grazed on lush grass. Other than his own ranch, this had to be the most peaceful-looking spot on Earth.

He smiled grimly. No more than large specks, people came and went through the villages. But they were far from peaceful. If they discovered his presence, they'd skin him for breakfast.

Suddenly, the hair on his nape lifted and his flesh crawled. *Scaring the shit out of yourself?* He frowned as the sensation grew. Apprehension slithered down his spine.

I'm not alone.

His heart stuttered at the thought, but he knew it was true. Someone was behind him, on the canyon's brink. The only place they could be. Not even a mountain goat could find purchase on the steep cliffs.

Deliberately, Matt placed his palms flat on the ground beside his shoulders. Not a sound marred the stillness, but he hadn't survived this long without developing the instincts of a predator himself. And predators knew when they were stalked.

He pushed himself away from the ground and jack-knifed to his feet. Whirling about, hand poised over the gun on his right hip, he half-crouched, ready to draw.

He didn't.

No more than ten paces away, an Indian stood directly in front of him. Had the situation not been so dire, he would have laughed. Brush sprouted from the warrior's headband and draped about his shoulders. He was so well camouflaged by native plants, Matt had walked right past him.

Sweat beaded his forehead when another bush rustled and rose. Then another and another.

Straightening to his full height, Matt looked into the obsidian eyes of ten warriors. If he was of a mind to attempt escape, his six-shooter couldn't get them all. Hell, one shot and half the Comanches and Kiowas in Texas would boil out of that canyon.

Brazen it out. He raised his right hand in the plain's age-old peace greeting.

" 'Lo, Chief. Looks to be a right nice day."

Chapter Fifteen

Hell's fire, that got as much response from the savage as from a stone. Careful not to make any sudden moves, Matt lowered his hand, keeping it well away from his .44. He glanced from Indian to Indian. Half a dozen stood about ten feet apart, ranged in front of him like a living, dangerous-as-hell shield. Hard to tell how many had moved out of his sight.

"Any of you fellas speak English? How about Spanish? *Hablan ustedes Español?*" His queries met silence. "Great." The closest man's eyes reminded Matt of a snake's. Didn't he ever blink?

Figuring he was on safe ground, he smiled. "Not one of you sons-a-bitches understands a word I'm saying. That makes it troublesome to find Eagle Feather." He tried Spanish again, working on the pronunciation. "*Aguila Pluma?* I'm Matt Conway, and I'm looking for Chief Eagle Feather."

In the next instant, he discovered what visiting hell was like. A rope dropped around him and jerked him

232

backward. He hit the ground with a grunt, the rock jarring his teeth.

Shit. Now he *was* in a pickle. Hogtied.

The first Indian, a half-head shorter than Matt, with skin the texture of leather, walked up to him, smiled evilly, and spat in his face.

So much for brazening it out. "That was damned inhospitable, you son of a bitch."

To the screech of war cries, Matt was dragged several feet. Well, how bad could it be? The men were afoo—

Oh, shit, he'd forgotten Trooper.

Mounted on the gelding, one warrior looped the rope around the saddle horn . . . and took off at a gallop.

Matt pitched, tumbled, slammed into the hard ground again and again. Searing pain took his breath as skin peeled off his shoulders and back. Blood pounded behind his eyes fit to explode through the top of his head.

Jesus!

He ate dust until he thought his lungs would burst. In the dim recesses of his brain, he heard the demented whoops and screams from the warriors running beside his flailing body.

Suddenly, he tumbled to a halt. No amount of blinking cleared the grit from his eyes. He might not be able to see it, but he sure as hell could feel the gash that extended down his left thigh from hip to knee. It stung worse than the other injuries combined, as if a hive of hornets swarmed there.

Hands clasped his upper arms and hauled him to his feet. He swayed, unable to see for shit. After a moment, an Indian shoved him from behind and said something. When Matt didn't move, another socked him in the gut, repeating the command.

The only way to protect his midsection was to stay bent, but he straightened anyway. Courage. Dutch courage, perhaps, but he'd not show fear. Indians respected nothing but courage in a white man. It could prove his only salvation.

Salvation? *Dim-witted fool.*

He spit dirt and snarled at the Indian. "Walk? That what you want? Okay, I'll walk."

He managed one step before he was jerked backward again. This time his head smashed against a rock, so hard his teeth clamped together. He tasted blood as he was hauled up and planted on his feet again. Jerked around just for the hell of it, he thought.

"Well, make up your mind, dammit!"

Blood spewed from his mouth. His tongue felt so swollen, he wondered if he'd bitten off a chunk.

Rather than whooping and screeching, this time several of his captors laughed. Matt realized he could see . . . barely. Every one of them was several inches shorter than he. In a fair fight, he could have whipped their asses one by one, but numbers were in their favor. Anyway, who said life was fair?

Matt glanced down and found himself dangerously close to the cliff's edge. His head swam. Then he saw a narrow trail slashed down the rock's face. "Fit for a goat, maybe," he muttered.

Trooper was already twelve feet below him, led by an Indian. They expected him to walk down, so he did, two warriors ahead of him in moccasins, sure-footed as mules, the rest following. Damn hard to maintain his balance with his arms pinned to his sides, but these bastards weren't about to make the descent easy for him.

It took a half-hour to plod down the switchback trail. Twice, his boots slipped on the rock and he went down hard on his butt. A third time, he slipped over the edge and dangled in midair. His blood smeared the sheer wall. His head, shoulders, and hips slammed into the rock as he twirled. He bit back a groan when jagged shale caught him in the back. It took three of the little bastards to haul him back up to the trail.

At least they hadn't taken his boots . . . yet. He figured himself lucky to have the rope around him. Of course, if luck had anything to do with it, he would have plunged to the canyon floor. Knowing the savages had far more gruesome pain in store for him didn't help his frame of mind or his reactions to their prods.

A couple of steps from flat ground, he whirled on the Indian who repeatedly shoved him. "Goddammit, push me again and I'll cut out your gizzard when I get loose from this rope!"

That show of defiance earned him a cuff on the side of his head that sent him sprawling. Then he was jerked into motion again. Trooper's hooves pounding the ground kept cadence with his body slamming into unforgiving earth. Inanely, it crossed his mind that it was a little softer down here than the caprock above. He tried to whistle to his horse, but dust clogged his mouth. As darkness crowded his vision, he knew he'd swallowed more sand than a body could hold.

A blast of water full in the face brought him to his senses. His head jerked up. Seated on the ground, legs sprawled, he was tied to a tree. His arms were wrenched painfully behind and around the trunk. Rawhide lashed his wrists so tightly, he couldn't feel his hands.

At least the water had washed enough of the grit from his eyes that he could see, but he couldn't breathe. He coughed. A glob of bloody dirt shot out of his mouth.

He looked up. Before him, stance wide, a warrior grinned and chattered guttural Comanche. The bucket hung from his fingers.

Matt tried again to communicate. "Eagle Feather? *Aguila Pluma?*"

The warrior kicked him in the long cut on his leg. In agony, Matt clamped his teeth together so hard, he expected molars to crack. But by God, he stifled a moan. The Indian strode away, apparently satisfied for the moment.

Matt surveyed his battered torso. Little was left of his shirt. Blood oozed through and between the shredded fabric; threads stuck to rapidly coagulating blood. Hell, much of his skin was scraped raw or gone. Not all of it, though. And the Comanches would take unholy delight in skinning the rest.

Don't think about that.

Water trickled nearby. The river might as well be on the other side of hell. He licked his dry lips with a swollen tongue. It would swell more for want of water, he knew, and eventually cut off his air. With any luck . . . He grunted, then groaned when pain ricocheted behind his ribs.

Luck? Stupid thought. But if there was any to be had, he'd be out of his head by the time he suffocated.

His eyes widened in surprise when he saw his gun still strapped to his right leg. He hadn't fired a shot; the cartridge was still loaded with six bullets. More ammunition, enough to reload a couple of times, was slotted in his gun belt. Didn't matter. He smiled grimly, knowing why the Indians had left his gun alone. He was helpless as a babe. Even if he could reach the pistol, it would be futile to fire.

Glancing up, his gaze swept the tipis, women, children, and countless warriors milling in the village. Yeah, they knew. Leaving his gun was their way of showing they didn't fear him. That he was at their mercy.

He wasn't surprised when more abuse was heaped on him. As the day wore on, warriors and women inflicted punches, pinches, and kicks. What really boiled his belly was the spitting.

He croaked Eagle Feather's name in English and Spanish to each one. None responded, though one fairly tall, young-looking brave frowned. He might have understood but said nothing.

Late in the day, two squaws attacked him with their fingernails, then spit in his face before they strolled away, giggling. Could have been worse. They could have come at him with knives. Hell, it was a foregone conclusion he'd be carved up before this was over. He might as well face it. He'd ridden in alone. He supposed he deserved what he got.

You're gonna die, you stupid son of a bitch.

237

* * *

A half-mile from his father's camp, Beaver Heart sat with friends. Two of them, older by several winters, were skilled at making arrows. Buffalo Hump smoked a pipe. Sees Like a Cat carefully wound rawhide around an arrow's shaft, securing feathers, fletching the arrow to fly true.

Ride the Wind, another friend camped farther toward the southeast, walked into the circle of firelight, grinning like a crazed coyote. "There will be much dancing and feasting this night."

Beaver Heart returned his grin. "You are offering for Swaying Tree?"

Ride the Wind puffed out his chest but shook his head. "Much sport comes with the sunrise. A white man will be tested."

"A white man? In Palo Duro?"

Sees Like a Cat chuckled. "He was captured this morning on the canyon's rim."

Beaver Heart wondered why his friend had said nothing until now. His father's warning again troubled him. "Is it not strange he is here? No white men other than priests of their god have traveled to Palo Duro before. Perhaps he is not alone."

"Warriors searched all day for more white men. None were found." Ride the Wind eyed Beaver Heart. "The great chief Eagle Feather vows white men will come to Palo Duro, but he said many bluecoats."

Beaver Heart bristled under his friend's disdainful gaze. His father's dire prediction was known far and wide in the encampment. Though his father was revered, other chiefs and many warriors did not believe it possible. Beaver Heart sat straighter, prepared to defend his father.

"This white man, he utters your father's name."

Ride the Wind's words pierced his heart with trepidation. "Not possible!"

"Con . . . wa, he calls himself. Your father has made a friend of this white man?"

"My father would not do such a thing."

Ride the Wind shrugged. "A puzzle, is it not?"

It was. Thousands of the People camped here. Why would this white man single out his father? How did he know his name? Beaver Heart leaped up to take the tale to Eagle Feather.

Though the sun had long since dipped to sleep below the horizon, heat still lingered in the canyon. Bright Star and Willow Branch rolled up the lower edges of Eagle Feather's tipi in a vain effort to catch a nonexistent breeze.

White Fawn sat at the edge of the circle and fretted. So many people had gathered around the cold firepit, their bodies added to the heat. Bright Star and Willow Branch sat behind Eagle Feather, who reclined on his backrest. Straight Arrow and Black Crow sat crosslegged on either side of their father.

Mind awhirl, White Fawn stared at Running Bear's broad back as he awaited her father's reply.

No, no, no! repeated in her head.

"What has changed your mind?" Eagle Feather asked.

After a moment's hesitation, he replied, "She is your daughter."

Eagle Feather nodded. "You asked for White Fawn as your slave when you were last here. Now you wish to take her to wife?"

"I would bestow that honor on her if you allow it."

Honor? The man was demented! Running Bear's condescension did not surprise her, but he certainly did not honor her. His own manhood alone mattered to him.

Though he had not laid a hand on her when she traveled with his war party, he had shown himself capable of great cruelty, great abuse.

Wildcat had slapped her, and she suspected he practiced the same treatment on his wives. He was, after all, Running Bear's younger brother, and had doubtless learned from him. He probably thought she deserved such treatment.

Eagle Feather was stern only when necessary. She enjoyed the freedom to express herself or rebel as few Indian women did. Laughter, even love, ruled this band.

"What need have you of a fourth wife, Running Bear?"

The warrior's back stiffened. "I can provide for her, if that is what you ask. My father will pass into the afterlife soon. As new chief, I bring many horses, many—"

Eagle Feather frowned. "The warriors of your band have already decided who will succeed your father?"

"It is our way," Running Bear snapped. "The warriors in our band are brothers, relatives to me. None surpasses my ability. I know this. They know as well."

"Hmm," Eagle Feather murmured.

"I have four hundred horses. I will gift you with an excellent one from my remuda."

"One? You would offer one horse for a chief's daughter?"

Her father's feigned surprise tickled White Fawn. The only Indian she knew with a sense of humor, he delighted in teasing people. One good horse was sufficient for an adopted white girl.

You sly fox, she thought with affection.

She could not glimpse Running Bear's face, but she could see his fisted hands. He wanted her because she was different. He wanted her because four wives would increase his standing with his people. A warrior who could provide for four wives and keep them breeding was big medicine indeed.

"I meant no disrespect, Eagle Feather. I shall bring a horse from my personal string."

White Fawn glanced at her mothers. Like her, neither had spoken. But Bright Star smiled ever so faintly when Eagle Feather turned to his son.

"Straight Arrow would go with Running Bear to look over his stock?"

An insult of the first order. An even greater insult than never bidding Running Bear to sit. Her father as much as said he did not trust Running Bear. Eagle Feather never faltered as he looked up at the man.

"If that is your desire, my father," Straight Arrow said.

The challenge had been issued. Now her father heaped dung on Running Bear's offer.

"I will speak with my daughter about the matter. If

241

she will have you, Straight Arrow will go to your lodge tomorrow."

Her father gave her a choice? White Fawn nearly keeled over with relief. As soon as Running Bear was out of earshot, she would refuse. She feared the man, and dreaded seeing the slave again . . . if she was still alive.

Running Bear bowed stiffly and turned to leave. She did not understand why Eagle Feather had chosen to make an enemy of the powerful warrior, but she was grateful.

At that moment, she heard pounding feet and glanced up. Beaver Heart ducked into the tipi. Out of breath, he stumbled sideways as Running Bear pushed past him. He frowned at the retreating brave and swiped his brow, then swiveled to face his father.

"My father, a white man has been captured and brought to a village near the south trail." Beaver Heart's chest heaved with each breath.

"I have heard the rumor, my son. Be seated. We have grave matters to dis—"

"It is true."

Preoccupied with watching Running Bear stalk away, White Fawn did not immediately absorb what Beaver Heart spilled out in such a rush.

"The white man spoke to Ride the Wind. He asks for you, my father."

Eagle Feather scowled. "I know no white man."

"That is what I said. But this Con . . . wa asked for you."

White Fawn blinked. Her heart pounded. "Conway?"

Every eye in the lodge turned to her.

Her voice rose to an incredulous squeak. "Matthew Conway is here?"

"Who is this white man?" Eagle Feather demanded.

Alarm slammed into her. Her vision! Conway tied to a tree, Indians milling about.

Had the man lost his mind? She leaped up, whirled from the lodge, and ran as fast as her legs would carry her. To come here was sheer madness.

Darkness had settled over the canyon by the time White Fawn found him. Had a fire not blazed, sending light dancing between circled tipis and beyond, she would not have seen him at all. Skidding to a halt, she clapped a hand over her mouth.

Slumped against a tree, head dipped as if he slept, he sat so she could not see his face. But the rest of his body told the tale of today's treatment. She stole forward and slid to her knees.

"Oh, Matthew," she wailed softly, her gaze darting over tattered clothing, scraped and cut skin. Dust coated his hair and entire body. He was splattered with ominous, mud-colored dirt where blood had dried. Blood still oozed from a jagged, open wound down his leg.

"Conway?" Hesitantly, she smoothed grit-encrusted hair from his bruised and scratched forehead. Bits of glass and beads tied in the fringe of her buckskin dress clicked in the faint breeze.

It was the only sound as he lifted his head to stare at her. One eye was swollen shut, his entire face was a mass of scratches. She realized he probably did not recognize her. Backlit by the fire, she was probably no

243

more than a form looming before him. His dark eye searched her shadowed face; then his cracked lips lifted in a half smile.

"Hello, White Fawn," he managed in a scratchy voice. "Didn't know if I'd found the right band."

Though his words were light, pain etched his face. Pain she knew he would deny until the Spirits claimed him.

"Why you here?"

"Oh, I just *dragged* on in for a visit."

She sucked in a breath. "No funny! In terrible danger!"

"Had the whole day to figure that out on my own, honey."

Though she was certain the endearment meant nothing, her heart nevertheless skipped a beat. Again, she surveyed the damage to his muscular body. Had he not been so strong, he might be beyond aid by now. Having his arms wrapped backward behind the tree must hurt like the devil. Perhaps he could no longer feel those corded limbs.

Though Conway had locked her in a room, he had never treated her cruelly. She had been tied, but only for one night and one day. And he had never tied her so tight she could not move. So tight the circulation was gone.

Without thought for consequences, she scrambled behind the tree, drew her skinning knife, poised to cut the ropes binding his arms. Strong hands plucked her up by her buckskin tunic and hoisted her in the air. She kicked and squirmed.

"What you think you do, woman?"

Strangled by the material cinched against her windpipe, she could only gurgle a response. The pressure eased when the warrior allowed her feet to touch the ground, but he did not release her. Unkind fingers bruised her arm when he spun her around to face him. A stranger.

So many bands were camped in the canyon, she actually knew very few of the People. Rubbing her aching throat, White Fawn glanced around and found several stern-faced warriors, none of whom she knew. Before she could gain her voice, the one who held her spoke again.

"Sheathe your knife or I take it from you. The white devil is my prisoner."

Recalling her cowardice in the face of Running Bear and Wildcat, she would not back down. Unaccustomed to manhandling, she glared at him. His stony expression did not change.

"He is not a devil! I know this man."

"How?"

The truth would doom Conway. Before she could answer, the warrior whipped her around so she faced the firelight. He looked her over, his gaze settling on her telltale violet eyes.

"You are a slave!"

"I am not! I am Eagle Feather's daughter. He will have your—"

"You lie!" He reared back to strike her.

Amazingly, Conway kicked the warrior's foot from under him. As he fell, the momentum wrenched his hand from her arm. She lost her balance and sat back hard on her bottom. The other braves lunged at Conway, knives drawn.

"No!" She scrambled in front of him and raised her hands in defense. "I know this man. You will not kill him!"

"White Fawn," Conway said behind her, "get out of the way before they hurt you."

"No!" She did not take her eyes off the warriors. "You will not kill this man!"

"Whatever you're saying, they don't give a shit, honey. Move away."

Two of the braves raised their knives and lunged at her.

"*Suvate!* Enough!"

The Indians froze in place, recognizing the voice of authority as readily as she did.

"Come!" the stern voice ordered in English.

Startled, Matt glanced up. The commotion had drawn a crowd. It took a moment to find the man who had spoken. He looked into black eyes clouded by age.

White Fawn leaped toward the imposing figure and spoke in rapid Comanche. The men who had been intent on attacking backed off. One after the other sheathed his knife in deference.

"Quiet!"

Matt understood because White Fawn was silenced as if her throat had been cut. This must be Eagle Feather. White Fawn's Comanche father. Though old, he was the most formidable-looking warrior Matt had ever seen. His bearing told the tale. He ruled with an iron will and, quite possibly, an iron hand.

Which didn't bode well for him.

As the old warrior gave each Indian a stern appraisal, Matt had a chance to look him over. Though his face was devoid of facial hair, no doubt plucked out as was the Comanche way, two braids extended to his knees, partially wound with beaver fur. Maybe five-ten, he stood straight, broad shoulders back. They appeared even wider draped with a robe that lay over one shoulder, wrapped around his back, crossed in front, and tucked next to his waist. A single eagle feather jutted straight up at the back of his head from gleaming black hair streaked with a little gray.

A larger amulet similar to White Fawn's hung almost to his waist. Bone earrings swung from his ears. Fringed buckskin covered his arms. A silver bracelet a full inch wide circled his wrist. His beaded leggings and moccasins bespoke wealth. One scarred hand clutched a war lance; the other was fisted, with the thumb hooked over the robe at his waist.

Matt's leg hurt like hell from downing the brave. The wound bled profusely again. Already weak, he knew it wouldn't be long before he passed out from loss of blood. Resting his head against the tree, he returned the old warrior's stare.

Get it over with, he said with his eyes. But nothing happened; no one moved. To a man, the Indians surrounding him were fierce and strong. Even unfettered, he'd never live through this. Besides, he'd come for White Fawn, and he wouldn't leave without her.

Looking at Eagle Feather, he wondered how the hell she could bear any affection for him. He certainly wasn't soft, not even amiable-looking. As a child, how had she managed to keep from dying of fright the first time she saw him?

Three warriors stood next to the old chief—one no more than a boy, the other two in their prime. Probably his sons. They bore similar features, especially the oldest, whose grim-faced visage mirrored his father's.

"What you do in Palo Duro?"

Matt's gaze flicked back to the chief. That the old boy spoke English might come in handy . . . if he lived long enough. Hurting too much to laugh, he still enjoyed the astonishment on White Fawn's face. Apparently she was as surprised as he that her adoptive father spoke English.

"I came to counsel with you." He figured a lie would serve better than the truth.

He hadn't fooled the old fox, though. His gaze rested on his daughter, then landed back on him.

"I know you not."

"True enough." Matt's glance moved from warrior to warrior. "No one does but White Fawn." He gathered his courage. Nuts, maybe, but he would have his say, by God.

"Your people are damned quick to condemn a man simply because he's white." His mouth kicked up in a half smile. "My welcome was a bit . . . extreme."

Silence reigned for endless seconds while Eagle Feather looked him over. Matt couldn't count the number of Indians now gathered around. Wavering shadows from the fire danced over faces, a forceful reminder that his death might come more quickly than he'd anticipated.

"Please, my father," White Fawn said in English, then switched to Comanche, locking him out of the rest of what she said, which irritated the hell out of him.

I could use a little help here, White Fawn.

Whatever she said earned a silencing, chopping motion from her father. Another half minute ticked by before Eagle Feather began to speak in Comanche. Given time, Matt could understand a little Comanche, but not under these circumstances.

Chaos erupted as everyone, except White Fawn's family, spoke at once. The Indian Matt had confronted first this morning yelled the loudest, until Eagle Feather again gestured for quiet.

While the chief spoke, Matt watched White Fawn, hoping her expression would give him a clue as to what was being said. Unfortunately, alarm clouded her beautiful eyes, then anger when she narrowed them at the warrior.

The harangue lasted long enough for Matt to figure he was in for it. Then the two older warriors with Eagle Feather stepped forward. One disappeared behind the tree. Matt didn't feel a thing, but a second later his hands flopped to the ground.

The son on either side hauled him to his feet. Blood galloped through him and feeling tingled into his shoulders and down to his fingertips. Circulation returned with a vengeance. Pain! *Jesus!*

He ground his teeth and hoped they'd give him a minute. His eyes popped open when fingers nudged against his belly. The young warrior he thought brother to the other two was unbuckling his gun belt.

249

The little pissant! Though the .44 would do him little good now.

Without warning, the braves holding him stepped forward, taking him with them, though stumbling and dragging his feet was more like it. He was weak and dizzy as hell; there was no way he could stand straight. If he could, he'd tower over the little runts. White Fawn stood, hand over her mouth, eyes wide with concern. Fear, maybe. It didn't matter.

There wasn't a spot on him that didn't hurt. He'd lost so much blood, he didn't know if he could survive anyway. *Bring on your worst, you bastards, and put me out of my misery.* His boot heel caught a rock and wrenched his leg. Pain searing the entire length of the jagged cut would have taken him to his knees if the braves hadn't held him up. They rattled exasperated-sounding Comanche to each other.

Then a wrenching thought slipped into his mind, and he dug in his heels. He looked at White Fawn for a long moment. This might be the last time he'd see her.

His gaze slid over her shining hair, her slim body enticingly clothed in buckskin. He drank in the loveliness of her sky-bright eyes. Had it been worth it?

Yeah, he'd do it again. He'd ride into hell to claim her. He didn't pause to examine the possessive thought because another bumped it aside.

You already have, you loco son of a bitch.

He smiled at her alarmed expression. He was going to die. And not pleasantly. He'd seen the remains of too many tortured men to think otherwise.

He tipped his head in farewell as the men wrenched him into motion again. Darkness rimmed his vision.

With a final sense of weightlessness, he sagged in their grips.

"Sorry, fellas," he mumbled. "Gonna have to carry on this little party without me for a while."

Chapter Sixteen

He swam in a sea of mud. The harder he tried, the heavier his legs and arms became. He couldn't see a damn thing, but he could breathe. Odd as hell, with his face sunk in mud.

He heard a clicking sound. Ever so slowly, he opened his eyes and discovered he lay on his back. Above him the sky was . . . tan? He cut his eyes to the left, met more of the color. Well, hell, it was hide, not sky. Blinking, he looked the other direction into a face.

He recoiled. "Jesus!" The movement sent pain slicing through every cell in his body like a ricocheting bullet. His left leg burned the worst, though. Maybe he lay on a bed of coals and didn't know it. He couldn't stop a moan.

When he ventured another peek, the face was still there. It smiled; two teeth to the left of center were missing. It spoke, in Comanche. A woman. She turned her head and said something over her shoulder. He heard movement but couldn't see past her. When the click came again, he realized it was her bone and silver bracelets as she rubbed some godawful-smelling gunk on his chest. It was cooling, but he wished she'd stop. No way did he want this crone touching him. Didn't matter what he wanted, though. The slightest movement nearly made him pass out.

"Preparing me for slaughter, are you?"

She grinned again but obviously didn't understand him. Never this close to a Comanche woman before, he looked her over. Must be at least fifty. Hard to tell.

Her face was smudged and lined, but her eyes were bright, and not a gray hair relieved the midnight black. Tousled to her shoulders, it looked as if she'd been in a windstorm. Obviously a comb or brush didn't meet that mess very often. The center part was painted vermillion as were the insides of her ears. Though faint with age, a small star was tattooed on each cheek.

He couldn't tell if she was fat or slim. Unlike White Fawn, this woman wore a wildly colored pink, blue, green, red, and white short calico dress. Beneath that, a gray-and-black-striped skirt was tucked around her knees.

He glanced back to her face when she spoke again and patted his hand as if she were soothing a child. Matt grinned back, thinking her the ugliest woman he had ever seen. Since she couldn't understand, he said so aloud.

At that moment, White Fawn's lovely face came into view over the woman's shoulder. Fire fairly shot from her lovely eyes; her lips thinned in a disapproving line. She was anything but pleased.

"Bright Star no ugly, Conway. See eyes. Kind like no other woman."

God, she's beautiful when she's angry.

His body leaped to life. How the hell could that be when he hurt like a son-of-a-gun everywhere else? Now his cock was heavy and ached, too! He didn't dare move his head, let alone contemplate bedding White Fawn.

You're not going to do that again. Remember?

Besides, he didn't have long to live. The savages would take particular pleasure in cutting off that throbbing part over which he had no control. The rest of him would undoubtedly be flayed like a fish.

"What's she doing?" He scowled. "Keeping me alive for everyone's entertainment?"

White Fawn blinked in confusion. "Entertainment?"

"Don't play dumb. No white man has ever walked away from Comanche capture. Hell's fire, looks to me like the whole population is camped here. You think I'm fool enough to believe I'll get out of this alive?"

Before she could answer, the Indian woman touched his arm. White Fawn knelt and spoke at length. Twice Bright Star frowned. Then, silent, both women stared at him.

"What?" Enduring the pain, Matt eased up to rest on his elbows.

The woman made a funny sound and patted his blanket-covered hip. An otherwise bare hip, he suddenly realized. His gaze darted from one to the other. "Where are my clothes? Who stripped me?"

When he didn't get an immediate response, he bellowed, "Dammit, White Fawn, answer me!"

She uttered a quick aside in Comanche, which got a

chuckle from Bright Star this time. White Fawn stared blankly, as if she were dumb as a sheep, then shrugged.

"Two questions, Conway. What I answer first?"

"Where are my clothes?" he grated through clenched teeth.

"Burned."

"What?" he yelled. Groaning, he sank back to the pallet skins. "What am I supposed to wear?" He pinned her with a glare. "Naked. The better for torture. Right?"

She shook her head, as she had when he'd first found her. "No. Not face that."

Matt raised his arm and gritted his teeth against pain that shot clear into his head. But what the hell. Circling a pointed finger around his forehead, he said, "Yeah, I see a pig flying, too." On a strangled laugh, he dropped his arm to his side.

The Comanche woman spoke, her expression fearful. White Fawn quickly replied, while the woman stared up into the tipi's ceiling and shook her head.

White Fawn addressed him. "She say sleep now. You drift in delirium."

"The hell you say. Bring me some clothes."

She shook her head. "No walk. Leg stitched. Move around soon, break open wound."

Matt flipped the blanket aside, exposing his left leg. It was wrapped in surprisingly clean cloth from his groin to below his knee. A lot of him had been seen by . . . someone. His narrowed eyes impaled White Fawn.

"Who did this?"

She motioned to Bright Star. At that moment, Matt

spied another woman seated across the width of the tipi. Though younger, she wasn't much better-looking. Dressed like the older squaw with paint, earrings, bracelets, and garish garb, this one had no tattoos but all her teeth. She smiled like a curious child.

"Who's she?"

"Willow Branch."

"That tells me nothing," he said wearily. It irked him to be so weak and helpless.

He lay back and started to cover his eyes with his hand until he saw his palm was smeared with the same gunk as his chest. He sniffed. Smelled like his outhouse on a hot summer day. He wrinkled his nose and told himself to look on the bright side: As long as he was cooped up in the tipi, the agony to come at the hands of the warriors remained at bay.

White Fawn smoothed the blanket into place, then sat back and folded her hands in her lap. She should be elated that Conway lay as helpless as she had been in his house. But she wasn't. He was injured. His wounds, the gash on his leg in particular, were grave. He did not know that he could lose it if the flesh became putrid.

She closed her eyes and willed the thought away. A strong man, surely he would heal and walk as well as he had before. She remembered his grace in the saddle, the way he moved so fluidly. His powerful body poised over her when they made love. She shivered and put that thought from her mind.

Bright Star had scared her silly when she'd first seen her, but now White Fawn knew better. Bright Star watched her patient with concern. Ugly? Perhaps to a white man. But her mother would not swat a fly. When she was not tending to her family, performing back-breaking chores, she was usually caring for the sick or wounded. Gifted, one might say.

When Bright Star began administering to Conway after Straight Arrow and Black Crow had taken him to White Fawn's tipi, she had sent White Fawn away. Though Willow Branch lacked Bright Star's gift, she was allowed to help, to fetch and carry because she was mated. White Fawn was not.

"I shall wash his entire body with turpentine to clean the wounds. He will be naked, daughter. You should not see your man helpless and unconscious."

She was glad he was unconscious. Turpentine would burn like the fires of the bad Spirit World. But that was not what she said. "Conway is not *my man*."

Bright Star chuckled. "No? Why has he traveled to our land so far from his own?"

This was a question White Fawn would like an answer to as well.

"To counsel with you," he had told Eagle Feather.

About what?

White Fawn had gone about her chores, though her gaze returned again and again to her tipi. It had been quiet for so long, she had feared the worst.

When finally allowed to return, White Fawn learned that after cleansing his entire body, Bright Star had stitched the ragged edges of his skin together and chewed peyote to make a poultice. The bandage would keep the area clean. Jimson weed was strong enough for the rest of the nicks and abrasions on Conway's sun-darkened skin. Just as well. Bright Star had been giddy from chewing so much peyote.

Eyes closed, Conway lay as still as stone. If he had drifted to sleep, White Fawn hesitated to wake him, but she wanted to put his mind at rest.

She leaned toward him and murmured loud enough for him to hear if he was awake. "Conway?"

His eyelids popped open. "What?"

"Bright Star give tea, you sleep." She shook her head. "My people no kill you. Eagle Feather bought—"

He lunged up, frowning ferociously. "Bought what?"

"Please," she pleaded, pressing him back.

He resisted but gradually lay back, his eyes pinned to hers. Conway had beautiful eyes, dark, liquid, framed by thick, spiky lashes. He was beautiful all over, she thought, her gaze flitting across his wide shoulders and muscular chest.

"Bought?" he demanded again.

"You free leave when well."

His laugh sounded rusty. "Now there're two pigs flying in the rafters."

She couldn't help smiling. "Pigs no fly, Conway. I no lie."

"What the hell would he buy my freedom with? And why?"

"Many questions, quick." She shook her head. "Tongue still. Listen. Why? I know not Eagle Feather's mind. Brothers gift ten horses. Each brave capture you get one."

He searched her face, clearly disbelieving. She worried that if he did not relax and sleep, his strength would be slow to return.

258

She motioned to Bright Star to give him the decoction that would make him sleep whether he wished it or not. Bright Star slipped her arm beneath his head and lifted.

He clamped his lips shut and glared at Bright Star. "What is it?"

White Fawn sighed. "Bad patient. You safe here, my lodge."

"Your lodge?"

"By all the saints!" she cried, then blinked in astonishment at her use of Father Anselmo's words.

Conway needed rest. Her heart ached at the thought that this man, this glorious man, might lose his leg—or worse, his life. She would not tell him that. Irrationally, she feared both might come to pass if she voiced her thoughts.

"Drink. All Spirits promise, better when you wake."

His lips curved in a little smile so endearing, she wanted to cry. His dark eyes never left hers when he pushed the bottom of the cup Bright Star held to his lips and drank deeply.

"All the spirits, huh? I hold you to that promise, White Fawn."

In mere minutes his eyes were glassy and unfocused. The same half smile curved his mobile lips. Lips she knew were firm but soft. Lips that had given her much pleasure. Lips she wanted to kiss. She remained motionless.

He lifted an unsteady hand and pointed to the smoke hole. "Think I'm gonna . . . join those . . . pigs." His eyelids fluttered closed. Shortly, his breathing settled to a regular cadence.

"He is a strong warrior, daughter. You have chosen well."

She stared at Bright Star, her heart grieving. "I did not choose him. Even if I wanted him, it could never be."

"You speak riddles."

"You do not understand the way of white men, Mother Bright Star. They would spit upon me. I can never return." She looked back at Conway. "I am Comanche. His world is not mine."

"Your heart is troubled. Think on it further. If he did not come to take you back to his world, why did he come? Tell me that, daughter."

Why, indeed? Would he explain when he awakened? It did not matter. She had fallen in love with Matthew Conway, but he did not return her love.

When he walked tall and straight again, Conway would leave. She envisioned the long years ahead. He would be gone from her life.

Perhaps they would make love again. No. She would not mate with a man she did not love, and she could not marry, the white man's way, the one she did love. Perhaps he desired her, but he did not love her.

She would take only bittersweet memories of him into endless time.

Eagle Feather reclined in White Fawn's tipi. Bright Star had brought his robes and backrest and set them in the place of honor beside the dead fire. Then Bright Star and Willow Branch went about their chores elsewhere. Woven mats covered the earth; the tipi's skirts were rolled up on two sides to allow air circulation. A balmy summer breeze caressed Eagle Feather's face.

White Fawn sat in attendance next to the man called Conway, his deep sleep doubtless the result of his woman's potion. Eagle Feather knew firsthand her healing and effective decoctions. Perhaps he would die soon, but for now most days he was free of pain.

His gaze settled on Conway. A shiver of apprehension shook his belly. White men towered over the Comanche, and this one was tall like a tree, strong like an oak. White Fawn bathed the muscled expanse of his wide, bare chest with cooling water.

The man lay oblivious to the proceedings around him. Just as well. Rest would restore him. Twelve suns had risen since Conway had arrived in Palo Duro Canyon. As soon as he regained his strength, Eagle Feather wanted him gone. Unwise, perhaps, but he would see this man returned to his life well and whole.

He glanced at his daughter. Her lovely eyes remained on the white man. Bright Star spoke truth: Though she denied it, White Fawn had found her warrior.

The pain of impending loss squeezed his heart, but he knew what must be done. When the man left, White Fawn would go with him. Soon he would no longer hear her sunshine laughter.

He must steel his heart, for she would not survive otherwise. As surely as Father Sun rose each day, Eagle Feather knew in his bones that his People's days were numbered. Though few had traveled this far north, Conway was the first to stumble upon Palo Duro Canyon. He would not be the last.

For many moons the warriors in his band had listened to his counsel, had raided very little, and had prospered. Though he was head man, *Atocknie*, Lone Tipi, the war chief, was restless. It was but a matter of time before he called the braves to raid again, and Eagle Feather could do naught about it. His own sons would likely ride along.

He smiled slightly when his thoughts strayed to his youngest son. Beaver Heart would join a raiding party without hesitation. Straight Arrow and Black Crow were fierce warriors, sons to be proud of. If they deferred to their father's wish, each risked the stigma of being called "weak woman." This they would not have. In their place and at their age, he would not either.

Finished with her ministrations, White Fawn sat back and folded her hands in her lap, her gaze still on Conway. She might deny it, but Eagle Feather was as convinced as Bright Star that she loved this man. He stared at Conway's sleeping countenance.

Did he return her love? How could he not? White Fawn was a beautiful maiden, a part of his family for many moons. Still, she was white. Crazed as a loon he might be, but Eagle Feather had decided that she would return to her people with this man.

As his mate.

She insisted she could not return to the white man's world. But as Conway's wife, married as the white man called a mated woman, surely . . .

Twelve moons past, Eagle Feather had followed White Fawn when she ran from his lodge at the mention of Conway's name. He had arrived in time to see him kick Ten Bears' foot, felling him with ease. Even bound, Conway lashed out to protect White Fawn. Recovered, standing on his own feet, Conway would be a formidable foe. Yes, he would protect White Fawn.

Suddenly, Eagle Feather's nape prickled. His gaze collided with Conway's dark, lucid eyes. The white man was awake and taking his measure. Dangerous, this one.

"Feel better?" White Fawn murmured.

The man's gaze snapped to her. His smile was boyish for such a big man. Slowly he sat up, windmilled his arms, testing their mobility. Muscles flexed over his upper body.

"Yeah. What was that stuff the woman gave me? I slept like a hibernating bear."

He does love her. Though he may be as dim in the head as she and deny it.

Conway moved his legs beneath the blanket. A gasp shuddered from him. White Fawn reached to halt his movement but did not touch him.

"Bright Star has gift like shaman. She give more potion this night."

"No," Conway said quickly. His eyes narrowed on Eagle Feather. "You didn't turn me over to your braves while I slept, but I think I'd better keep my wits about me from here on out." Then he asked of White Fawn, "What do I wear?"

"Nothing. Stay in blankets. You—"

"Bullshit! I'm leaving this bed even if I have to do it naked. Find me something to wear!"

Eagle Feather watched the exchange and suppressed a smile. Matthew Conway was as determined as a mule, doubtless used to having his own way in all things. But White Fawn could be mule-headed, too. She spit back at the man like a cornered cat, kitten size, but feisty.

"No, you not!" She leaned up on her knees and pressed his shoulders as if she could hold him there with her slight weight. "Stitches pull loose!"

Conway grabbed her wrists and put her away from him, though he did not release her. "I'll say it only once more. Find . . . me . . . something . . . to . . . wear. Now!"

Though he enjoyed the battle of wills, Eagle Feather knew White Fawn had the right of it. The sooner Conway healed, the sooner he could travel. Roaming about now might slow his recovery.

Intervening, he said, "Quiet yourself, white man. Release my daughter."

Conway glared at him but released her wrists. White Fawn dropped a hand to the mat to catch herself from falling against him.

"She's not your daughter, Chief. She's as white as I am. Where did you learn to speak English?"

Eagle Feather scowled at Conway's rapid-fire speech. He stared back as fiercely as the white man glared at him. "You would do well to listen to my words. Quiet yourself. My *daughter*"—he suppressed another smile when Conway's eyes sparked at his emphasized word—"will do *my* bidding. You will be civil if you wish to rise and walk about."

"My father—"

"Leave us, daughter." He spoke Comanche simply to irritate Conway. "Ask Straight Arrow for a pair of buckskins. They will be short for the white man's long legs, but it is the best we can do for him."

"He must not lea—"

"Find a stick," he interrupted again. "He is stubborn and unwise. But if he wishes to walk about, he will need something on which to lean."

She sat still, biting her lower lip. He put out his hand and patted hers. "Go, child. I would speak privately with your Conway."

"He is not *my* Conway!"

"As you say," he replied, but couldn't keep a smirk from his lips.

Though in a huff, she rose gracefully and slipped outside.

"What was that all about?" Conway asked, his tone surly.

"You have short sticks that flame quickly."

Conway frowned blackly; then he grinned without humor. "If you're saying I have a short fuse, you're damn right there, Chief."

Eagle Feather stared at him for a long moment, though Conway was not intimidated in the least. Most white men who found themselves surrounded by Indians would quake in their boots. Not this man.

"You say you have come to counsel with me. Speak now."

Conway waved his hand. "You have another one of those?"

Eagle Feather's brow creased. "Of what do you speak?"

"Your backrest. I could use one."

"Ah."

Since neither of his wives was close at hand, Eagle Feather rose and went to Black Crow's lodge. Returning, he placed the hide-covered furnishing behind the tall man, then regained his own comfortable seat.

Conway gingerly leaned back. Bright Star's poultice had already worked wonders on the cuts. But for his leg wound, Eagle Feather doubted not that Conway would be up and causing trouble by nightfall. As long as he remained, he would pose a danger.

Without preamble, Conway said, "I came to take White Fawn—Rebecca—back where she belongs."

Action edged with impatience sat on Conway's shoulders like a watchful eagle, ready to fight at the first opportunity. Unlike himself and his People, this man would be hard pressed to deliver long-winded, respectful, even eloquent speech.

Eagle Feather ignored Conway's abrupt manner and assumed his own. "Many seasons ago," he began, "a white girl-child was brought to my village. She did not cry. She did not beg to be saved. She asked for nothing and would have died. I took pity on her. This white child I took to my heart and gave her a Comanche name, White Fawn. I made her my daughter. You speak of 'where she belongs'. White Fawn is a *naduah* of the *Nermernuh*, woman of the People. She is of an age to mate and bear Comanche braves."

"Over my dead body," Conway snapped.

Eagle Feather's lips tightened in a humorless smile. "I can arrange that."

"No doubt. I'm at your mercy here. Where is *here*, exactly? Palo Duro Canyon?"

Conway had known of his People's camping place? He should not be surprised. Many times men of the black robes had traveled here, preaching of their god.

266

The People had turned deaf ears to their words, but the men had been allowed to leave unmolested. They were holy men.

The canyon had been a winter home, a safe place for many seasons. Even during the season of the summer sun, the People camped here before taking to the plains when falling leaves heralded a good buffalo hunt.

His strength grew each day in this restful place. He hoped it would not fail him when his band moved north. This time, though, he would urge his People to travel into the high mountains and reside there. In safety, he prayed. Perhaps then his spirit would be at peace to move on to eternity.

"Palo Duro was campground for my ancestors and is home to my People." He would not tell this man of his plans.

"How many Comanches are here?"

"What do you ask?"

"The number. A thousand, two thousand?"

"Ah. I know not this number you ask. As many as the leaves on a tree, perhaps."

Conway chuckled. "Not that many. But more than enough to do me in."

"Your words are strange. 'Do me in'?"

"Butcher me," he said grimly. "Kill me. Send me to the Spirit World."

At that moment, White Fawn reentered the tipi. Eagle Feather was surprised to see she carried Straight Arrow's ceremonial leggings, a breechclout, and a quill-decorated shirt. Surely she would not have taken them without permission.

She dropped the garments and laid a long stick fashioned into a crutch next to Conway.

"Open leg wound. Bleed to death. No care," she said petulantly.

Eagle Feather smiled inwardly. She cared. The man made her angry, but she loved him. His glance slid to Conway and awaited his retort.

He said nothing. Only looked at her . . . with desire. Yes, he recognized desire for a woman when he saw it in another man's eyes.

Conway wanted her. That would make Eagle Feather's proposal easier. Tomorrow, perhaps the next day, he would again speak with Conway. Two concessions he would gain from him before granting him the right to take White Fawn back to his world.

If Conway was allowed to leave, he must swear never to reveal the exact location of the canyon. The second promise involved White Fawn. She did not want to mate. Not with Running Bear. She did not like him, and neither did he. But she did need a man's protection.

Was it truth or speculation that caused White Fawn such fear of returning to the white world? He did not know the answer. But if she was protected by Conway . . .

As he stood to leave, he hid another smile from the young people. A gleeful one. It would be a simple matter to threaten Conway's life if White Fawn continued to refuse to marry him in the white man's way.

To what lengths would she go to save the man she loved?

Chapter Seventeen

Frustration battered Matt as he watched the chief exit the tipi. *Damn!* Though he'd insisted he would get up, he knew that was a near impossibility. Just leaning against the backrest taxed what little strength he had. But he wanted this settled.

He eyed White Fawn through lowered lashes. Maybe she was telling the truth. Maybe he wasn't about to be skinned alive. If not, why not? He'd believed for so long that Comanches scalped and mutilated whenever the chance arose. Why should Eagle Feather be any different?

"This white child I took to my heart."

Eagle Feather's words echoed in Matt's head. Could the old goat really be kind? Even love someone? Confusion roiled in his mind. Okay. The chief might love White Fawn like a daughter, but he would have to give her up.

Matt gazed at her for long minutes. Arguing with her would gain nothing, but by damn he *would* have his way. He'd take White Fawn when he left or die trying.

Suddenly, another thought chewed at him. *"She is of an age to mate and bear Comanche braves."* He cringed. The old man meant it. Just like that, he'd give her to a warrior.

"Not if I can help it."

"What?" White Fawn asked.

"Nothing."

"Wily old goat," Matt muttered.

White Fawn heard him and frowned, but he didn't care. She might hold the Indian in high regard, but he sure as hell didn't have to. She belonged to . . . in Austin. At the orphanage, where she could meet . . .

White Fawn stood, distracting him. Damn, she looked so good. Though she was dressed in buckskins again, it made no difference to him. He'd destroyed her other clothes, so this tunic was new and clean. She was lovely, trim as a willow, graceful as a . . . swan. *Poetic?* That potion must have addled his wits.

"Where are you going?"

"Carry backrest to Father's lodge."

"Why?" Couldn't he carry his own? He'd brought the one Matt rested on. Though gaunt-faced, he looked strong as a horse, and he was a man, for God's sake.

"Eagle Feather no do woman's work."

Matt grabbed her hand. A mistake. Just as when she'd pressed her hands on his shoulders, desire cannoned through him clear to his loins. Dammit!

"Your *father* is a fraud if you believe he can't carry a backrest."

She nodded. "He carry. Choose no do. My place carry his possessions."

"You're not his woman!"

270

She sighed. "Bright Star, Willow Branch my father's women. Me, daughter, my duty."

Two wives? "Oh, go on. You will anyway." He didn't attempt to hide his surliness.

Just as she'd run away from the Rocking C, she'd do as she pleased now. And that was exactly what had put him in his present predicament, in the clutches of more savages than he'd ever seen.

Matt gingerly lifted the blanket to examine his wounded limb. He didn't have to be told he was in trouble. The slightest movement sent pain shooting into his foot, up his hip, arrowing through his body to set his teeth on edge.

He heard a giggle. Glancing beneath the rolled tipi's hide, he met a child's dark eyes. Two others squatted next to him, all three naked as the day they were born. No more than four years old, he guessed. All three were grinning. Tousled, dirty hair framed round, equally dirty faces. The first boy pointed and said something, then clapped his hand over his mouth when another giggle erupted.

Matt looked down at his limp penis. As limp and powerless as the rest of him. For some reason, it looked as funny to him as it had to the youngsters.

He grinned at the boy. "Not very awe-inspiring, is it?" They didn't understand him, but he pointed at the boy's inch-long member. "It's got a helluva lot more fire power than what you're sporting between your legs, though."

That earned him a chorus of giggles and more Comanche jargon. Then all three sprang up and ran. He watched them go, the smile lingering on his face. Kids were kids, he supposed—until they learned to kill.

271

He adjusted the blanket for modesty's sake and began to untie the bandage to get a better look at what he was dealing with.

White Fawn stepped into the tipi, her eyes rounding in alarm. "What you do?"

"What does it look like? I want to—"

"No!" She slid to her knees and clasped his hands to still them.

Again, heat sizzled through him, but he gritted his teeth. "You say that too damned often, woman! I'm not a boy you can order around. Get that through your—"

"No act like one!"

He stilled and spoke in a dead-soft voice. "Let go, White Fawn." *Before I throw you down and devour you.*

Her gaze darted to his face. She snatched back her hands and settled on bent legs. "Please. Do damage, you disturb Bright Star's poultice."

"Maybe. But I want to see what she's done."

White Fawn raised a staying hand, but she did not touch him again. "I tell. Want lose leg, Conway?"

Her roughened, breathy voice carried the ring of truth. She believed he might actually lose his leg? A sobering thought. Scary as hell, in fact. He frowned at the bandage that made his leg appear twice its size.

"Okay. Tell me."

"Muscles, tendons, no damage. Stitches inside and outside. Flesh gone. Scar never leave."

"I don't give a shit about a scar. What else?"

She took a steadying breath. "Clean wound with turpentine, then stitch. Poultice on top."

"What's the poultice made from?"

She shook her head. "Know not."

"White Fawn . . ." he warned.

"I know not! Peyote, one thing. I speak truth, Conway."

Yeah, probably. And she was worried. Her beautiful eyes were bright as if tears—of frustration or concern—lurked. If concern, it was a new experience for him. Well, that wasn't entirely true. If he didn't show up on the Rocking C, Lupe and Xavier would be concerned, too.

If he couldn't walk, couldn't defend himself, the Comanches would make mincemeat of him, Eagle Feather's wishes be damned. But he'd go down fighting. If he could stand. At the moment, that appeared highly unlikely. He moved his leg slightly and amended that thought. Unlikely, hell. He'd pass out between one heartbeat and the next if he tried.

He frowned, eyeing the garments she'd brought earlier. He couldn't gain his feet, but he could put on clothes. Sharing laughter with kids was one thing, being really vulnerable another. He picked up the shirt.

"What you do?"

Matt smiled. "Well, honey, I'm going to wear this Indian garb you so thoughtfully provided."

"Why you no rest? Gain strength soon, then wear clothes."

"What's the matter, darlin'? Can't bear for me to cover my naked body?"

Her cheeks flamed.

Oh, hell. What a bastard. All she wanted was for him to heal. Okay, he'd wait to wrestle into the breechclout and leggings, but he'd wear the shirt. Helpless he might be, but he didn't like being so exposed.

He retied the bandage and drew the shirt over his head. Surprisingly, when he smoothed it down over his chest, the shirt fit as if it had been made for him. His brow furrowed, wondering where she'd found it. Settling against the backrest, he crossed his arms over his chest.

"How long have I been here?"

She raised both hands and stuck her fingers in the air, then shrugged. "More, maybe. Hungry now?"

How would he control his desire for her while cooped up in such close quarters? "Yeah. Come to think of it, I could choke down a bite."

She left and returned shortly carrying a bowl with a bone spoon stuck in a stew mixture. He sniffed. Smelled all right. He dipped in the spoon and took a bite. Surprise rounded his eyes. Damn good!

"You like?"

He took another bite and chewed with appreciation. "Yeah. What is it?"

"Buffalo meat, onions, potatoes."

"Where—"

"*Comancheros* come village. Trade."

He knew that. Like most Texans, he didn't like it one bit. Not only did they trade everyday goods, but the damned Mexicans supplied Indians with guns. That made his life much more dangerous. Bows and arrows were deadly in an Indian's hands; add guns . . . He finished the stew and set the bowl aside.

"Why you here?"

Because I want you. The thought leaped into his mind, but he wouldn't tell her that. He wasn't going to act on it, either. By God, he would not be led by his damn cock. *Oh, yeah?*

"To take you back to Austin," he finally answered. He hadn't revealed that to her before, but she deserved to know what he intended to do with her. If he got out of this canyon alive, he *would* do it.

She frowned. "Why?"

"There's an orphanage—"

"No go Austin. Happy here."

Was she really happy with these people? He now suspected she'd lived most of her life with the Comanches. Maybe she'd never readjust. But he had to try.

He'd lain on the pallet for three endless days. His troubled gaze left Bright Star, who tended his wound, to stare morosely at the stick that taunted him. It had taken all the strength he could muster to walk his hands up the tree limb and pull up his protesting body. That was as far as he'd got. Nausea roiled in his stomach and he pitched to his knees. And that earned him waves of pain that sliced from the wound clear to his head. He hadn't passed out, but he'd come close.

The pain stayed with him for hours, but he'd refused the crone's potion. No, sir, he wouldn't allow her to snuff him out like a candle again. Concentrating on just breathing from one moment to the next had relieved his other problem . . . until dark, anyway.

The days had been long, but the nights ticked by even slower. Why had they put him in White Fawn's tipi with her sleeping a mere six feet away? Every breath she took purred along his nerves. By morning he was nearly berserk with need.

He hadn't had a woman since that night with White Fawn. He grimaced with disgust. Even if he wanted to go back on his word not to take her again, he was too damn weak. That set his teeth further on edge.

"Ouch!" He gave vent to his frustration.

Bright Star made a sound of sympathy in her throat. He looked closely at her. Maybe she enjoyed every wince, every jerk of his quivering flesh as she spread fresh, pulpy goo over the wound. He watched her quick hands.

That was unfair. Not by word or deed had the Comanche woman delivered a callous act or deliberate hurt. She feathered her fingers over his skin as gently as she could. Not her fault his flesh was so sensitive. The wound was healing more rapidly than he'd hoped.

As primitive as her medicine was, she knew how to prepare and use what she found at hand. He doubted Lupe could do better. Contrite at his ill thoughts of her, he watched her passive face for a bit, then looked outside.

Ever since he'd stopped drinking her decoction, the rolled-up tipi skirts afforded a view of the village all the way to the river that twisted through the canyon.

This morning he'd finally struggled into the breechclout. Still couldn't get the leggings past the thick bandage, though. Unbelievably strong for her size, Bright Star had helped him out behind the tipi to take care of his needs. She'd positioned him by a tree so he wouldn't fall, then left him alone for a few minutes. Perhaps today he'd try the damn stick again.

It was still early, the sun had barely risen, but the village was already a beehive of activity. Squaws' fires leaped beneath iron kettles. Indian bread baking on rocks close to the fires sent a delicious aroma into the air. His mouth watered.

Through this whole ordeal, he'd maintained an appetite. Unless he'd refused food from pure cussedness—which he'd done at noon yesterday—he'd eaten heartily each time White Fawn brought him a bowl. She'd prepared the food herself, as good a cook in her own way as Lupe.

Matt spied White Fawn at the fire near Eagle Feather's tipi. His second wife, Willow Branch, worked with her. His stomach clenched when he heard White Fawn laugh. He ignored the smile that touched his own lips.

What would it be like to wake every morning to her smile as she lay beside him? His cock jumped at the thought, and gooseflesh pebbled his skin. His gaze snapped to Bright Star. He had to stop thinking of White Fawn like that.

Bright Star murmured something in Comanche and slipped her hand beneath his knee. He dutifully slid his foot back and cocked his leg so she could rewrap the bandage. Finished, she patted the material as she might a child, with a show of affection.

"Thanks," he said, meaning it, even if she didn't understand.

She spoke for several seconds as White Fawn arrived with his breakfast. He looked up at her questioningly and wished he understood their language. As difficult as it sounded, he wouldn't feel so helpless if he knew what they were saying.

"Lower leg, Conway. Bright Star say walk more today. Heal better." She knelt and placed the food within his reach.

"I will. I'd like to bathe."

White Fawn spoke rapidly and got an equally quick response. "Yes, before sun sleeps. She say wound need new bandage then."

"How long will she have to smear this stuff on me?"

"Two suns, perhaps."

Bright Star gathered the soiled bandages and the peyote mixture. White Fawn started out of the tipi behind her.

"Wait."

She looked over her shoulder. "Eat."

"I will, but I want to speak with Eagle Feather. The old go—" Oops, better not call him that. "He left and hasn't been back."

In fact, he hadn't seen hide or hair of him, though warriors came and went from the chief's tipi. White Fawn had confirmed that the three warriors he saw most often were indeed Eagle Feather's sons. Her brothers, she defiantly stated, daring him to contradict her.

A commotion outside brought Matt's head around. A warrior walked toward Eagle Feather's tipi leading a handsome paint pony. The brave wore equally handsome buckskins, lavishly quilled and beaded. His hair shone with bear grease and two long braids adorned with skins and tin bangles dangled below his waist. The man was obviously decked out for something important.

Though Indians gathered, they left a wide path for him. Without exception, all pointed to the horse, talking and laughing among themselves. The brave himself looked neither right nor left.

He stopped before Eagle Feather's tipi and pulled a war ax and a stake from his belt, then pounded the wood into the ground. After tying the horse, he turned and walked back the way he had come, head high, the same haughty expression gracing his features.

His brow creased, Matt looked at White Fawn. "What's going ..." The question died when he saw her face.

Slightly bent to exit the tipi, she froze in place, her expression so telling it took his breath away. Fear? He glanced outside again, catching a last glimpse of the warrior before he disappeared behind a tipi.

"White Fawn?" he questioned as she slowly straightened.

She didn't answer. Instead, she backed up one careful step at a time until the tipi's hide wall stopped her. She sank to her blankets, her eyes locked on the horse.

Jesus, Mary, and Joseph, what's wrong with her? He'd never before seen such abject fear. Oblivious to his pain, he crawled toward her.

"White Fawn?" Settling next to her, he clasped her hand. It was like ice. He chafed her fingers between his own warm hands. "Hey, darlin'." He used the endearment without thinking. "Speak to me."

When she remained mute, he glanced around for assistance and found Straight Arrow inside the tipi. He hadn't heard the other man's approach.

"My father would speak with my sister," he said ... in perfect English.

After his momentary surprise, Matt erupted. "Dammit, what's going on? She's scared witless." He raised White Fawn's hand clasped tightly in his, as if to show of whom he spoke. "I want to know why. Now!"

279

As worried as he was, he rose to his feet, oblivious to the pain, and took a menacing step toward the brave. He would pound him into the ground if he didn't get an answer. He stood a half head taller than the Comanche, his reach longer, his chest wider.

Not the least bit intimidated, Straight Arrow calmly returned Matt's angry stare. No wonder; he had several hundred to back him up if Matt was addlepated enough to take a swing at him.

"My father has received a bride price for White Fawn."

Bride price? "He'd sell her?" He knew of this practice but couldn't believe it was happening. Not to White Fawn!

"Running Bear wishes to mate with White Fawn," Straight Arrow said.

Matt shook his head as if he hadn't heard right. He glanced at White Fawn. She had risen to her feet, wide-eyed with fear. And, perhaps, shock?

Straight Arrow beckoned. "Come." He turned and ducked out of the tipi.

Though pale as a dove, White Fawn dutifully followed.

Matt bit back a protest. Nothing he could do. Hell, he could barely stand. Running away with White Fawn was impossible right now.

Straight Arrow had smiled at her, though. Which made him wonder if the brave might really care for White Fawn. Savage he might be, but dammit, the Indian bled. Maybe he cried, and maybe he even loved her.

Matt slowly hobbled to the blankets and sank down as best he could. He stared at the bandaged leg and realized that he'd taken robust health for granted. Though he was strong and unrelenting in many ways, this injury had laid him as low as a snake. He didn't like it one bit, but he had no say in the matter. Only time would heal the damn gash.

Suddenly, he felt a touch as soft as thistledown on his shoulder. Bright Star stood next to him, her expression as anxious and concerned as any white woman's. She said something.

Damn, he wished he understood the words, but he clearly heard anxiety in her voice. She knelt and touched the bandage, then shook her head.

He clasped her hand. "It's all right." If the wound had reopened, he'd know it. Impossible to get that across to her, so he didn't try. He shook his head and said curtly, "Leave it."

She glanced from his face to the bandage, then back again. Matt did something then he never would have thought possible. Had any white acquaintance seen him, they'd have stuffed him in a straitjacket, locked him up, and thrown the key into the Gulf.

Smiling, he touched her knuckles with his lips. Those hands, as callused as any man's, had nursed him gently. She was a kind, gentle person, despite the life she led.

He couldn't help chuckling at her bewildered expression. Then she rose and left.

Matt's gaze settled on the tipi across the way.

What the hell was going on in there?

Chapter Eighteen

White Fawn entered her father's tipi on Straight Arrow's heels. She cast a baleful look at her brother as he seated himself.

Though her legs shook with fear of what was to come, she paused before her father. She had a bone to pick with him as well as Straight Arrow before her situation was discussed. Casting courtesy and caution to the winds, she addressed Eagle Feather before he could speak.

"Why did you never tell me you and Straight Arrow speak English?" Accusation rife in her glance, she eyed the entire family. "How many others speak the white man's tongue?"

Seconds ticked by as Eagle Feather stared at her, impassive as a stump. Bright Star shook her head in warning. White Fawn waited . . . and waited, then began to fidget before her father deigned to speak.

"You would overstep your place and raise your voice to your father?"

She had, but now thought better of it. Provoking Eagle Feather was, at best, unwise; at worst, it was fool-hardy in the extreme. Yet he sounded surprised rather than angry.

She backed down rather than push him to ire, and sank to the floor, glowering at her lap. She felt as helpless as a small child. Though not really contrite, she nevertheless thought it prudent to apologize.

"I beg your forgiveness, my father. I spoke out of turn and from . . . frustration."

For many seasons she had feared every moment when left alone. Tears burned the backs of her eyes as she remembered how she had cowered inside the tipi. She had lain awake nights fearing Yellow Bird would come at her again with the vicious knife. Not until she grew older did she realize the woman dared not touch her again.

"You have been brought to me for a momentous purpose, daughter."

Disappointment hitched her breath. Eagle Feather had chosen to ignore her outburst and would not enlighten her regarding his and Straight Arrow's ability to speak English. Perhaps it mattered not. In truth, she was far more concerned about the handsome war pony shuffling just beyond the tipi's entrance. She had hoped that discussion could be put off . . . for a little while.

She remained quiet. In his own good time, her father would doom her to a life of servitude with a man she feared and despised. A man who arrogantly offered a one-horse bride price for a chief's daughter.

"Many moons have passed since I took you to my heart, daughter. Since then, you have grown to be a strong Comanche woman."

When he paused, she glanced up to find a rare smile

283

on his lips. *Taken to his heart?* She had thought so, but at this moment she doubted his esteem.

"You have grown the span of ten hands since I first set eyes upon you, but that is not to say you are much taller than the fawn for which you are named."

Bright Star and Willow Branch, ranked behind their husband, smiled at her. From the corner of her eye, she saw that her three brothers, expressions grave, attended their father's every word.

"You have reached an age when it is your duty to take a husband and bear strong children."

He paused again, as if waiting for her to speak, but she doubted it would do her any good to say she hated Running Bear. That she feared him like no other.

The horse he'd presented was strong and well-proportioned. She should know after following its every step across the *Llano Estacado*. Most likely Running Bear's favorite war pony. Eagle Feather must covet it. What warrior would not?

He gestured at the horse. "Running Bear has offered for you. He is a strong warrior. Perhaps destined to be chief of his band. You would do well to think on that. It is a great honor for a maiden to lie with a man such as he, to bear sons in his likeness."

Matthew Conway's image rose in her mind's eye. *Bear sons in his likeness.* Oh, Spirits of the People, she would gladly bear sons if only . . .

Conway did not love her. Yet, somehow, without welcoming it, love for him had crept into her heart. If he loved her in return, if he asked for her, she would fly into his arms with gladness. But he would not marry. He had said as much.

"Will you accept this man, daughter?"

Wrapped in thoughts better left in the past, she glanced up, spearing her father's age-dimmed eyes with her own. *Do I have a choice?* The question clamored in her head, though she feared to ask it aloud. Had she misunderstood?

"Daughter, you may not put off Running Bear's offer without response. You insult him if you do not say yea or nay."

Eyes wide, she licked dry lips. She could read nothing in her father's expression. Why could he not ease her way in some manner? A smile . . . No. She had seen few smiles from him. Oddly, when his humor flashed, he was usually sober-faced.

"My father," she began, "I should feel the honor you speak of, but . . . May I speak my heart, Father?"

Surprise lit his features. "I would not expect otherwise."

He glanced at his sons, drawing her gaze to follow his. Each one of the people she had come to cherish as family stared at her expectantly. Hope, faint as it was, fluttered in her breast. She looked back at Eagle Feather.

"I rode with Running Bear and his warriors. He was not as you are, my father. He is not like my brothers."

"Explain," Eagle Feather demanded.

"Cruel," she said, now anxious to make her father understand what could be viewed as timidity on her part. "I fear this man rather than revere him. I believe he would treat me as he did when he thought me a slave."

She hoped with all her heart that the flare in her father's eyes was anger. Though adopted and a mere girl, she prayed he still felt insulted that Running Bear had offered to buy her.

"May I speak?" Straight Arrow asked. At his father's nod, he continued. "White Fawn must think about the future. You, my father, no longer hunt. I am honored, as are Black Crow and Beaver Heart, to supply meat for our cookfires. Running Bear is an excellent hunter and will bring plentiful buffalo to his wife for food and robes. White Fawn could do worse than accept him as her mate."

Her brother brought up a problem she had not considered. It was past time that she look for a man to be responsible for her.

Unfortunately, her brother wasn't finished. "Running Bear is a hard man, but fair, I believe." He looked directly at her. "He would not beat you unless you deserved it."

Though unsure if that was laughter dancing in his dark eyes, she was certain that his words outraged her. "Beat me? I would run away if he did such a thing!"

"Is that what your Conway did?"

Eagle Feather's question came out of the blue, so surprising she could only squeak, "No!"

"You lived in his lodge."

She nodded. "He never beat me. He would not! He was . . ." Kind? Not exactly. But he had not hurt her apurpose. Had he not brought her ecstasy?

"What?" Straight Arrow persisted.

She did not need her brother's mischievous intervention.

"Protective," she finally replied. No one needed to

know that Conway's protection meant he kept her locked up every night.

"Ah," Eagle Feather said, sounding as if he read something into the word that she had not meant. "Whatever your Conway—"

"He is not *my* Conway!"

Light similar to that in Straight Arrow's eyes gleamed in her father's when he gestured with two fingers near his mouth.

"I do not speak with double-tongue, my father."

Signaling he had had enough, Eagle Feather said, "My daughter, it is past time to untie Running Bear's gift. Loose the stallion or lead him to my remuda."

A choice! Relief unlike any she had ever known washed over her. Whether Conway believed it or not, Eagle Feather was truly a compassionate man. She rose and extended her hand in a gesture of thanks.

"I shall begin to think on finding a mate, my father."

"It matters not. When next I decide a man is worthy, you will accept him, daughter."

She quaked at his determined expression, could not help wishing for the man she wanted. Still, with a much lighter heart, she walked outside and untied the horse. He whipped around and galloped through the village, back the way he had come. Good riddance.

As she returned to the fire, her gaze skipped over several women and men watching her. Avoiding the men's fierce expressions, she read dismay on the women's faces. In their eyes she was loco. She bent to her task, fervently hoping it would be a long time before her father found a man he deemed *worthy*.

She looked toward her own tipi but could not see Conway. Rapidly healing now, he gained strength each day. Soon he would leave the village. And this time he would disappear from her life for good.

Matt wondered what the release of the stallion meant. But he wasn't about to call to her for an explanation and draw attention to himself.

The damned chief had not been back. He suspected Eagle Feather was avoiding him. He needed answers, and by God he intended to have them. He took in a deep breath and rose, determined to begin exercising seriously.

Day by day, walking became easier. A week later, though still limping, he was gratified to throw away the stick.

During his daily walks, the Comanches disabused him of some of his beliefs. They did bathe. Not every day, but several times a week. Their lingering odor came from unwashed clothes. Probably didn't have many garments.

Warriors spent an inordinate amount of time fussing with their hair. As they repeatedly combed their thick hair, he thought they'd pull every last strand from their heads before separating it into two sections. Binding them with hide and beads, they wove in loose hair so the ends trailed to their waists. He would not speculate where the loose hair came from.

Unmolested on his walks, he could have traversed the length of the canyon had he wished. Remudas galore ranged in back of many tipis, all the way to the base of the canyon's walls.

One day he spied Trooper grazing in the midst of a couple hundred mounts. He whistled, then grinned when the gelding lifted his head and ambled over.

Scratching the horse's poll, he murmured, "Hello, old son. Who owns you now?"

Glancing at the other steeds, he also saw Pepper. Probably Eagle Feather's possessions. Though they were not fenced, there was space between the groups, as if each band had claimed an area.

The Comanches ate well. Secure in the stronghold, braves hunted frequently and always returned with deer or antelope. The women did the gutting, cleaning, and cooking. White Fawn worked as long and as hard as the others.

Lupe worked hard, too, but neither he nor Xavier would think of dropping a heavy carcass into her hands and expect her to carry the damn thing, then prepare it and the smoke fire to dry the meat.

Night after night he listened to White Fawn's soft breathing and yearned to close the distance between them. But he didn't.

After one of his trips to the river to bathe, he sat in the tipi, fuming in frustration. Since Eagle Feather wouldn't come to him, he wanted to go to the old man. But one of his sons always lurked close by, giving Matt the impression that the chief's tipi was off-limits.

When White Fawn entered, he glanced up. Still wet from her own bath, her hair glimmered in the firelight, a shining curtain down her back. The fragrant soap she used smelled like an armload of wildflowers.

Need slammed into his chest with the force of a sledge. *Stick to your vow!* "Do you have to do that?"

he grumbled, shifting uncomfortably to accommodate his body's response.

Confusion crinkled her brow. "What?"

"Bring springtime into the tipi." Now he sounded demented. Before she could reply, he asked, "Why am I housed in your tipi, anyway?"

White Fawn sank gracefully to her blankets and poked the fire. She was fussing over it for no good reason, he thought. Before long she'd let it die for the night.

"I know not. He say brothers bring here. No question Eagle Feather."

"I noticed," he mumbled, lowering his face to hide the desire that surely shone in his eyes.

"Leg better. No much limp."

And I'm out of here as soon as I figure a way to get to Trooper and take you with me. The miracle of all miracles.

"Bright Star say look at wound."

She hadn't been around all day. Funny, he missed her. Over the past weeks he'd taught her to say "good morning," "hello," and "good-bye."

"What's wrong with her?"

White Fawn put a hand on her stomach. "Little pain."

"Has anyone looked at her?" And who would that be? A shaman?

She shook her head. "Slight pain come sometime, moon cycle."

Of course! A woman was a woman. Lupe had moped about occasionally but had never taken to her bed. Matt had secretly smiled at Xavier's morose behavior

290

some days. When he was like that, Matt knew as well as he knew his own name that his friend enjoyed no bed sport at night.

White Fawn scooted toward him and sat on her folded legs. "Look at wound?"

His every nerve sprang to attention at her scent. Desire sliced right to his loins. "I don't think that's a good . . . idea."

Too late. She touched him.

He seized her wrist and captured the other when she tilted off balance. Then she fell against his chest, her breath whooshing over his jaw. Matt froze, wondering if he could burn any hotter.

Her face was just inches from his, and he saw desire cloud her violet eyes. Holy . . . She wanted him, too. Why should he deny himself? Why should he deny her?

"God, sweetheart, I'm a weak man." He claimed her lips in a searing kiss, something he'd wanted to do for weeks.

His fingers tangled in the silken, damp hair, he held her in place as he wrapped his other arm around her and sank back on the blankets. Her slight weight atop him felt so good, so right.

She moaned ever so softly when he slanted his lips, deepening the kiss. She parted hers, offering access to her sweet mouth. The moist heat set him aflame.

After moments of hot torture, he jerked his mouth away to find her throat, then licked and nipped his way down the smooth column to her collarbone. Traveling back up the other side of her swanlike neck, he suckled her earlobe.

Between flutter-soft kisses, he said, "I can't stop myself. I need you."

In answer, her moist lips pressed against his throat. She, too, nipped several times, soothing each spot with the tip of her tongue.

God, she learned fast! He rolled her beneath him, again capturing her lips before her teasing made him lose control entirely.

Indifferent to the twinges in his thigh, Matt ripped her doeskin dress over her head and released his loincloth. Her hands slid up beneath his shirt, a silent invitation to remove the barrier separating bare skin from bare skin. He lifted his arms as she tugged upward. Recapturing her lips, he settled between her legs and sighed. This was where he belonged, with her smooth thighs wrapped around his hips.

He slid inside her. Slick, tight, hot, she was ready for him. But he wanted to savor her, give her pleasure beyond what she'd experienced before. No pain this time. He reined in his need to thrust before he lost himself in pleasure.

He softened his assault on her tender mouth, then kissed his way down her throat again. Grazing the tops of her breasts, he cupped one globe. It filled his hand perfectly. He kneaded and soothed, then lowered his head and captured the puckered nipple between his teeth.

She gasped when he gently bit, then laved the nipple with his tongue. He gave the other equal adoration. So damned sweet, so willing, and his . . . for these glorious moments. *Forever.*

"Oh, Matthew."

The sound of his name on her lips worked like an aphrodisiac. He burned hotter still.

She tangled her fingers in his hair and pulled him closer.

Never one to look a gift horse in the mouth, Matt groaned when she moved her hips, urging him to motion. His slow assault escalated into deep thrusts. His muscles tensed as he savored the heat inside her. God, if ever a woman had been made to receive him, it was White Fawn.

When her contractions began on his shaft, he realized she wouldn't take her pleasure quietly. Mouth open, he captured hers as she erupted into a near scream. She bucked and trembled as spasms shook her.

Unable to deny himself the exquisite pleasure any longer, he thrust deep and felt the back of her womb. That sent him flying into the abyss. Shudders racked his body so hard he moaned almost as loudly as she screamed.

Matthew was heavy, but she didn't care. Though he rested a portion of his weight on his bent arms, his lower body pressed her into the soft robes. More relaxed and fulfilled than she had ever thought possible, White Fawn lazily stroked his silken hair. Such a beautiful, big man.

If only she had met him long ago. She loved him. But this fleeting ecstasy was all she would have of him.

Eyes closed, she bit her lip. He would leave.

Eagle Feather had saved Matthew Conway from sure death at the hands of the other Comanches. Yet he

293

owned a ranch, had friends, a life far removed from Palo Duro Canyon. Far from her.

"You're going with me." Conway raised his head and looked at her. A crooked, endearing smile curved his sensuous lips.

His statement was so quiet, it took her a moment to understand his words. "No."

His smile vanished.

She would hug these moments to her heart, remember in her mind this time with him.

"We're back to that, are we?" He frowned. "I'm leaving as soon as I can figure a way out of this canyon without my hair being lifted. And, by God, you're . . ."

She placed trembling fingers on his dear lips, then raised her head and kissed him. Did he not know she would give everything to do as he said? Why did he badger her? Though he did not wish to be contradicted, somehow she must make him see the error of his thoughts.

He enjoyed making love to her. But he despised her people. He would never reconcile himself to the fact that she was Comanche in every way but birth. She would rather be dead than endure the scorn, the hatred of his friends.

Hoby Varner might have changed his opinion, but Conway could not protect her every moment for the rest of her life. What folly to think, even for a moment, that she could return to his world.

She used the same seduction on him that he had used on her. She touched his lips with her tongue. Feathered her hands over his muscled back. Dug her nails into his shoulders and knew deep satisfaction when his body trembled. After a moment he groaned and gave her what she sought.

Make love to me, Matthew. "Please," she murmured aloud.

He did. As thoroughly and enchantingly as he had before.

Chapter Nineteen

Just past daylight, from one heartbeat to the next, Matt came awake and sat bolt upright, automatically slapping his hip. Damn, no gun.

Crouched at the foot of his blankets, Straight Arrow's teeth flashed in a grin. Voice hushed, he said, "You do not value your scalp, Conway. While you sleep, I could add it to my lance."

God's truth! Dammit, had he lost his edge? He wouldn't admit it, not to this arrogant Comanche. Straight Arrow's gaze shifted to White Fawn, asleep at Matt's side. His gaze swung back, the grin still plastered on his face.

"What do you want?" he asked in an equally soft tone, mindful of waking White Fawn. He didn't give a good grunt what Straight Arrow thought of her presence in his bed. Now that he'd healed, he might welcome a fight with the brave before he left the canyon.

"My father would speak with you."

About time! Eagle Feather had left him cooling his heels long enough. "I'll be along shortly."

Straight Arrow left as quietly as he'd entered. Matt peered at the end of the blankets. So, that's what had wakened him. He reached for folded garments the Indian had left draped over his blanket-covered feet. New, butter-soft shirt and buckskin trousers. Why would they give him this gift?

He pulled on the clothes in record time and stepped outside to relieve himself before heading to Eagle Feather's tipi. The village folk had begun to stir, a few fires were already kindled. The smell of newly cut cottonwood drifted in the air. Braves headed toward horses, quivers slung over shoulders, bows in hand.

He nodded at Willow Branch as he paused before the open flap of the chief's tipi. She smiled shyly and gestured him inside, following behind.

Matt ducked through the opening, straightened to his full height, and glanced around. Except for White Fawn, the whole family sat inside.

Eagle Feather reclined on his backrest. Holding court, Matt thought cynically. A small fire crackled in the circle of rocks. The chief's expression was grave, his thoughts masked. He motioned Matt to sit on folded robes to the left of the tipi's entrance.

Enduring the chief's disquieting, mute perusal, Matt wondered why the devil he'd been summoned. If the old goat had something to say, why the hell didn't he get on with it?

Arms folded over his barrel chest, what passed for a smile lifted his lips when he finally nodded. "You have taken my daughter to wife."

"What?" Matt's eyes rounded in astonishment, then narrowed. "You're kidding. Right?"

Eagle Feather frowned. "What is this word, kid-ing?"

"Joshing me. Pulling my leg." When that further perplexed the chief, Matt said, "Speaking with forked tongue. Untruth."

That got a reaction in one helluva hurry. Eagle Feather reared back as if he'd been slapped. "My tongue speaks straight!"

Matt glanced around at the family. The two women cowered, but not the men. No, sir. If looks could scald him, he'd be in a pot over a fire right now. He'd committed an unpardonable sin, called the man a liar. He understood their confusion, but dammit . . .

Oh, hell, he'd better smooth their feathers a bit. Maybe Eagle Feather wasn't so inclined, but all three of his sons looked as if they'd gladly gut him if he didn't say something, and quick.

"Look, Chief, what I mean is, there's no preacher here to say the words, so I can't be married to White Fawn."

"She shares your blankets," Straight Arrow snapped.

"Yeah. But that doesn't mean—"

"Comanche way say she now your mate, Conway," Eagle Feather insisted.

He shrugged. "Our ways are different. I'm not getting married."

"You do not want a Comanche maiden?"

"She's not Comanche! She's as white as I am. I'm taking her to an orphanage in Austin."

"What is this or-fan-age?"

Damn, would he ever get through this ridiculous . . . "That's where children stay when they don't have parents."

"White Fawn is not a child," Eagle Feather said.

Matt could attest to that in the most intimate way, but . . . He frowned. What if he accepted the Comanche way while here? God knew, he wanted her in his bed. As soon as he was away, he'd do as he pleased.

And what was that, exactly?

Lupe and Xavier got along just fine. Marriage agreed with them.

A wife? Nope, you aren't going to leg-shackle yourself.

Would that be so bad? He shook his head, trying to clear his thoughts.

Matt remembered a conversation he'd had with Eagle Feather. "We'd need a priest."

"Ah. A black robe must say words for you to take a wife?"

"Yeah." That took care of that problem. There wasn't a priest within a hundred miles of Palo Duro Canyon. Now, maybe he'd find out exactly where he stood with these people.

"Look, I don't know what your game is, but you haven't gutted me yet. Are you going to release me or what?"

"My thoughts are unclear." Eagle Feather gave him that irritating grimace again. "Leave me."

"Unclear? Dammit, stop this pussy-footing . . ." Hell, that would only confuse the chief further.

Eagle Feather didn't ask what he'd meant; instead, he clamped his mouth shut.

Straight Arrow and his brothers rose. The first-rank warrior motioned him outside.

"What the hell?"

"My father will speak with you again."

He'd had a gut-full of these arrogant men. "And when will that be?" He was ready to ride right now.

"My father will decide, Conway."

Matt glanced from face to face. After sitting on his butt for days, Matt knew that Eagle Feather wouldn't say another word until he was damn well ready. He glared his displeasure but left. Not much else he could do. The Indians had him neatly boxed in.

When he got back to White Fawn's tipi, he lit into her. "If you hadn't run off, you'd be safe in Austin, and I'd be preparing for a cattle drive. It's your fault I'm in this mess!"

She knelt before the fire, apprehensive and confused. Then she frowned, too. "What mess you speak, Conway?"

"Just because we've slept together, Eagle Feather says we're married."

"No." Her head wagged from side to side. "You no my mate. I no marry you."

"Tell that to . . ." He felt a stab in his gut. *You won't marry me?* "Why the hell not?"

She rose and faced him, her expression confused. "What?"

"Why won't you marry me?" *Hell's fire, she agrees with me for a change.*

White Fawn lowered her chin, long lashes veiling her eyes. But not before he glimpsed . . . hurt.

"It matters not. I no marry you. I speak to my father."

"You do that," he snapped. He suddenly felt a sense of loss. Emptiness hollowed his chest.

* * *

Eagle Feather inspected each of his sons. Straight Arrow and Black Crow practiced patience, awaiting his command.

Beaver Heart's eyes flashed angrily. "Did she not return to us? She does not want to mate with a man."

"Hear my words, my son. White Fawn dwells in my heart like a daughter, and she is a woman of the *Nermernuh* in many ways. Though she is white, when the bluecoats come, that will matter not. Your sister will be like dirt under their feet. Rape, the white man calls the degradation that will be visited upon her until she no longer has breath."

"Is this not the fate that awaits my mothers as well?" Beaver Heart asked.

"Perhaps. More likely they will be shot on sight. Your sister will be punished because she lived among us rather than die."

Eagle Feather's heart was heavy that he must be so blunt. Fright dwelt upon his gentle wives' faces. But his visions had been too clear not to know what would befall them when the bluecoats came. Though his sons and brothers in the band still questioned his vision, he knew that one day the *Nermernuh* would be no more.

"A priest must be found."

"You would have us bring a black robe here?" Black Crow asked with astonishment.

Eagle Feather nodded. "They have been here many times, my son. Ride now, and make haste. Conway grows impatient. Disaster brews the longer he remains in the village."

Beaver Heart persisted. "White Fawn does not wish to mate with any man."

301

"Have you not seen the way her eyes follow Conway? You think she would let him die?"

All three sons frowned in confusion.

"White Fawn fears living in Conway's world. But I believe he will protect her. He says he will not mate, but I shall tell him he may not take my daughter unless he marries her the white man's way."

"He will not—" Eagle Feather's sly smile stopped Beaver Heart's protest.

"He does not know whether he will live or die at my command. He wants her. He has mated with her. He will marry her if a priest is found, for I shall make him believe she will be given to another warrior."

"But—"

Impatient, Eagle Feather sliced the air with his hand. "White Fawn is stubborn, but she loves him. Though it is not my way, I will speak with forked tongue. I will tell her Conway dies if she refuses to marry him."

He repeated, "You think she would let him die?"

Except for Beaver Heart, slow smiles of understanding lit his sons' features.

Matt lay on the ground, hot, dirty, tired. And exhilarated as hell. He hadn't wrestled in years. At the moment, Sleeps in the Saddle had him pinned, his bare chest grinding against gravel.

Though Matt couldn't understand his words, he knew Sleeps in the Saddle asked if he would yield.

He shook his head. "No."

The Indian pushed his arm higher behind his back. Hurt like a bitch. Damn, the little runt was good.

Two dozen or so braves circled them, egging on their *compadre*. Though Matt doubted any of them wanted him to win, he was sure some had bet on him.

Suddenly, the brave's long hair slipped over Matt's right shoulder. He grinned, tangled fingers in the greasy, dusty strands, and planted his knee in the dirt. Pulling and pushing, he flipped Sleeps in the Saddle to the side, dislodging the grip on his wrist.

Matt rolled and sprang to his feet. He whirled and fell atop his opponent, knocking the wind from him. Clutching the brave's long hair in both hands this time, he jerked his head off the ground, then slammed it down. "Yield?"

Getting no answer, he did it again, to cheers and hoots all around. He didn't want to kill the man; he simply wanted to win the match. Damn, the Comanche had a hard head.

Then, out of the corner of his eye, he saw Sleeps in the Saddle's hand wave weakly. He looked into the black eyes inches from his own. The Indian gave him a crooked grin and dipped his chin a fraction.

Matt grinned back and pushed himself to his feet. When he extended a helping hand, the brave accepted it. Several men patted both their backs, chattering a mile a minute. Sleeps in the Saddle swept his hand in front of his body, then pointed to the river.

Matt nodded. Yeah, both needed a bath. Thank God he'd shed the buckskin shirt and pants. They were the only clothes he had. As he moved toward the river, he caught sight of White Fawn. His gut clenched just looking at her.

To counter Eagle Feather's pronouncement that he'd

married White Fawn the Comanche way, Matt had moved out of her tipi and now slept next to the river. He hadn't yet figured out how to leave, but he was working on it. That was what he told himself, anyway.

He hadn't made love to her for a week. And he wouldn't. That way courted disaster. She might already be with child.

Would that be so bad?

He walked faster . . . to escape that wayward thought. He ripped off the breechclout and plunged into the cold water, Sleeps in the Saddle right behind him. A few minutes later, the brave leaped ashore, gave Matt a friendly wave, and left.

Matt lingered awhile, floating, watching the play of light on the leaves above him. Though the days were still hot, the tips of some of the leaves had begun to turn. A change in weather was right around the corner.

He jumped up on the bank near his blankets, shook himself like a dog, then pulled on the trousers, leaving his chest bare until it dried. Wouldn't be long until supper. After the strenuous exercise, he was starved.

As he reached for his boots, he came face-to-face with . . . "Pastor Anselmo! What are you doing here?" Not Catholic as the Cruzes were, he used pastor when he met up with a priest.

"I visit the Comanche whenever I can," the priest said. "More important, Matthew, what are you doing here?" He smiled deprecatingly. "I still haven't convinced most Comanches they should not kill white men. I'm amazed you have survived in their midst."

"I wouldn't have if it weren't for Eagle Feather." He motioned for the priest to be seated.

Older than Matt by a number of years, but not as old as Eagle Feather, the man nevertheless grunted a bit as he lowered his rotund body. He laughed. "I fail to see why Indians have not adopted chairs."

Matt grinned as he sank to his other blanket and pulled out one of the cigars a brave had given him a couple of days earlier. He offered one to Anselmo, who declined. Wine he would accept, but he didn't smoke.

"So, you visit the Comanches." Matt snapped his fingers. "You taught Eagle Feather and his family English!"

Father Anselmo nodded. "The chief and Straight Arrow were apt students."

"White Fawn speaks English. Not as well as the chief and his son, but—"

"I could not spend much time with the girl. Though most of the women are smart, Comanche culture does not recognize women's worth. Cooking, heavy work, bearing children: That's their place in the Comanche world."

He'd noticed. And he didn't like it. The one time he'd cut wood for a fire and taken it to White Fawn, she'd been appalled. Men didn't do that!

"My friend tells me you have wed White Fawn in the Comanche way."

The words dropped like blows into Matt's stomach. Hell's fire! Anselmo was one of the men of the cloth he'd mentioned to Eagle Feather. He had no hope that the wily old goat wouldn't remember. And facing this pious man made him uncomfortable. Still, he protested.

"I don't know about their customs, pastor, but I don't intend to marry. I couldn't live through seeing another massacre."

The priest knew about his heartache. He and Pastor Sebastian had happened by the ranch the very afternoon Matt had found his family dead. They'd helped him bury his kin, then said a few prayers over the graves.

"Matthew, Eagle Feather says you mated with White Fawn. Do you believe you can now walk away from the girl and not look back?"

"I have to. She could be killed like Ma."

"We cannot foretell the future. We can only pray, my son. And in my opinion, more destruction will be visited on the Indians than on white men."

Maybe so, Matt thought. And if he left, would he ever see her again? Probably not. Not ever knowing what happened to her, how she fared, would . . . eat at him. *Oh, hell, at least be honest with yourself!* He wanted White Fawn in his bed. Damn weak. But there it was.

I love her, he finally admitted.

Eagle Feather gasped for breath as pain again pierced his belly. He would welcome death to escape this affliction, but not today. He must be strong for what was to come.

"Prepare your decoction," he ordered.

"You must sleep, my husband," Bright Star argued, her brow creased with concern.

"Time enough to sleep when I join the Spirit World."

"Please," she wailed softly. "If you will but rest—"

His hand sliced the air. "Do as I say. Now."

Straight Arrow entered, then stared pointedly at his father. "You do not fare well this day."

"No. Did you find a priest?"

Straight Arrow nodded. "Your friend, Father Anselmo."

Eagle Feather took the cup from Bright Star. "Good." He drank deeply, closing his eyes for a moment. "Fetch White Fawn. I would speak with her."

When Straight Arrow left, he asked, "Have you made the garment for White Fawn?"

"Yes, my husband. A white doeskin, as you wanted."

White Fawn swept into the tipi, her eyes worried. "My father, bad spirits plague you today?"

"It is nothing," he lied. "I have summoned you to speak of another matter." He waited a moment while another pain lanced through his body. Thank the Spirits and Bright Star's potion, it was not as daggerlike.

"Daughter," he said softly, "you have taken Matthew Conway to your blankets. You have chosen him as your mate. It is time to take him the white man's way as your husband."

Tears welled in her glorious eyes; her lips trembled. "I cannot, my father. Conway does not want me."

"His eyes speak differently when they follow you."

"White people would spit upon me, maybe kill me."

"Conway could not protect you?"

If she said he could not, then she would be saying he was less than the man she knew him to be. That Eagle Feather knew him to be.

"He could, yes, but he would not care. Conway does not want me as wife."

"You are mistaken."

307

She shook her head.

"Hear my words, daughter. Your Conway is a strong man. He has endured much and he wants you, or he would not be here. Perhaps he fears what may befall you, but he would protect you with his life. Tomorrow I send him on his way."

Alarm clouded her face. She sucked in a shaky breath.

"Your heart does not swell in your breast for this man?"

She did not answer. Instead, she cast down her eyes, long lashes hiding them from him. But he knew. Her heart ached for the man.

"I cannot guarantee he will find his way home unmolested. He may die."

Fear for him shone in her eyes. "Could you not . . ." She did not complete the question, the answer to which was in his power to grant.

"I must look to my own people. We travel north before the next full moon."

He had decided to wait until the sun had risen ten times to allow time for his sons to escort White Fawn and Conway from harm's way. When they returned, and if he still lived, he would ride at the forefront of his band, his face looking north when the sun rose on the eleventh day. The plan was written in his mind and soul.

"But if we leave here, Conway would never find—"

"You," he said softly. "That is true, my daughter. If you marry him, he will become part of my family. I will protect him as I do my people, until the two of you are safely away."

308

Hope brimmed in her eyes, then dimmed. "But he does not want me."

Eagle Feather chuckled. "You do not understand the way of men. Be assured, he wants you."

Though still reluctant, White Fawn acquiesced. If Matthew Conway asked for her, she would marry him the white man's way.

Eagle Feather was pleased he had not been forced to lie to her. He had no intention of killing Conway, nor would he allow his brethren to do so.

Matt sat on the river bank, chucking small rocks into the water. He'd donned the elaborate shirt, combed his hair as best he could, and now waited for the priest to return.

He'd looked at the situation six ways to Sunday, but his convoluted thoughts always circled back to the same conclusion: He wanted White Fawn. And fight it though he might, he loved her.

He'd watched her day after day, working, laughing, playing with children. There was a . . . dignity about her. A quality possessed by both Bright Star and Eagle Feather. Especially Eagle Feather. His sons, too. He couldn't help respecting the way the Indians went about their daily lives as his own people did. How hard they worked just to survive. He'd come to admire them in a strange way.

An unseen woman tittered downriver. A male voice murmured. Having a roll in the blankets, he imagined. Which took him back to last week. That incredible night he'd shared with White Fawn.

M-a-r-r-i-a-g-e. The word crawled into his mind, undulated, curled like a snake, and settled in his belly. He snorted at the image of a coiled rattler, head dipping and swaying, tongue flicking, tasting the air, tail straight up, rattles buzzing. He bit back a laugh at the fanciful image. "Oh, for God's sake," he chided.

"My father would speak with you."

Matt looked around, silently cursing. Damn. Far too often, Straight Arrow caught him off guard!

The Indian stood tall but relaxed. Like his father, he wore one eagle feather in his hair. Unlike his father, the son's hair was not adorned and braided, but hung straight down his back to his shoulder blades.

Matt brushed his hands free of dust. "Glad to hear it. I would speak with him, too."

Take that. Two can play the intimidation game.

Chapter Twenty

White Fawn nervously fingered her beaded doeskin dress. Bright Star had insisted she don the new garment for the marriage ceremony. To Matthew Conway.

She loved and wanted him, but he did not love her. Why could her father not believe her and leave well enough alone? Instead, he insisted she stand before Father Anselmo and take Matthew as her husband in the white man's way.

Bright Star had assured her that Conway had agreed, but he would doubtless feel he had been forced. She wondered how he would treat her once they were gone from her village. She feared that Xavier, Lupe, and the men on his ranch would shun her.

She brushed a tear from her cheek. If only Conway had asked for her right away. Her spirit would soar and she would marry with gladness in her heart.

Night had fallen, leaving her in darkness inside the tipi. Outside, her entire family had gathered around a large fire a few paces from the entrance to Bright Star's tipi. Stands Tall Woman and several other women sat beyond the circle of light. Warriors arrived, including Running Bear and Wildcat and their wives, to witness her humiliation.

Matt followed Father Anselmo into the light of the blaze. He scanned the dark, solemn faces around him. To a man, the braves carried bows and arrow-filled quivers.

He couldn't control his grin. He'd heard of shotgun weddings, but this beat all. Unnecessary, too. He'd battled through his own misgivings. Hell, he was eager to wed White Fawn.

He searched but didn't see her anywhere. Maybe she'd flown the coop. He wouldn't put it past her. She wasn't inclined to marry him. Inclined, hell—she was adamantly against it.

"You're a wily one, Eagle Feather. I didn't know you knew a priest. Should have guessed. Who better to have taught you English than Pastor Anselmo?"

He shrugged. "After thinking on it, I'm ready. Time to tie the knot."

Eagle Feather dipped his head but said nothing. He probably didn't know what *tie the knot* meant, Matt thought, hiding a smile.

"You will take my daughter to the white man's world and honor her?"

"The honor is mine, Chief." He blinked, realizing it was true. More words as natural as breathing spilled out. "I will stand against any man who looks upon her with less than honor."

White Fawn's voice came out of the darkness. "No speak promises you no keep, Conway."

He spun to face her as she stepped from the shadows.

His breath hitched to a dead halt. *Jesus, Mary, and Joseph, she's beautiful!* Firelight haloed her indigo hair with silver. A wide band encrusted with colored beads and pieces of silver circled her forehead.

His admiring gaze traveled her length. He'd never seen such fine white doeskin, the bodice beaded in a sunburst design, the sleeves fringed down to her wrists. The dress caressed her luscious curves to midcalf, the fringed hem dusting the tops of equally fine beaded moccasins.

His body roared to life with a need he wouldn't deny even if he could. But his eyes narrowed when they met hers. Her gaze was troubled, even sorrowful, dark as the night with emotion. The flickering firelight reflected in their depths.

Stalling for time, he licked his lips, then allowed them to curve in a half smile. "You calling me a liar, White Fawn?"

Airing their differences before a passel of curious Indians wouldn't have been his first choice, but perhaps she needed reassurance. He took measured steps until she had to tilt her head back to look him in the eye.

"I no call you liar. But you no want to marry."

"A man can change his mind. Besides, you refused to marry me, too." His glance flicked her length again. "Now you're dressed in Sunday-go-to-meetin'. You change your mind, as well?"

He turned completely around, meeting the gazes of the warriors, until he faced her again. "Or maybe you plan to mate with one of these fellows."

"No!"

His gazed never wavered. "No, what? You aren't

marrying one of these men, or no, you still don't want to marry me?"

Her shoulders lifted in a heavy sigh as she cast down her lashes, hiding her eyes. "I marry you, Matthew Conway."

"Why?" He wanted to know. He wanted her change of mind to be for the same reason his had been. Yeah, right; she'd never mentioned love. *You haven't, either.*

"Because I . . . must," she whispered.

He wasn't going to get the words he wanted to hear. Hell's fire, he'd never given her a reason to have tender feelings for him. Indifference, maybe. *God, not that.*

Abruptly, he turned to Eagle Feather. "I'm ready, Chief. Let's get it over with." He grinned at the priest. "Come on, *padre,* open your book and get started."

"Conway, you not—"

"Shut up, White Fawn." None too gently, he seized her hand and drew her next to him. "We're marrying here and now, so say the proper words when the preacher bids you to."

A short time later, Matt looked into her troubled eyes as the priest asked, "Wilt thou take this man to be thy wedded husband?"

Tears swam in her eyes. "I will," she murmured.

Will what? Run from me again? Hate me rather than love me? Yeah, that might be her way to make his life miserable. And damn, maybe he deserved it.

Wedding days were supposed to be joyous for a woman. She looked as down in the mouth as a hound. And why shouldn't she? Not once had he uttered the words a woman wanted to hear.

A few moments later, he lowered his lips to her trembling ones, a fleeting kiss to seal the bargain. Shackled until death. He loved her, but he wouldn't say the words. No, sir. He wasn't about to give her the chance to grind his heart into the dust.

Now she knew exactly what Eagle Feather meant when he said his heart was heavy. Unshed tears clogged her throat. Mounted on Pepper, she rode behind Matthew Conway and Straight Arrow. Beaver Heart and Black Crow followed, honoring her father's word to protect Conway while yet on the *Llano Estacado*.

Her husband.

Not once had he touched her since their brief kiss four nights past. Many times she had found him staring at her with troubled eyes. Doubtless he regretted the forced marriage.

"Wilt thou love, honor, and cherish her?" Father Anselmo's words played over and over in her mind. Matthew had stared into her eyes and replied, "I will."

He did not love her.

Nevertheless, she was relieved he was on his way home. A home she would probably never be able to truly call hers. Perhaps one day she would go her own way. Never to experience love like Eagle Feather shared with his wives, his family, did not bear thinking about. Despair lay at the end of such a path.

She tipped back her head to view the white clouds scudding across the azure sky. "Buttermilk sky," Lupe had called the lacy cloud formation. Sometimes it foretold rain. The weather was a bit cooler in these waning days of summer. Before long cold wind would whistle down from the north.

"We stop here."

Straight Arrow's statement silenced her thoughts.

"It's a bit early to camp for the night," Conway said.

"You ride on. We return to our father now."

Conway looked at him, then scanned the south. "It took me weeks to find your canyon, Straight Arrow. How much farther until we leave the Staked Plains?"

"Before the sun sleeps, you will see country you recognize, Conway. From what you have said about your land, it is another four, maybe five suns south."

"You mean to tell me I spent over a month looking for you, and now I'll arrive home in ten days because we've ridden more or less straight as the crow flies?"

Straight Arrow smiled and nodded.

Matthew shook his head, a slow grin turning up his lips. "I could have probably ridden this alone if you'd pointed me in the right direction."

"My father say you are now part of his family. He protects his family. We ride until you are out of danger from other bands."

Matthew cast another quick glance at White Fawn, then said, "Part of his family, huh?"

Straight Arrow nudged his mount closer to Conway's. Astonished, White Fawn watched him offer his hand. Conway lifted his, and her brother clasped his forearm in friendship.

"We will never cross paths again, Conway. Go in peace."

White Fawn's heart thudded. Her father had uttered those same words to Conway when they'd departed the village.

Then he had turned to her. "Go, my daughter. Let

your heart be glad you will live with your man. Bear him many fine sons."

Eagle Feather and Bright Star had stood rigid. They did not touch her, did not smile. Only Willow Branch had shed a few tears and embraced her before she mounted and rode away.

She did not look back. If she had, she feared she would have begged to stay with the only people she knew as parents.

Straight Arrow looked at her now, a faint smile lighting his features. "Obey your man, White Fawn. May the Spirits protect you."

She could not speak, only watched as he touched his mount's flanks and rode north. Black Crow pressed a fist to his chest in salute, nodded, and followed his brother.

Beaver Heart sidled close. "I do not agree with my father's decision to give you to this man, White Fawn, but I can do nothing. You will live in my heart, sister, until the day I pass to the Spirit World."

He touched her face with gentle fingers. "Maybe someday we will cross paths again. I will not forget you." The single feather Beaver Heart wore swayed as the breeze caught his long hair, sending strands across his mouth.

She would not forget him, either. None of them. This image of him would dwell in her heart. He whirled and kicked his horse to catch up with his brothers. Profound silence settled around her. For endless moments she watched, until her brothers were no more than specks, and then lost in the waving grass.

Ducking her head, she shuddered, a desperate attempt to hold back tears. She had not heard him approach, but suddenly Conway's arm came around her waist to pluck her off her horse, and settle her back against him.

"Cry, Rebecca. It'll do you good," he said softly, his breath caressing her temple.

She shook her head. If she started, she feared she would not stop. His gentle understanding sent shivers through her. She forced a reply through trembling lips. "My name White Fawn."

He chuckled. "Back to that, are we? Well, you're going to have to get used to it, darlin'. You are Rebecca Conway now."

"We'll camp here."

Conway's deep voice shattered the silence. Of a sudden she heard the faint sough of the wind. Doubtless it had blown all day but, engrossed in her thoughts, only now did she hear and realize twilight neared.

She dismounted and scanned the spot, which was protected by a small grove of trees. On the far side of a narrow gully, she could barely see above the grass north, east, and west.

"I'll bed down the horses. Would you start a small fire?" He took Pepper's reins from her.

"Of course." It was the least she could do.

Though he had asked, not ordered, Conway's countenance was as closed as if he stood behind an invisible wall.

An hour later, she forced down a last bite of succulent rabbit, wondering whether she would ever be hungry again. Whether Conway would ever speak more than a few words, ever smile again. Ever acknowledge her presence other than to issue orders.

Mostly embers, the fire licked in tiny flames. She gathered up tin plates and cutlery and went to the narrow thread of water where he had tethered the horses on long leads so they could drink.

Conway's voice came out of the darkness behind her. "Watch your step, Rebecca. That gully is probably alive with snakes."

Snakes. That conjured images best forgotten. An eternity had passed since she'd stared down the barrel of his gun, and a moment later felt his arms clasped tightly around her.

His kiss.

Gooseflesh spread the length of her arms, down her spine. Heat sluiced through her and unerringly settled at the juncture of her thighs. Would they ever make love again?

When she returned, he sat on his blanket, back against his saddle. His gun belt lay close at hand.

As she stowed the gear, he patted her blanket, spread next to his. "We need to talk, darlin'."

Anxious, she approached and sank to her knees, but not close enough that he might touch her. She spoke before he could. "You no want marriage, Conway. I go . . ."

"Whoa. Hold your horses."

Her brow creased. "I no have horses."

Expression exasperated, he speared fingers through his hair. "Just an expression, darlin'. Listen: You don't know me at all if you think I could be forced to do something I didn't want."

319

"You no—"

He raised his hand. "Let me finish. I changed my mind. I told you that. I wanted you. I still do."

"You no lo . . ." She could not say the word.

He extended his hand. "Come here."

She stared at his callused, open palm. Shook her head. Not a good idea to touch him, remember his hands on her body, the ecstasy . . . No longer able to hold them back, she felt tears trickle from the corners of her eyes.

He clasped her upper arms, settled back, and dragged her against him. Though she made no sound, Matt felt her chest hitch with suppressed sobs.

He'd seen the suffering in Eagle Feather's face. Matt didn't doubt that the old man loved White Fawn. Maybe that was why he'd sent her away. He wouldn't be able to protect her much longer.

Since her brothers' departure four days past, Matt had wondered when she'd break. A strong girl, she'd been uprooted from the only family she knew, forced to marry a man she hardly knew, and now he was taking her into the white world she feared.

God, her heartache was enough to break his own. He caressed her back, turned her so she sat more comfortably on his thighs. Unable to help himself, he kissed her hair. His body roused. Dammit, couldn't he just this once offer comfort and put his own needs in abeyance?

"Shh. It's going to be all right."

She took a shuddering breath and leaned back to look at him.

"You send me Austin. I no argue."

"Think again. I've got you. I'm not giving you up."

She tilted her head, her eyes wide and questioning.

320

Hell's fire, he'd have to say it. Though she still might not believe him. He bracketed her face between his hands. "I didn't see it coming, but . . . I've fallen in love with you, White Fawn."

She blinked several times, searching his eyes, then gripped his wrists and pulled his hands toward her chest. "Feel heart, Conway."

He splayed both across her chest and felt the fast flutter as he returned her unwavering stare.

"It beat for you. Many moons."

He exhaled the breath he'd held for God knew how long, then kissed her; deep, searching. The next thing he knew, she lay beneath him on her back, her hands tangled in his hair.

Propped on his elbows, he pulled away and allowed a faint smile to turn up his lips. "I take that to mean you love me, too."

She nodded. "Make love to me, Con . . . Matthew."

He didn't have to be asked twice. Within minutes he had them both naked, sprawled on the blankets, panting for release, and finally . . . finally . . . finding it.

She shuddered awake the next morning to find lips on her breast, teeth teasing a nipple. How long Matthew had been caressing her, arousing her, she did not know, but her body was ready, straining, wet between her thighs. *Magical.*

"Matthew," she gasped as he rose above her and sheathed himself with one thrust.

"God," he gritted through his teeth. "I thought you'd never wake up."

A climax seized her. Stars showered; rainbow colors

exploded before her eyes. She rode the spasms for several minutes of pure bliss, felt his powerful body tense as his seed filled her.

It was some time before he lifted his head and looked at her. An endearing smile lifted his lips.

"You okay?"

"You wake me like this . . . all time?"

"With pleasure, sweetheart."

She wrapped her arms around his neck and pulled him close to nuzzle his mouth. "Get attention quick." She grinned, then nipped his bottom lip.

"Two can play at that game." He flipped her over so she lay atop him. He stilled, searching her face as if he had never seen it before. "You're beautiful, you know that?"

"Love you." She needed to say it again and again to make herself believe she had the right.

He took a deep breath, caressed her hair once more, then pushed her up to sit. "I'm tempted to stay here all day and make love, Rebecca, but—"

"White Fawn my name."

He claimed her lips, then pulled back. "Yeah, and I love that name, but I gotta remember to call you Rebecca." He narrowed his eyes. "And you need to get used to hearing it."

She sighed. He was right. But she had never liked the name Father Anselmo had bestowed upon her. Still, there was no other white name she liked better, so . . . She nodded agreement.

As they broke camp, Matt told her they would be back at the Rocking C by nightfall. Rather than take time to cook, they ate the last of the pemmican and a strip of hardtack each.

The sun burned brightly on his hair as he handed over Pepper's reins, then turned to mount Trooper.

Everything happened so quickly. She heard the report of a gun. Saw the hair at Matthew's temple flick out just before a streak of scarlet spattered her tunic.

He staggered.

"Matthew!" She reached for him as he sank to his knees, hand to his forehead.

"Hell's fire, I'm shot!"

And a bit disoriented, she thought, as he settled back against a tree trunk. Footsteps approached.

A man's voice. "I got the son of a bitch!"

Without thinking, she ripped Matthew's gun from the holster.

His hand waved drunkenly in the air. "Give it over, White Fawn."

"I do this." She cocked the hammer.

That tiny sound halted the footsteps. Two men, both white. One, rather young, held a rifle in his hand, but he did not raise it. Not with Matthew's gun clutched in both her hands, pointed dead at his chest.

"Hey, little . . . lady." He sneered the word. "Don't be hasty."

"Isaac?" Matthew questioned behind her.

The young man scowled and craned his head to see around her. She took one step forward. The older one eyed her warily but did not move.

"Come close, I shoot."

"Rebecca," Matt slurred. "He's a friend."

"Cap'n?" the younger man croaked.

"Holy shit," the older man snapped. "It's Conway!"

The man Matthew had called Isaac dropped his rifle and raised both hands. "I thought you was an Indian! She's . . ." He peered at White Fawn. "She is. Ain't she?"

"My wife."

"Wife?" both men yelped.

Isaac took a step. "Cap'n—"

"Stop!" White Fawn ordered.

He did, his face turning red. "I didn't know it was Cap'n Conway . . . uh, ma'am." He kept his hands raised, eyes on the weapon she held in surprisingly steady hands. "Cap'n, would you ask her to point that gun somewheres else afore it goes off? By accident, like?"

"Rebecca—"

She shook her head, the gun wavering a bit. "No. He shoot. I no let him."

"He won't do it again, darlin'. Put the gun down."

Her eyes narrowed.

Isaac's widened. "She's got blue eyes, Cap'n!" His gaze traveled her length. "But she looks like an Indian."

"So do I." Matt struggled to his feet. "That's why you took a bead on me." The dizziness nearly passed, he touched his temple. His fingers came away crimson. "Damn, Isaac, a fraction closer and I'd be a goner."

Now beside White Fawn, he clasped the gun's barrel and forced it down. "Let him pass, darlin'. I promise, he's a friend."

She glanced up at him, terror clear in her violet eyes, but she'd stood her ground against two armed men.

Partly to brace his wobbly knees, he put his arm around her shoulders. Squeezed. "I'm proud of you, sweetheart."

Rigid as a frozen steer, she almost vibrated with the terror still churning inside her. Then he felt her slight tremor of relief. But she stiffened again when Isaac leaned to pick up his rifle.

"It's okay," he murmured. "Fellas, this is my wife of just a few days, Rebecca." He tilted his head toward the two men. "Isaac Bettencourt and Cecil Barnes."

She didn't acknowledge the men. Instead, she turned to him. "I tend wound now."

Isaac offered to tie Trooper and Pepper; then all three men sat down, Matt's back again supported by a tree. While White Fawn washed and bandaged his head, he explained where he'd been and why they wore Indian garments. He didn't tell them White Fawn had been reared by Indians. They could suspect what they wanted; they had no proof.

"Ridin' with Isaac, that mean you've joined the Rangers with him?" Matt asked.

Cecil shook his head. "No. Didn't like kowtowing to a superior in the Army, don't plan to do it again." He glanced at Isaac and shrugged. "We just keep bumping into each other. Fact is, I'll probably head south for a while. Warmer down there when winter comes."

After she finished, White Fawn sat next to Matt and eyed his two friends suspiciously. There was nothing he could do about that. And secretly, he didn't care if she remained wary of all white men. For a while, anyway. Except him, of course.

Well past midmorning, Matt convinced Isaac and

Cecil he didn't need their escort. In familiar territory, he figured they would make it home just after supper. Traveling after dark presented no problem.

He extended a hand to White Fawn and smiled. "Shall we try again, darlin'?"

She placed hers in his and smiled shyly. "Love you. No let man shoot again."

He couldn't resist. He nuzzled her ear, then took her lips in a deep, heady kiss that almost had him putting off the trip until morning. Finally, he chuckled shakily and lifted her into the saddle.

He mounted and took her hand. "Let's go home, Mrs. Conway."

Home. As she gazed into Matt's dark eyes, she prayed to the Spirits: *Grant my wish that it be so.*

Matt squeezed her fingers, then let go and took up his reins.

She offered him a brilliant smile. "The Rocking C. Our home."

Her heart soared as she rode south beside the man she had come to love beyond reason.

THE MOON AND THE STARS

CONSTANCE O'BANYON

Caroline Richmond started running on her wedding day—the same day her husband died. Her solitary life is filled with fear of her malicious brother-in-law always one step behind her. She thought she'd found a shred of peace in Texas. But when a mysterious bounty hunter comes to town, she knows the wrath in his amber eyes is meant only for her. He finds a way to be everywhere she is, making her nerves hum in a way she thought she'd conquered.

Wade Renault came out of retirement for one reason: to see a deceptive murderess brought to justice. But when he meets the accused woman, he senses more panic than treachery. She lives too simply, she seems too honest and scared. Someone had deceived him, but he will wait to get her right where he wants her, beneath...*The Moon and the Stars.*